"Hello, Felix. Yo⸺⸺⸺⸺⸺⸺⸺ie closed the garden door be⸺⸺⸺⸺⸺⸺ped him up in her arms. The⸺⸺⸺⸺⸺⸺wn. "Why did you not bring him with you? You could have carried him under your coat."

Richard laughed. "He's not cold, Maggie, and he has no need of my coat. He has his own and I'd wager to say it's far warmer than mine."

"Just so!" Maggie conceded the point with a smile. "But what is this? Someone has hung a small box on a ribbon around his neck."

"They have?"

Richard's expression was perfectly guileless, but Maggie noticed the glint of mischief in his eyes. "Why did you tie this box around his neck, Richard?"

"Perhaps you should open the box, Maggie. It is obviously intended for you."

Maggie laughed in delight as she slipped the pink ribbon from Felix's neck and retrieved the small box. It was wrapped in a square of pale pink paper with her name inscribed on the top. "You should not have given me a gift, Richard. I am not certain that it is proper for me to accept it."

"But I did not give you a gift, Maggie. It is clearly from Felix. All I did was wrap it for him."

"Of course." Maggie giggled. She loosened the pink paper and lifted the lid of the small box. What she saw inside made her gasp.

"Felix would like to know whether or not you approve of his choice. He informed me that he spent hours debating the wisdom of blue eyes versus green."

Maggie was so surprised, she could not speak as he drew out the small brooch nestled inside the box. It was fashioned of gold and shaped like a cat viewed from the side. Its back was curved up in a graceful arch and one large eye sparkled with a gleam of blue light. "It is the loveliest brooch I have ever seen! And the most clever! Is this a . . . a sapphire?"

"I do believe it is. Felix told me that it put him in mind of your lovely blue eyes."

"Oh, Richard!" Maggie was so delighted by this thoughtful gift, she did not stop to think. She acted on impulse, throwing her arms around his neck and kissing him soundly on the cheek.

—from *A Family for Felix* by Kathryn Kirkwood

WINTER KITTENS

KATHRYN KIRKWOOD
JUDITH A. LANSDOWNE
JEANNE SAVERY

Zebra Books
Kensington Publishing Corp.

http://www.zebrabooks.com

ZEBRA BOOKS are published by

Kensington Publishing Corp.
850 Third Avenue
New York, NY 10022

First Printing: January, 1999
10 9 8 7 6 5 4 3 2 1

Printed in the United States of America

CONTENTS

"A Family for Felix" by Kathryn Kirkwood   7

"Rescuing Rosebud" by Judith A. Lansdowne   103

"Four-Penny Cat" by Jeanne Savery   187

A FAMILY FOR FELIX

KATHRYN KIRKWOOD

CHAPTER ONE

"Come back here, Artemis, you naughty girl." Margaret Pendleton's bright blue eyes twinkled with amusement as she removed the small kitten from the rose velvet draperies that graced the windows in her aunt Lenora's library. This was no easy task as the kitten's sharp claws were tangled in the threads, but Maggie managed to achieve it, extricating one small paw at a time without doing damage to the fabric. Laughing at the tiny creature's antics, she resumed her seat and settled Artemis on her lap. "You've heard what they say about curiosity, have you not? I declare that you have already used two of your nine lives this morning!"

Artemis, her explorations put to an abrupt end, gave a wearied yawn and closed her eyes. A moment later, she was asleep, nestled comfortably in the folds of Maggie's skirts. Maggie regarded her with a fond smile and then rose again, to place her in the large basket by the hearth where the other five kittens slept.

"They are a handful, are they not?" Maggie addressed Felicity, her aunt's tabby, who was the mother of this lively brood. "If you had given a care to what should result from your *tendre* for their papa, I doubt that you would have welcomed his attentions.''

Felicity began to purr, staring up at Maggie with unblinking eyes. The expression on the cat's face was one of supreme contentment, and Maggie reached out to stroke her soft fur. ''On the other hand, I cannot deny that their papa is a superb father. If he adheres to his schedule, he should arrive to pay his afternoon call before the clock strikes two.''

No sooner had Maggie uttered the words than the great carved clock that had belonged to her uncle struck the hour. Before it had concluded its second strike, there was the sound of scratching at the French doors that led to her aunt's pleasure gardens. Maggie walked quickly to the doors and opened them with a smile. Papa was here to see his kittens.

''Hello, Papa. You are prompt, as usual.'' Maggie stepped aside so that the huge orange cat could enter the library. ''Did you bring a friend with you today?''

Papa responded by rubbing up against her skirts, and Maggie reached down to pet him. He immediately started to purr, a deep rumbling in his throat to show his pleasure at her attentions.

''Perhaps you will find me a friend tomorrow.'' Maggie smiled at the father of Felicity's kittens. ''I should not like you to think that I do not enjoy your company, for I do very much, but I must admit that I long for human companionship.''

The huge cat nodded his head as if he understood and then he padded into the room. He glanced over at the basket, where Felicity and the kittens awaited him, and turned back to Maggie.

''Very well, Papa. I shall play the part of the butler and announce you.'' Maggie approached the basket to address her aunt's cat. ''Your gentleman caller has arrived, Felicity. I shall pour the tea for you, as you are otherwise occupied.''

While Papa was nuzzling each of his six offspring and paying like attention to their mother, Maggie fetched the two bowls and the pitcher of milk that sat on the tea table.

She carefully poured a bit of milk in each bowl and set them down in the alcove that housed her uncle's collection of maps. "Your tea is served, Papa and Felicity. It is still slightly warm, just the way you prefer."

Papa moved back to give Felicity room and she sprang nimbly from the basket. Soon the two cats were lapping up the milk from their bowls, Papa's loud rumbles joining Felicity's higher pitched purrs in a melody that clearly bespoke their enjoyment. Maggie returned to her seat to watch the two cats, an amused smile upon her face. She had enjoyed very little contact with felines in the past as the mere presence of a cat in his vicinity had caused her dear father to wheeze most dreadfully. Her father's sister, however, had always kept cats, claiming that one could not maintain a library without some method of keeping down the mice. Maggie had seen evidence of this a sennight past, when Felicity had proudly presented her with the tail of a mouse.

Maggie giggled, remembering the occasion. She had finished her breakfast and then entered the library to join Felicity and her kittens. They had been reposing quite contentedly in their basket and Maggie had taken up a book, intending to spend the remainder of the morning perusing an account of life in ancient Greece.

The moment that Maggie had seated herself quite comfortably, Felicity had leapt up on her lap, a thin, whip-shaped object secured in her mouth. Curious as to what her aunt's cat had found, Maggie had taken the object to examine it more closely and discovered, to her shock, that it was the tail of a mouse.

After ringing for Spencer, Aunt Lenora's butler, the library had been thoroughly searched for the remainder of the creature. No traces had been found, and Spencer had told Maggie, in the most delicate of terms, that it had most likely been the greater part of Felicity's last meal. He had also warned her that Felicity was a skilled mouser and that Maggie should prepare herself to accept further evidence of her proficiency in future.

Once Maggie had conquered her initial revulsion, she

had praised Felicity and braced herself for further develop-
ments. To date, Felicity had presented her with no less
than six thin tails, one each morning. Spencer had mentioned that her aunt Lenora had seen fit to reward this
behavior with a portion of warm milk, and it was to this
end that Maggie had requested a pitcher of warm milk
with her tea tray.

When the bowls were empty, Maggie collected them and
placed them on the tea tray, knowing full well that all but
her aunt should doubt her sanity for serving milk tea to
her feline guests. Felicity returned to the basket to tend
her kittens and Papa padded over to nuzzle each of them
once again. He spent a moment with each, beginning with
Athena, who resembled her mother most closely. Aphro-
dite, the most affectionate of the females with a lovely coat
of golden fur, was next, followed by Artemis, the curious
hunter who was fond of stalking a bit of yarn and climbing
the draperies to peer at the world outside the library windows. Hermes, the smallest and swiftest male, was the next
to claim Papa's attention, and then Apollo, the large
golden male whose mewing was undeniably melodious.
When Ares, who tended to scrap with his fellow littermates,
attempted to bat at him playfully, Papa parried the thrust
of his tiny paw most adroitly and picked him up by the
scruff of his neck to place him more securely in the basket.

"Perhaps I should call you Zeus," Maggie addressed the
father of the kittens, "since Aunt Lenora chose to name
your kittens after his offspring."

Papa turned to gaze at her, his yellow eyes wide, and
Maggie began to smile. "What is your name, Papa? I am
certain you have one, for it is quite evident that someone
sees to brushing your coat and feeding you well."

The huge orange cat opened his mouth to favor her
with a melodious yowl, and Maggie burst into laughter. "I
see. You are telling me that your name is Raoul."

Papa answered her with a deep rumbling purr that
sounded surprisingly like a chuckle and then he padded
to the garden door. He flicked his tail impatiently, and
Maggie hastened over to gather him into her arms.

"Just a moment, Papa. I have something for you." Maggie patted him affectionately as she retrieved the toy she had made from a bit of cloth. "I made this for you, Papa. It is intended to resemble a mouse."

Papa stared at the toy in Maggie's hand, his yellow eyes regarding it soberly. Then he reached out to take it into his mouth, the braided tail flopping comically out to the side. The moment Maggie opened the doors again, he ran down the path and leapt over the garden wall, Maggie's gift held securely in his mouth.

"Good-bye, Papa." Maggie closed the doors and returned to her seat with a sigh. The most exciting moment of her day had passed. She would have no other visitors, as her aunt Lenora was her only acquaintance in London. As bad luck would have it, on the very day of Maggie's arrival, her aunt had been called away to a dear friend's sickbed and had set out immediately to a location many miles to the north of London. There had been no opportunity to meet any of her aunt's friends and Maggie had been bitterly disappointed.

Aunt Lenora had written to Maggie of the weekly soirees that she held. There were poets who came to read their new verses and artists who exhibited their newest paintings on the easel in her aunt's drawing room. There were also scientists, inventors, astronomers, physicians, and a diva or two among the ranks of Aunt Lenora's friends. Politics was often the topic of converse at these gatherings, and several high-ranking members of Parliament came to consult Maggie's aunt on matters of considerable importance. Lady Lenora Worth was well known as a bluestocking, but she was forgiven this aberration by virtue of her highly placed friends.

A carriage rumbled past on the street outside and Maggie jumped up from her seat. Was it possible that one of Aunt Lenora's fascinating friends had failed to receive notice that she was away and had come to call upon her? But the carriage did not stop and Maggie sat down again with a heavy heart. She would be alone again today.

If Maggie had been a young miss with aspirations to ton

affairs and a penchant for buying expensive items in the fashionable shops that lined Bond and Oxford streets, she should have been most overset by her aunt's untimely absence. As an unmarried miss, new to London and not yet presented, it was unseemly for Maggie to venture out alone. But Maggie had accepted her confinement with good grace and occupied herself with exploring Aunt Lenora's home in Parkhurst Square and its surrounding gardens until such time as her aunt returned.

In truth, Maggie was not unhappy. Felicity and her six kittens provided much amusement, and Papa arrived to pay a call upon them every afternoon without fail. Maggie also enjoyed reading volumes from her aunt's extensive library and she knew she should be quite content if only she should be permitted a caller or two. Maggie had attempted to discuss such important matters as the moral consequences of the peninsular wars and the fairness of the proposed window tax with Felicity and the kittens, but the converse was, by nature, one-sided. This exercise was quite satisfying in one respect, as Maggie had received no argument as to the validity of her opinions, but she longed for an honest human response to her views.

Maggie had never had cause to lack companionship in the past. Before her brother, Stephen, had left home to join the military, his commission kindly secured by one of Aunt Lenora's influential friends, they had spent many hours in the cozy vicarage parlor, reading aloud and discussing passages from their favorite books. Maggie's father had frequently entertained the members of their small congregation and Maggie had acted as his hostess. They had amused themselves, on these happy occasions, with musicales, tableaus, and games of charades. Even on the rare evenings when Maggie had found herself alone with her papa, they had enjoyed themselves immensely by discussing the subjects that had intrigued them. Maggie had thought that they might go on in this way for many years, but an event transpired that had rendered her further efforts on her father's behalf quite unnecessary.

John Pendleton, the Vicar of Stonebridge, had remarried.

Maggie had nothing but approval for this match. Her new stepmama, a widow who had long been a member of their small congregation, had been one of her mother's dearest friends. Maggie had been quite delighted when her father had announced that they planned to marry, but after her father's new wife had established herself at the vicarage and assumed her wifely duties, very little had remained for Maggie to do. Though both her father and her new stepmama had assured her that she should always have a home with them, it had not taken Maggie long to realize that her continued presence was no longer essential to her father's happiness.

Aunt Lenora's invitation to join her in London had arrived as if in answer to Maggie's prayers. Her father's sister had offered to send a carriage for her, and she had stated that Maggie would be welcome to stay at her home on the fashionable West End for as long as she desired. Maggie had accepted this kind offer by return post, grateful for the opportunity to experience the world beyond her small rural community of Stonebridge.

The weeks preceding Maggie's journey had been filled with preparations, but at last the day of her departure had arrived. Maggie had dressed in the new traveling ensemble her stepmama had commissioned for her and surveyed her appearance in the glass. With her chestnut-brown hair arranged in soft curls that framed her face, and her blue eyes sparkling with excitement, Maggie had voiced the thought that she looked almost attractive.

"But you *are* attractive." Maggie's stepmama had smiled at her, reaching up to pat a curl in place.

Maggie had been put to the blush at her stepmama's compliment, thanking her nicely, but then dismissing it out of hand. She had assessed her reflection many times in the past, and though she regarded herself as presentable, she had never thought to claim beauty as one of her attributes. She possessed too much height to fit the current pattern card of beauty and her figure was regrettably slight.

Maggie had readily admitted, however, that the new gowns her stepmama had chosen for her did much to conceal her faults.

"I have no doubt that you shall find your match in London, Maggie." Her stepmama had regarded her fondly. "Your father and I have discussed this possibility and we both agree that it is time for you to marry and begin a life of your own."

Maggie had turned away to hide the sorrow that clouded her eyes. She, too, wished for marriage and a family of her own, but thus far no one had offered for her. Perhaps it was due to her education, which far exceeded that which was available to the young men of Stonebridge. None had the courage to marry a wife who could best him in an argument or correct him when he was wrong. Even though Maggie was properly modest about her abilities, the simple fact that she enjoyed studying her father's books and could figure the number of bushels an acre would yield without benefit of paper or ink intimidated even the staunchest of suitors.

Keeping her private thoughts to herself, Maggie had followed her stepmama down the stairs. In the bustle to load Maggie's baggage and provide her with a hamper of food for her journey, there had been time for only one caution from her father's new wife. When a gentleman came to call upon her, Maggie should take a care to guard her tongue. She must needs remember that most gentlemen, unlike her dear papa, did not regard educated ladies with favor. To that end, she should never disagree with a gentleman's opinion, even if he was in error. Instead, Maggie should listen to his words with interest and compliment him on his discerning views.

As Maggie recalled her stepmama's warning, an ironic chuckle escaped her lips. At least she should not fall victim to that particular foible. It was quite impossible for her to disagree with a gentleman's opinion when the only gentleman who had come to call was the huge orange cat who had fathered Felicity's kittens!

CHAPTER TWO

Richard Bromley, Marquis of Larchmont, leaned back in his chair and glanced at the clock. It was already two in the afternoon and he had risen less than an hour ago. Since he had come to stay at his sister's home on Parkhurst Square, he had been breaking his fast at a later hour with each successive day.

"Should you care for more tea in the library, Lord Larchmont?" His sister's butler raised an inquiring brow.

"Yes, thank you, Hobbs." Richard favored him with a smile and rose from his chair, exiting the breakfast room with a sigh. He had been in London for less than a fortnight and he had already attended seven balls, an equal number of dinner parties, three routs, and countless assemblies and breakfasts. They called this the "little" Season, and Richard hoped that he should not have occasion to remain for the true Season, which coincided with the opening of Parliament. This did not commence until sometime in April, as most gentlemen of the peerage were avid hunters and would not consider leaving the country until the frost was out of the ground and the foxes had begun to breed.

Richard should have been quite content to stay at Larch-

mont Park, the favorite of his country estates, but his sister
had begged him to spend the Little Season at her London
home in Parkhurst Square. It seemed that Alicia was eager
to accompany her husband on one of his diplomatic journeys and she had been unable to find anyone to see to
the care of her cat.

"But you have a staff to do that sort of thing." Richard
had stared at his sister in shock when she had first broached
the subject on one of her infrequent visits to him.

"This is true, dear Richard." His sister had given a most
convincing sigh. "But poor Felix shall be so desperately
lonely. Aunt Seraphina has always come to stay with him
in the past, but she is not free. You will come to keep him
company, won't you, dear? I should not rest easy for a
single moment if I left him in the care of the servants for
such a long time."

Richard had never been able to resist his sister's tears,
and when he'd seen Alicia's deep green eyes begin to fill
with moisture, he had reached out to hug her tightly. "I'll
take care of your cat, Allie, but there is no reason for me
to come to London. I'll just send a man to fetch him and
keep him here until you return."

"But that will not serve at all!" Alicia had announced
with a noticeable quaver in her voice. "Felix does not like
to travel, you see, and he should be most uncomfortable.
Please, Richard. You must come to London. If you will but
do this one small thing for me, I shall never ask another
of you, I promise!"

Richard had stared at his sister for a moment, fighting
his urge to do as she wished. And then he had uttered the
words that had sealed his fate. "All right, Allie. If it means
that much to you, I will come."

When Richard had arrived in London, his sister had
regaled him with instructions and admonitions. Richard
was to take Felix to the library each morning and read the
papers to him. It would not do to change his routine, for
Felix enjoyed this interlude immensely. At luncheon, Felix
was to have fresh fish, prepared especially for him by Alicia's French chef, and once her cat had eaten his fill, he

should be brushed by the head footman who was particularly adept at this task. Immediately before retiring, Richard should order a saucer of warm milk for Felix's enjoyment and he must promise to sleep with his door ajar in the event that dear Felix desired human companionship in the wee hours of the morning. Alicia's most important instruction was that Felix be confined to the house. He had wandered off several times in the past and had returned quite chilled and bedraggled.

Richard had bit back a smile and valiantly refrained from remarking that Felix was undoubtedly the most cosseted feline in all of England. Instead, he had exchanged a conspiratorial wink with Alicia's husband and vowed solemnly to do exactly as his sister had asked. But then Alicia had offered one final instruction that had caused Richard to suspect that he had fallen into a deception cleverly conceived by his sister and mother, combined.

"You will go to parties, won't you dear?" Alicia had called down from the window of the carriage. "Felix simply adores to hear the news of the ton, and I would not wish to deprive him of that pleasure. I have heard tell that the new debutantes are very beautiful, and it is even possible that you shall meet your perfect match while we are away."

Richard had laughed long and hard as the carriage containing his sister and brother-in-law had rumbled off round the corner. Alicia had just elicited his promise that he would look for a wife. It was what his mother desired above all things, and it appeared that his sister shared this sentiment.

Realizing that he had been thoroughly duped, Richard had embraced the inevitable. He was not averse to marriage, and perhaps his mother and sister were right. He was only a few months shy of his thirty-first birthday and it was past time for him to set up his nursery.

The day after Alicia and her husband had departed, invitations for Richard had begun to arrive. With the aid of Hobbs, his sister's most exemplary butler, Richard had sent off the appropriate responses and his foray into the glittering world of the ton had begun.

Richard had enjoyed his pick of the lovelies, as he was considered a prime catch. His holdings were vast, his title was old and respected, and his family was one of the finest in England. Though he did not regard himself as handsome, the young debutantes had been quick to differ. Richard had been complimented on his height, tall enough to suit even the tallest lady, and his figure, which was strong and athletic. One young miss had claimed that his full head of dark, curling hair was most handsome, and another had praised his finely chiseled features and his dark-green eyes. These compliments did not turn Richard's head, as he was well aware of their purpose. He had no doubt that the mamas of these young ladies had instructed them to praise him lavishly in an effort to gain his approval.

Any one of the young ladies he had squired should have been delighted to accept his declaration, but Richard had offered for none of them. The reason for his reticence was simple; though he had danced and conversed with scores of attractive young misses, they all seemed quite interchangeable. He had yet to meet even one who truly piqued his interest.

Richard pushed open the pocket doors to his brother-in-law's library and took his favorite chair in front of the windows. No sooner had he settled himself than a footman entered with his tea. Richard motioned for him to pour and then dismissed him. He needed time alone to gather himself for yet another social engagement this coming evening.

A frown appeared on Richard's brow. He wished for a night to himself, but it was too late to send an excuse to his hostess. Barring death or an equally drastic circumstance, he was obliged to attend. Rather than anticipate yet another boring evening, Richard picked up the paper. He unfolded it, crinkling the page, and waited for Felix to appear.

"Felix?" Richard crinkled the paper again. "Where are you, boy?"

There was perfect silence in the room and Richard began to frown. Felix was a huge cat and there were not that many places for him to hide. He got up to check beneath the settee, but there was no sign of his sister's orange cat. A search of the spot behind the draperies that Felix often frequented yielded no result, and Richard crossed the room to ring for Hobbs.

"You rang, Lord Larchmont?" The butler appeared so quickly that Richard suspected he had been hovering in the hall, waiting for his summons.

"Yes, Hobbs. Felix appears to be missing."

"Yes, my lord." Hobbs nodded. "Felix often disappears for an hour or two of an afternoon, but I assure you that he shall return before three. That's when Mrs. Jarvis gives him his afternoon tea."

"His tea?" Richard raised his brows, a smile hovering about his lips.

"Yes, Lord Larchmont. Felix has a bowl of warm broth with a bit of biscuit crumbled over the top."

"I see." Richard nodded. "Do you know where Felix goes when he disappears?"

"Out, Lord Larchmont. Precisely where, I couldn't say."

Richard frowned. "But I thought my sister gave orders for the doors and windows to be closed."

"They are, my lord. We are most conscientious in following Lady Ainsworth's instructions, but Felix still manages to escape us. He is quite clever at it, sir."

"No doubt he is." Richard chuckled. He had noticed that his sister's cat did precisely as he wished. "You are certain that he will return?"

"Yes, indeed, Lord Larchmont. Felix is most punctual when it comes to his tea. At precisely ten minutes before the hour of three, he will appear at the garden door and scratch to be admitted."

Richard glanced at the ormolu clock that sat upon the mantelpiece. If Hobbs was correct, Felix should return within a few minutes. "I shall open the door myself, Hobbs. I wish to have a word with him."

"Certainly, my lord." Hobbs's formal manner underwent a subtle change. His eyes took on a decided sparkle and his lips began to twitch. "Shall you ask him where he has been, my lord?"

Richard nodded, biting back his own smile. "Indeed, I shall. Felix must learn that he cannot leave without first informing me of his destination."

"And if he will not tell you, sir?" Hobbs's voice shook slightly with suppressed laughter.

"Then I shall be forced to discover his secret in another way. Thank you, Hobbs. That will be all."

Hobbs turned and walked to the door, his shoulders quivering. To the man's credit, he managed to control his mirth until he had closed the pocket doors behind him.

Richard gave a chuckle, himself, and then he settled down to peruse the papers. He had finished the *London Times* and had just picked up the *Gazette* when he heard a scratching upon the garden door.

"Ah ha! The renegade returns!" Richard jumped up to open the door. "If you do not tell me where you have been, it will go badly for you."

Felix stared up at Richard with unblinking yellow eyes, not in the least intimidated. Then he turned to glance at the garden door, which was still open wide.

"Yes, indeed. It is quite chilly outside and I shall close it." Richard returned to the door and shut it securely. "And now you must give up your secret, Felix. I wish to know where you have been."

Felix walked a bit closer to the fire that had been lighted in the grate. He shook his massive orange head and Richard noticed a strip of red cloth hanging out of the corner of his mouth.

"What have you there, boy?" Richard reached down to scoop up his sister's pet. He gazed at the object in Felix's mouth and raised his brows. "Someone seems to have given you a toy shaped like a mouse. Have you found a new friend?"

Felix purred happily for a moment, butting his head against Richard's chest. Richard scratched him beneath the chin and then he smiled as a familiar scent wafted up from his fur.

"Attar of roses?" Richard raised his brows. "I begin to understand why you are so reluctant to divulge your whereabouts. You are involved with a lady, are you not?"

Felix's purrs grew into a loud rumble of confirmation and Richard laughed aloud. A lady who favored attar of roses had come into close and recent contact with his sister's cat. No doubt this same lady had given him the toy, and it was quite apparent that Felix had gained an admirer.

"Who is she, boy?" Richard found himself curious as to the identity of Felix's newest acquaintance. Since Alicia had moved here quite recently, she had not yet met any of her neighbors and it would be good for her to have a friend nearby. "Does this lady live in one of the surrounding houses?"

Felix stopped purring abruptly and glanced at the clock atop the mantelpiece. He cocked his head, staring at it for a long moment, and then he wiggled from Richard's arms. Placing his toy carefully down on the hearth, he headed straight for the door to the hall. When he reached it, he gave a demanding yowl that caused Richard's brows to shoot upward in surprise.

"I do not believe that you can tell the time, Felix." Richard shook his head in disbelief. "Alicia mentioned that you are a particularly intelligent cat, but surely this feat is impossible!"

Felix yowled again, raising one paw to scratch at the door. Then he turned back to Richard almost as if he were asking why Richard did not come to open it for him.

Richard laughed. "You have outsmarted yourself this time, boy. If you are intelligent enough to tell the time, you should be able to contrive some way of opening a door by yourself."

Felix gave him what appeared to be a disdainful glance and then he turned his attentions to the door once again. After a long moment of staring at the wooden surface, he stuck out his paw and scratched at the bottom edge of the door. The well-oiled panel slid open slightly and Felix turned to rub against it with the side of his body. This created even more of an opening, wide enough to accommodate his body, and Felix pushed through to pad down the hall in the direction of the kitchens.

Richard stared after his sister's pet in shock. If Felix could open a door, it was little wonder that Alicia's staff had experienced so much difficulty in confining him. This caused Richard to wonder what other miraculous tricks Felix could accomplish. Though he was not well acquainted with cats and their habits, Richard doubted that many could tell the time and open doors for themselves.

There was a smile on Richard's face as he bent down to retrieve Felix's toy to examine it more closely. It was a charming little creation of bright blue satin, shaped like a mouse and stuffed with cloth. The stitches were even, and it had obviously taken some time to complete. The ears were fashioned from folded bits of red satin and the long red tail was of the same material, braided from three long strips. The features were drawn directly on the material, and the creator of this whimsical creature had given it a pair of laughing eyes and a mouth that was set in a devil-may-care smile.

As Richard held the clever toy, his curiosity about its creator grew. She was obviously a woman. In addition to the delightful scent that had clung to Felix's fur, the mouse, itself, had a hint of sweetness about it. She was also young, for the toy had been fashioned of brightly colored satin, a popular fabric for ball gowns. The very fact that the gown was of such a bright hue eliminated the possibility that it had been intended for a dowager or a widow.

Richard grinned. He knew one more fact about this young lady, one that pleased him greatly. She possessed an admirable sense of humor. The features on the face of the mouse were comical, and a young lady who lacked humor should never have thought to draw them.

Felix's friend was also kind and generous, as she had given Felix the mouse in the first place. And she must be clever as well, for the toy was ingenious.

A smile spread across Richard's face. He should like to make this young lady's acquaintance, for she seemed to possess all the attributes he sought in a wife. Hobbs had stated that Felix disappeared for an hour every afternoon, presumably to visit this admirable young lady, and Richard resolved to follow him on the very next day.

Once he had returned the toy to the hearth, where Felix should find it when he returned, Richard cautioned himself not to count too heavily on the outcome of this endeavor. It was possible that he should be disappointed. He was not a detective and some of the assumptions he had made could very well be erroneous. But Richard was grinning as he turned away, imagining Alicia's delight if he should meet his perfect match through the auspices of her cat!

CHAPTER THREE

Maggie had awakened to leaden skies that threatened yet another bout of chill winter weather. She had dressed in a cheerful gown that was patterned with blue and yellow violets in an effort to stave off her depression, but before she had taken a sip of her morning chocolate, the fog had begun to gather in a dense cloud that quickly obscured the view beyond the windowpanes.

Her morning ritual had been no different from those of other mornings. Maggie had descended to the breakfast room, taken her chocolate and a bit of toast, and adjourned to the library. There she had greeted Felicity and the kittens, and proceeded to read the newspapers.

Luncheon, an excellent shepherd's pie that Cook had made especially for her, had been most satisfying. After sending her compliments to the kitchen, Maggie had retired to the library again, to occupy the afternoon hours with several volumes from the shelves. She was reclining on her favorite leather-covered chaise longue, deeply involved in one of John Howard's treatises on prison reform, when Aunt Lenora's youngest footman came in with the tea tray.

As the footman placed the tray on a table, Maggie glanced over at her uncle's standing clock. It was half past one and a smile spread across her face. It was almost time for Papa's daily visit.

"This came for you in the post, miss." The footman presented Maggie with a letter. "Mr. Spencer instructed me to bring it to you immediately."

As Maggie glanced down at the letter and recognized her aunt's familiar hand, her heartbeat quickened in excitement. Perhaps Aunt Lenora had written to say that her friend had recovered and that she was returning to Town.

Almost afraid to open the letter for fear that her hopes should be dashed, Maggie dismissed the footman and stared at the envelope for a moment. Then she took a deep breath, drew out the letter, and unfolded the single sheet of velum.

Long moments passed as Maggie attempted to decipher her aunt's words. They had been written in haste and the lines were crossed in a most untidy manner. It seemed that Aunt Lenora's dear friend had taken a turn for the worse on the day that she had arrived and a physician had been summoned. At this writing, her friend was improving, but recovery would be slow and tedious. The physician had warned Aunt Lenora not to anticipate a full return to health for at least six weeks. Aunt Lenora apologized profusely for leaving Maggie alone for so long, but she had promised her dear friend that she should remain at her bedside until such time as she was well again.

Maggie glanced at the date on the letter and her spirits plummeted. It had been written only two days ago. She could not expect Aunt Lenora's return until the beginning of March, at the earliest. This meant that Maggie should have to endure another month and a half of solitude, a prospect that was daunting in the extreme!

As Maggie stared down at the letter, the standing clock began to strike the hour. Almost immediately, there was a scratching at the garden door and Maggie's frown quickly turned to a smile as she rose from her seat to open it. Papa was here, and she was very grateful for his company upon this particular afternoon.

"Alone again, Papa?" Maggie stepped aside so that the huge orange cat could enter the library. "I begin to suspect that you do not know any suitable companions for me."

Papa looked up at her and gave a short yowl. And then he closed one eye in a decided wink.

"You are telling me that you do?" Maggie giggled at his comical expression. "Then you must fetch him straightaway, Papa, before I grow so old that I can no longer appreciate an intelligent conversation."

Papa's eyes twinkled as if he had a delicious secret, and this caused Maggie to burst into laughter. Without Felicity, Papa, and their darling kittens, she should have had a most dismal day, indeed.

Richard shielded his eyes from the swirling fog with one gloved hand and stared at the spot where Felix had disappeared. For such a large cat, Felix was amazingly agile. He had leapt over the garden wall with no regard for the slippery moisture that clung to its surface.

His friends would think him insane for venturing out on such an inclement afternoon. Richard grinned and adjusted his scarf so that the chill air should not creep under the collar of his greatcoat. Felix had led him on a merry chase thus far, leaping over three successive sets of garden walls. Richard had followed him from house to house, remaining on the street and peering through the fog to catch glimpses of his sister's orange cat as he crossed from one wall to the next. Felix had begun with the house next door, jumping over its wall to the garden. He had darted around to the back of the dwelling and emerged once again to jump the far wall into the next garden.

Richard stamped his feet to warm them and hurried past the house whose garden Felix had just entered. He was grateful that Alicia had not chosen a gray cat, for it should have been impossible to follow a cat of that color in the dense clouds of fog. Despite the poor visibility, Felix was quite easy to spot. His orange coat contrasted well with the thick, grayish brown haze that surrounded him.

Though Richard stared at the far wall of the third house for a minute or two, Felix did not reappear. He watched for another few moments and then he began to smile. This was it. Felix had undoubtedly gained entry. Now it was up to him to do the same.

With a most resolute expression upon his face, Richard walked up to the front door and employed the knocker. He had already decided upon what tactic he must use to explain his presence. When the door was answered, he went into his prepared speech.

"I am sorry for the intrusion, but I fear this is an emergency. I am Lord Larchmont. My sister's residence is but four doors from here and she is depending upon me to take care of her cat while she travels the Continent with her husband. A few moments past, he ran off and I followed him here, to this very garden. I have come to retrieve him if any in your household has been kind enough to allow him entrance."

"Would this be a large orange cat, my lord?" A flicker of a smile crossed the butler's face.

"Yes. My sister prizes him above all things and she should be quite inconsolable if any harm were to come to him."

The butler's smile widened perceptively. "I assure you that your sister's cat is quite unharmed. Please follow me and I shall show you to the library. You will find him there."

Richard allowed a footman to divest him of his outer clothing and then he followed the butler down the hall. The man knocked once upon the pocket doors, and then opened them to a massive room whose walls were completely lined with books of all sizes and shapes.

"What an impressive library!" Richard was not aware that he had spoken aloud, until he heard a delighted chuckle from across the room. He turned to the source of the charming sound and his eyes widened in appreciation as a tall, slender lady rose to her feet to greet him.

"Miss Pendleton, may I present Lord Larchmont?" The

butler performed the introductions. "It seems his sister's cat has gone missing while in his care."

"Miss Pendleton." Richard nodded, his senses reeling. The lady was quite attractive and she was obviously unmarried as her butler had introduced her as a miss. "Please pardon my intrusion, but my sister is inordinately fond of her cat. I should be in the deepest of waters imaginable if he is still missing when she returns from her travels."

"No doubt you should be, for he is a most extraordinary creature." Miss Pendleton smiled, her eyes twinkling. "You must set your mind at ease, Lord Larchmont. Papa merely dropped by to visit his family, as he does every afternoon at this time."

"Papa?" Richard raised his brows.

"Yes, indeed." Miss Pendleton's smile was as bright and golden as the ribbons that trimmed her most attractive gown. "I had no way of knowing his name, you see, and Papa seemed appropriate, given the circumstances."

"The circumstances?" Richard's brows shot up again. "Which circumstances would those be, Miss Pendleton?"

Miss Pendleton laughed again, a charming sound with no artifice. "He *is* a papa, six times over. Do have a look in that wicker basket by the hearth and you shall see for yourself."

Richard walked quickly to the basket and stood staring down in utter shock. There were six small kittens inside, curled together in the center of the basket and fast asleep. One little ball of fur looked exactly like Felix in miniature, proving that he was indeed, the father of this brood.

"I apologize, madame. I had no idea that my sister's cat should . . . should . . . be so irresponsible as to . . ." Richard stopped, not knowing quite what to say. How did one tender an apology for a cat?

Miss Pendleton giggled at his obvious embarrassment and crossed the room to his side. "There is no need to apologize, Lord Larchmont. These things do happen, even in the best of families, and creatures of the feline persuasion are not required to follow the same conventions as we do."

"I am aware of that, Miss Pendleton, but . . ." Richard stopped in midsentence once again as the humor of the situation struck him. He laughed long and hard and then he turned to face the charming lady at his side. "I am not certain what my sister's responsibilities should be in this situation. It seems most unfair to expect you, as the mother cat's owner, to shoulder the entire burden for the welfare of these kittens."

"I am not the mother cat's owner, Lord Larchmont," Miss Pendleton corrected him. "Felicity is my aunt's cat. I am merely seeing to her care in my aunt's absence."

"Why, that is even more unfair! Perhaps the father of these kittens, or rather, the *owner* of these kittens' father, should settle a small monthly stipend . . ."

"Oh, this is absurd!" Miss Pendleton collapsed into rollicking laughter. "Truly it is not necessary, Lord Larchmont. Felicity is perfectly capable of taking care of her kittens without our assistance, and there is no cost involved at this time. It is not as if they need clothing or shoes, you know."

Richard broke into laughter once again at the thought of a kitten dressed in breeches and boots. "Yes, but there is still a certain responsibility, I should think. My sister shall be delighted, of course. She adores kittens. But six of them seem quite a few for you to take on alone, Miss Pendleton."

"They are, indeed." Miss Pendleton nodded. "But they are a welcome diversion, and Felicity has them well in hand. Let us go on this way until your sister and my aunt return, and then we shall see."

Richard nodded his agreement. "That seems the best course, I suppose. But I do not see my sister's cat or the mother of these charming kittens. Where are they, Miss Pendleton?"

"Taking their tea." Miss Pendleton smiled. "Come with me and I shall show you."

Richard followed her to an alcove and a grin spread over his face as he caught sight of Felix and a beautiful gray tabby lapping liquid from two china bowls. Turning to her, his eyes twinkling, Richard asked the obvious question. *"Tea,* Miss Pendleton?"

"Warm milk. I am the only one who truly takes tea. Should you care to join me?"

"I should be most grateful." Richard nodded quickly. He was enjoying this brief visit with Miss Pendleton and found that he did not wish it to end. She intrigued him much more than any other young ladies of the ton. "I have been following my sister's cat for quite some time now. He leapt over three sets of garden walls before he arrived at your aunt's home."

Miss Pendleton broke into laughter again. "And you say that you *followed* him, Lord Larchmont?"

"Not over the walls, no." Richard chuckled. "I simply stood on the street and watched for him to mount the next wall. When he did not appear on your far wall, I assumed that your aunt's home was his destination."

Once they were seated and enjoying an excellent cup of tea, Miss Pendleton turned to him again. "What is Papa's real name, Lord Larchmont? I have been most curious about it."

"His name is Felix."

Miss Pendleton nodded. "Your sister named him after the Latin *felis domesticus?"*

"I sincerely doubt that! My sister is quite intelligent, but she knows nothing of Latin. I am certain that the name originated with my brother-in-law, as Alicia should assume that *felis domesticus* was some type of decoration for the home."

Miss Pendleton laughed at his quip, but she quickly sobered. "Perhaps you do your sister a disservice, sir. Since Latin is at the root of our language, it is possible to become familiar with many of its words without being aware that one is utilizing that ancient tongue."

"Quite so." Richard smiled in delight. Miss Pendleton was not just another attractive young miss. She was knowledgeable as well. "But Latin is not the sole language we English have purloined."

Miss Pendleton laughed. "No, indeed. Why, hardly a

moment of the day passes that I do not borrow heavily from foreign origins."

Richard gave her a challenging smile. "Do go on, Miss Pendleton."

"I commence this borrowing when I *wake,* which has its origin in Old Norse. I *wash,* a word derived from the Dutch, and *dress,* which is Anglo-French. Then I break my *fast,* a word of German extraction, with a hot *beverage,* which is another Anglo-French word, and peruse the *newspaper,* which is a joining of the Middle English *newis* and the Latin *papyrus.* You see, Lord Larchmont? I have used words from six different languages already!"

"I beg to differ, Miss Pendleton." Richard grinned at her. "You spoke of a hot beverage. Was it tea, or chocolate, or coffee?"

Miss Pendleton laughed with great appreciation. "Very clever, sir! I should gain one additional language regardless of which beverage I choose. Tea should be Chinese, chocolate should be Spanish, and coffee should be Arabic."

"You are very nearly correct, Miss Pendleton." Richard grinned at her. "But it is obvious that you have not studied Italian. Coffee is an Italian word."

"It is, sir. The Italian word is *caffè.* But the Italians merely borrowed this word from a much older language."

Richard shook his head. "I do not believe you are correct, Miss Pendleton."

"But I *am,* sir. It descended from the Turkish word *kahve,* which came from the Arabic word *qahwah.*"

"Are you certain, Miss Pendleton?" Richard raised his brows.

"Very certain. I found that word of particular interest as I am exceedingly fond of coffee."

Richard shrugged. "Then I bow to your expertise, Miss Pendleton, and I shall consider myself corrected. Tell me how you come to know so much about languages."

"It is my father's influence." Miss Pendleton gave a tinkling laugh. "He is a scholar of ancient tongues, which is not an unusual diversion for a vicar, but I fear he knows nothing of raising a daughter. My mother died when I was quite young, you see, and my father gave me leave to pursue any subject that claimed my interest. By the time the ladies of the church realized that I was not being properly trained as a young lady, it was too late to correct the situation."

"Then you do not sketch, or sing, or play the piano-forte?"

Miss Pendleton seemed rather surprised at his question. "Why, yes, Lord Larchmont. I do those things as well. But my father taught me to think for myself and it is far too late to correct that."

"Then you hold strong opinions on various subjects?" Richard's eyes began to twinkle. Miss Pendleton was intriguing, to say the least.

"I do. And I do not suffer fools gladly. Why, right before I took leave of my stepmama, she warned me that . . ."

"What is it, Miss Pendleton?" Richard leaned forward in alarm as she suddenly stopped speaking and clamped a hand to her mouth.

"Oh, dear! As a gentleman, Lord Larchmont, I must ask you not to mention what we have discussed here today."

Richard stared at her in some confusion. "Of course, Miss Pendleton. I give you my word on it. But I can think of nothing improper that we have discussed."

"The words themselves have not been improper, but I fear I cannot say the same for my behavior." Miss Pendleton sighed deeply. "You see, Lord Larchmont, I have done precisely what my stepmama told me not to do!"

Richard lifted his brows. "And what, exactly, is that?"

"She warned me that I must listen to what a gentleman has to say and agree with him completely, even if he is incorrect. And I have argued with you, sir. I should have held my tongue and not corrected your erroneous impression of the word *coffee.*"

"I see." Richard bit back a grin. It was true that Miss Pendleton had corrected him, but he had thought little of it at the time.

"You are the very first London gentleman of my acquaintance and I've argued with you on our first meeting." Miss Pendleton sighed again. "My stepmama had the right of it. I am thoroughly hopeless at conversing with a gentleman. But . . . but you *were* wrong and I . . . I *was* correct!"

Richard fought to keep his laughter under control, but it was of little use. He chuckled a bit at first and then he began to chortle. This gave way to a guffaw of laughter that threatened to bring down the ceiling. Miss Pendleton joined in, her giggles of mirth turning into a full gale of riotous laughter until they both were left holding their sides and gasping weakly for breath.

"Are you angry with me for correcting you?" Miss Pendleton took the square of clean linen he handed to her and dabbed at her eyes.

"Not in the least." Richard shook his head. "I find you utterly charming and most erudite."

"Thank you. But my stepmama warned me that most gentlemen should not appreciate conversing with a bluestocking."

Richard nodded. "There is truth in that. But I am not like most gentlemen, Miss Pendleton. If something I say is incorrect, I wish to know about it so that I shall not make the same mistake twice."

"My sentiments exactly!" Miss Pendleton gave him a happy smile. "But my proclivity for having the last word will not sit well with other gentlemen, will it?"

Richard winced, but he knew he must be truthful. "No, Miss Pendleton, it will not. Your stepmama is quite right on that score."

"Oh, I shall never get it right!" Miss Pendleton sighed again. "I have been thoroughly spoiled by conversing with none but Felix and Felicity since I arrived in London. They accept my word on all matters, you see, and I am able to expound on my theories without fear of being contradicted."

Richard laughed. "Then you must practice your polite converse with me. Shall we pretend that I am an ordinary gentleman who has but recently made your acquaintance?"

Miss Pendleton raised her brows in surprise, but then

she nodded. "Yes, please. That should be most helpful to me."

"Let us proceed then. I shall say, *coffee* is an Italian word. And you shall say . . . ?"

"Do tell, Lord Larchmont." Miss Pendleton widened her eyes quite convincingly. "I had no idea that *coffee* was Italian. I am most grateful to you for enlightening me from your vast store of wisdom. I am but a poor female, after all, and I do not have the benefit of your fine education. Alas, all I am able to accomplish is to arrange a few flowers in a vase, sketch inane subjects quite prettily, and accompany myself whilst I sing several charming selections on the pianoforte for you."

Richard nodded, his eyes twinkling. "That is quite acceptable, Miss Pendleton. I am convinced that you have all the requirements to make a superb match. Will you demand a noble title?"

"Most certainly. I should prefer to marry into the royal family, but their numbers are few and I fear I shall not have the opportunity. I have therefore resigned myself to accepting the position of baroness, if the baron is handsome enough."

"Am I handsome enough for you, madame?" Richard could not keep the teasing note from his voice. He had not told the butler his title and there was no possible way that Miss Pendleton could have learned it.

"Indeed, sir, you are most pleasing in appearance. But alas, you are not a baron. I fear I could not settle for anything lower, you see."

"But my ranking is higher than baron."

"It is?" Miss Pendleton's perfectly shaped lips rounded in surprise. "Then you are a viscount, sir?"

Richard shook his head. "No, dear Miss Pendleton. My ranking is higher than a viscount."

"An earl?" Miss Pendleton's brows shot up.

"No, indeed. I am a marquis, and I am also far richer than Golden Ball."

"You do not play fair, sir!" Miss Pendleton burst into laugher, her eyes twinkling. "You did not mention that you were pretending to be a marquis. Now I shall have to change my game, for I should never have occasion to meet a marquis in my aunt's circles."

"And why is that, Miss Pendleton?"

"I am not to be formally presented. I shall meet my aunt's friends, of course, but I sincerely doubt that any among them shall rank that highly."

"But you have met me, and I *am* a marquis." Richard's grin grew wider.

There was a moment of indecision as she stared into his eyes. Then she laughed, and color flooded her cheeks. "You are pretending!"

"I am?" Richard grinned. He had not felt this light-hearted since he had become a marquis.

"Of course you are." She nodded quickly, her eyes twinkling. "You could not possibly be a real marquis."

"And why is that, Miss Pendleton?"

"Because a marquis should be haughty and impressed with himself. And you seem so . . . so normal!"

"I am anything but normal, according to my mother and my sister." Richard laughed a trifle ruefully. "I beg you to ignore the differences in our stations and think of me only as a friend. I should like to have one friend in London with whom I can be myself. Will you be my friend, Miss Pendleton?"

Miss Pendleton considered it carefully and then she nodded. "Yes, we are friends, most truly. I feel as if I have known you for a very long time."

"And we shall tell each other our secrets?" Richard prompted.

"Perhaps." Miss Pendleton laughed. "I have already told you that I am a bluestocking, so now it is your turn."

"Then I shall think of a secret to tell you." There was a yowl from the far corner of the room and Richard saw that Felix was pawing at the garden door. His tail was flicking impatiently and Richard grinned. "I must take my leave now, Miss Pendleton. Felix appears anxious to return home. Weather permitting, should you care to join me for a ride through the park tomorrow afternoon?"

"Oh, yes! I should adore it!" Miss Pendleton's eyes began to shine with excitement. "I have been confined to this house since my aunt was called away and there is so much of London that I wish to see. But . . . should it be proper, Lord Larchmont, when we have not been formally introduced?"

Richard considered it carefully and then he shook his head. "No, Miss Pendleton, it should not. Though we have a feline family in common, that will not be enough to satisfy the tabbies of the ton. If I can arrange a proper introduction before this time tomorrow, will you accept my invitation?"

"Indeed, I shall!" Miss Pendleton nodded quickly.

"Very well then. You may expect me to call upon you tomorrow, Miss Pendleton."

Miss Pendleton rose from her chair to ring for the butler and Richard was again struck by her elegant figure. She was almost as tall as he was and yet she was strikingly feminine. "Until tomorrow, Lord Larchmont."

She extended her hand and Richard took it quite formally. "If we are to be friends, you must call me Richard."

"Richard." She nodded. "And you must call me Margaret . . . or Maggie, if you prefer. My friends call me Maggie."

"Maggie it is then." Richard repeated her name with a smile. He raised her hand to his lips and smiled at her, holding it just a bit longer than was necessary.

Several minutes later, garbed once again in his greatcoat with Felix tucked securely in his arms, Richard arrived at his sister's house. He tossed his coat to Hobbs and carried his sister's cat to the library.

"You have triumphed, old boy." Richard grinned as he set the huge cat down on the carpet. "Whether by accident or design, you have found the one young lady in London who I am most eager to see again. And to make this even more enjoyable, she doesn't even believe that I am a marquis!"

CHAPTER FOUR

Maggie gazed down at the card that Spencer had presented to her and began to frown. The corner was turned down, quite properly, to signify that her visitor had arrived in person. "Are you certain that the baroness has come to call upon me?"

"Yes, miss." Spencer nodded gravely. "When I advised her of your aunt's absence, she informed me that you were the person she had come to see."

Maggie frowned, uncertain of the protocol in such a situation. "Is it proper for me to receive her, Spencer?"

"Yes, miss. Indeed, it should be most improper if you failed to do so. I should suggest that you entertain them in the gold drawing room."

"Them?" Maggie eyes widened as Spencer nodded. "How many are there, Spencer?"

"Just two, Miss. Lady Pierce and Lord Larchmont. If you will recall, he is the gentleman who came to collect his sister's cat."

"Oh, yes." Though Maggie struggled to maintain her outward composure, a delighted smile spread across her face. Richard was here and he had brought Lady Pierce to introduce them properly. "Thank you, Spencer. Will you please order the tea tray?"

Spencer nodded and then he stepped a bit closer. "Perhaps it is not my place to mention this, but Lady Pierce is known for speaking whatever enters her mind. Your aunt finds this quality delightfully amusing, but it can be quite disconcerting for the uninitiated."

Maggie thanked him for warning her and hurried down the hall to the gold drawing room. She was delighted to see that a fire had been laid in the grate and that the chamber appeared both cozy and commodious. She took a seat on one of the chairs that were arranged in a grouping near the fire and clasped her hands tightly on her lap to keep them from trembling. She had dressed in her best gown this morning, a deep rose muslin trimmed with Belgian lace, as Richard had promised to call.

There were sounds of footsteps in the hall and Maggie rose to her feet. A moment later, Spencer opened the door and announced the baroness and Lord Larchmont.

"My dear girl! What a treat this is!"

Maggie tried not to stare as an imposing woman, dressed in a flowing purple gown with a turban of the same material, sailed into the room. There was a wide and genuine smile on her face and Maggie could not keep from smiling back.

"Your dear aunt has told me all about you and I feel as if I know you already. What a pity Lenora had to be called away on the very day of your arrival! If I had known of your unfortunate situation, I should have come to your side straight away. I have been told that you have been languishing here for a fortnight without anyone to amuse you, and that is simply unfathomable!"

Maggie's smile grew wider. In addition to saying whatever entered her mind, the baroness also seemed prone to exaggeration. "You are too kind, Lady Pierce. Really, it has not been so dreadful as that."

"But you must have been bored to tears, my dear!" Lady Pierce crossed the distance between them and Maggie quickly found herself the object of a most enthusiastic hug.

"Lenora mentioned that you had the habit of putting the best face on things. But why she did not call upon me to see that you were properly entertained, I shall never know!"

"There really wasn't time, Lady Pierce." Maggie did her best to explain. "Aunt Lenora and I had only a brief moment together before she set off on her journey."

Lady Pierce released Maggie with a smile and took an adjoining chair. "It is of no matter, my dearest girl, for we shall correct this unfortunate situation immediately."

Richard cleared his throat rather loudly and Lady Pierce turned in his direction. He was standing by the fireplace, his arm draped casually over the mantel and regarding her with some amusement.

Lady Pierce gave an exasperated wave in his direction. "Yes, yes, dear boy, but you are far too impatient. The amenities must be observed, you know."

"You have done that, Aunt." Richard glanced pointedly at Maggie.

"I have, indeed, and rather well if I do not say so myself." Lady Pierce smiled as she nodded. "I shall introduce you now, Richard. Miss Pendleton, may I present my dear nephew, Lord Larchmont?"

"I am delighted to make your acquaintance, Lord Larchmont." Maggie dipped her head to acknowledge him, the color rising to stain her cheeks.

"What a pleasure to meet you at last, Miss Pendleton." Richard dipped his head in return and a smile tugged at the corners of his lips. "I have been desirous of making your acquaintance for an inordinately long period of time."

Lady Pierce frowned at him sharply. "Really, Richard! You know full well that you met her only yesterday, and in a most improper manner at that! There is no need to attempt to wrap it up in clean linen for me. Now say something nice about Miss Pendleton's appearance or I shall box your ears for you."

"Yes, Aunt Eustace." Richard grinned at Maggie and closed one eye in an almost imperceptible wink. "Your gown is most charming, Miss Pendleton. So clever of you to choose a hue that precisely matches your complexion."

Lady Pierce sighed and gave Maggie an apologetic glance. "You must not mind Richard's jokes, dear. It was inheriting at such a young age, no doubt. Swelled his head, made him think he did not have to learn his manners. And the young ladies only served to give him an exaggerated sense of his own worth. You have no idea how many mamas wished for their daughters to become his marchioness!"

Maggie nodded quickly, doing her utmost to hide her shock. Richard had told her the truth in their game. He *was* a marquis!

"Of course their ploys did not succeed, for Richard saw through them all. What was the name of that fair-haired young miss who tried to hide in your carriage, Richard?"

"I believe that would have been Miss Mapleby, Aunt. But I see no . . ."

"Cecelia Mapleby." Lady Pierce interrupted him. "She chose the wrong carriage and spent the night in the Larchmont stables. Caught a dreadful chill and had to forgo several lovely parties."

Richard began to frown. "Please, Aunt Eustace. I doubt that Miss Pendleton is interested in something that happened so long ago."

"It was only four years past. And the year after that there was the dark-haired termagant who actually possessed the audacity to—"

"Aunt Eustace!" Richard interrupted her with a scowl.

"All right, dear boy, though I am certain that Miss Pendleton should be very interested, indeed." Lady Pierce turned to Maggie. "You *are* interested, are you not?"

Maggie raised her brows and searched for something to say. "It is most interesting, Lady Pierce, but I should rather not hear about it if it causes your nephew distress."

"Nicely said, Miss Pendleton." Lady Pierce favored her with a smile of approval before she turned to Richard. "This one is a lady, Richard, a far cry from those silly debutantes who try to lure you into the garden each year and—''

"Aunt Eustace!" Richard's scowl deepened and Maggie had all she could do not to burst into laughter.

"Never fear, dear boy. I shall hold my tongue. But it only proves how foolish the young debutantes have become. There is not one grain of sense among them, and I . . ." Lady Pierce stopped speaking and turned to Maggie in some alarm. "Oh, dear! *You* are not a young debutante, are you?"

Maggie burst into laughter. "No, Lady Pierce. I am neither young nor a debutante. I am twenty-four, the daughter of a vicar, and have no plans to be presented. I can set your mind at ease on another score, as well, by assuring you that I desire only friendship with your nephew."

"How marvelous, my dear!" Lady Pierce laughed gaily. "The tabbies of the ton shall be at sixes and sevens when they find that someone so unsuitable has managed to captivate Richard. Twenty-four? And the daughter of a vicar? They will be stricken, to say the least! Lenora told me that you were a wit, but I had no idea that you should be quite this charming."

"Thank you, Lady Pierce." Maggie acknowledged the compliment, even though she was not entirely certain that it had been intended as one.

"It is Miss Pendleton's demure manner that captivates me, Aunt." Richard spoke up, his smile completely guileless. "She accepts my superior wisdom without question, though I am certain that she should wish to disagree with me on this point. Is that not correct, Miss Pendleton?"

Maggie opened her mouth to tell him just what she thought of his statement when she realized that he had boxed her quite neatly into a corner. If she agreed, she should be accepting his superior wisdom. And if she disagreed with his assumption that she should disagree, she should actually be agreeing with him. He had placed her in a position where she could not utter a word!

"Really, sir . . . you are . . . you *are* incorrigible!" Maggie sputtered for a moment and then she burst into laughter at the smug expression on Richard's face.

Lady Pierce stared at Maggie for a moment and then she patted her hand again. "Pay him no mind, my dear. Richard is baiting you, and that means he likes you very well, indeed. And now that I have accomplished what my dear nephew has begged of me, I must take my leave."

"Please wait just a moment, Lady Pierce." Maggie glanced at the ormolu clock atop the mantelpiece and noted that it approached the hour of two. "Someone has just arrived and I am certain that you should like to make his acquaintance."

"But your butler has not announced another visitor." Lady Pierce appeared perplexed.

"This particular caller does not arrive in the usual manner." Richard caught Maggie's meaning immediately. "Come with us to the library, Aunt Eustace, and we shall introduce him to you."

Richard glanced over at his passenger as he negotiated the narrow streets and saw that Maggie was smiling with unconcealed delight. "What is it, Maggie? You put me in mind of a starving waif who has just been presented with a whole roasted joint."

"That is precisely how I feel, Richard." Maggie laughed at his comment. "It is so wonderful to be out in the world once again. Oh, do look at the splendid livery that footman is wearing!"

Richard grinned as he spotted the object of Maggie's fascination. The footman in question was dressed in quite ordinary livery, and it was apparent that Maggie had never been a guest in one of the finer homes. He could imagine her awe if she ever set foot in Larchmont Hall, or the elaborate town mansion that he kept here in London for his mother's use. She might even enjoy his ancient castle in the north, which dated back to Norman times. It now sported a hodgepodge of styles, one tacked on after the other, as each former marquis had attempted to render it more commodious.

The edges of the park appeared before them and Richard smiled. "Shall we take a turn around Rotten Row?"

"Rotten Row?" Maggie's expression turned to one of dismay. "But that is where all the fashionable ladies and gentlemen go, is it not?"

"Yes. I thought you might like to observe them."

"I would, but is it wise?" Maggie looked very concerned. "I cannot help but recall your aunt's comment. I am not a suitable companion for you."

Richard sighed, wishing that he had managed to find someone other than his aunt to perform their introduction. Aunt Eustace had not meant to be unkind. Indeed, she should have been quite mortified to realize that she had given Maggie cause to doubt her worth. But his dear aunt did manage to discombobulate all who were not accustomed to her.

"Aunt Eustace has always possessed a tongue that has no connection to her senses." Richard reached out to take Maggie's hand. "You are a perfectly suitable lady for me to escort."

Maggie still appeared doubtful, but she gave him a brave little smile. "If you are certain . . ."

"I am."

"Good." Maggie's smile grew wider and then she gave a most charming giggle. "I *am* the granddaughter of a baron on my father's side and my mother was the third daughter of one as well. No one can find fault with my family. And it is not as if I were a paid employee, like a governess, or a lightskirt, or an opera dancer."

Richard shot her a startled glance. "Lud, Maggie! What do you know of lightskirts and opera dancers?"

"Very little, I fear." Maggie shrugged. "I happened to hear the squire mention them once, in conversation with my father. He seemed concerned that his eldest son had hired several such ladies in London at great expense."

"I see." Richard bit back a grin. "And what, precisely, did you assume they were?"

"I would surmise that a lightskirt is a lady who prefers gowns of thin silk or lace. The squire spoke of entertainments, so perhaps she is some sort of hired hostess for unmarried gentlemen at social events."

Richard chuckled inwardly, all the while attempting to maintain a sober expression. "And an opera dancer?"

"She is most likely a performer upon the stage who is for hire at private gatherings and soirees. Do I have the right of it, Richard?"

Richard could not hold his composure any longer. He chortled and chuckled as he guided his team into the entrance of the park, his shoulders shaking with mirth. When he had managed to contain some of his laughter, he turned to Maggie with a grin. "If I tell you what they truly are, will you promise not to mention them again?"

"Yes, of course I will." Maggie nodded quickly. "What are they, Richard?"

"They are . . . well . . . actually they consist of . . ." Richard stopped, uncertain of how to proceed. Maggie was gazing at him inquiringly and he chuckled again. "I fear there is no way to put this delicately, Maggie."

Maggie nodded again. "That does not signify, Richard. Please continue."

"You must never tell anyone that I explained this to you, Maggie." Richard felt his hands beginning to perspire inside his driving gloves. "Do you promise?"

"Certainly. But I do not understand why you are so reticent. Surely the terms are quite common, for you recognized them immediately."

Richard began to laugh again. "Yes, Maggie. The terms are quite *common,* indeed!"

"Then it is your duty to impart them to me. I expect to meet many of my aunt's acquaintances while I am in London, and some of them may very well be lightskirts or opera dancers."

"Oh, no they will not!" Richard chortled again, fighting to keep an even hand on the reins. "I sincerely doubt that your aunt knows a single lightskirt or opera dancer."

"How do you know? She has friends from all walks of

life. Why, there are artists, and musicians, and poets, and physicians, and scientists, and . . ." Maggie stopped speaking suddenly as the curricle lurched from side to side. "Really, Richard! You cannot possibly drive this fine pair when you are so convulsed with laughter."

Realizing the truth of what she said, Richard slowed the horses and wheeled the curricle far over to the side of the path. When he had stopped them, he gave way to a riot of laughter, tears streaming from his eyes.

"What on earth is the matter with you?" Maggie regarded him with some alarm. "If I have made a joke, Richard, I wish to know what it is."

Richard opened his mouth to attempt to explain, but he could not seem to stop laughing. Maggie watched him for a moment, bristling somewhat, and then she, too, began to giggle.

Several equipages passed them by, their occupants peering with curiosity at the gentleman and lady who were laughing so uproariously. When Richard and Maggie had calmed at last, holding their sides and bursting into only an occasional volley of giggles, Maggie turned to him.

"Will you please explain it now? Truly, Richard . . . I must know what caused you to laugh so."

Richard took a deep breath and looked into her lovely eyes. Strange, but he had not noticed how much they resembled sparkling sapphires before. "I will attempt it, Maggie, but I have never been required to explain these particular terms to an innocent young lady before."

Maggie nodded. "Just proceed, Richard. I am growing older by the second, and I fear I shall expire of advanced years before you see fit to satisfy me."

"*Satisfy you?*" Richard chuckled again, manfully curbing his impulse to shout out with glee. "Oh, Maggie. I haven't laughed this hard in all my life!"

"I am happy to be such a source of amusement for you, Richard, but you must attain some measure of control. How difficult can it be to explain two such terms to me?"

"It is exceedingly difficult." Richard swallowed to

restrain his urge to laugh again. "All right, Maggie, but you must not think ill of me."

"I promise you, I shall not. Perhaps I should ask you a question just to get you started. Do the terms lightskirt and opera dancer possess similar definitions?"

Richard nodded, beginning to chuckle again. "Yes, they do."

"Excellent. And they do involve some manner of position?"

Richard burst into laughter, so long and uproarious that he was forced to gasp for breath. When he could speak again, he nodded. "Yes, Maggie. A *position* is definitely involved."

"Ah ha!" Maggie looked pleased. "From what I overheard, these lightskirts and opera dancers must be well paid for their efforts. Is that not correct?"

Richard nodded quickly. "Some are paid quite handsomely."

"But others are not?"

"That is correct." Richard bit back another volley of laughter.

"Then I must assume that excellence is the key. The more proficient the lightskirt or the opera dancer is at performing her duties, the more she should be paid. Is that also correct?"

Richard nodded, struggling manfully to contain himself. "Yes, Maggie. You are entirely right."

"Let us move on to experience." Maggie leaned closer, entering into the spirit of this questioning. "Is an excellent lightskirt or opera dancer a highly experienced individual?"

Richard chortled, his face turning red. "Oh, yes. She must be highly experienced."

"Does her position require her to work long hours?"

Richard bit the inside of his cheek in an attempt to control his mirth. "On occasion. She is . . . uh . . . expected to be available whenever her . . . her employer has . . . uh . . . need of her services."

"What an odd position this must be! Shall we go on to the tools of her profession?"

"Oh, no!" Richard collapsed into gales of laughter. "Please, Maggie. Let us not discuss that!"

"But we must if you want me to guess, although I do not see why you cannot simply tell me and have done with it. You are doing me a great disservice, Richard. What if someone made me an offer of this particular position? I should want to know all about my duties before choosing whether or not I should accept!"

"Oh, Maggie." Richard groaned with the effort of laughing so hard. "If someone offered you this position, I should immediately plant them a facer. You must believe me when I say that you do not want to become a lightskirt or an opera dancer."

"But why?"

Richard sighed and pulled her close to him. Then he took his flagging courage in hand and whispered the words in her ear.

"Oh, my!" Maggie's face turned a bright shade of pink. She stared at him in shock for several moments and then she did something so unexpected, Richard could scarcely believe his eyes. She started to laugh, clutching at her sides and rocking back and forth in a paroxysm of glee.

"Maggie?" Richard winced as he watched her slight body shake with laughter. Had his most improper revelation driven her round the bend? "Are you quite all right, Maggie?"

His question brought forth another round of laughter so intense that the curricle jounced on its springs. "Y-yes, Richard. I'm . . . I'm perfectly fine!"

It was a full minute before Maggie stopped laughing and Richard reached out to take her hand. "Do you understand now why I did not want to tell you?"

"Yes." Maggie giggled again. "But, Richard . . . I am so very glad you did!"

Richard stared at her closely. She did not appear to be overset, but politeness required that he ask. "Are you angry with me, Maggie?"

"Oh, no! If I am angry with anyone, it is with myself for not guessing the answer. It is no wonder that Squire Younger was worried about his son. And it is also no wonder that his son resisted when the squire demanded that he return home immediately."

"Is it safe for me to assume that you do not aspire to this particular occupation?" The words were out of Richard's mouth before he realized just how inappropriate they were. She had every right to slap him for his impertinence, but Maggie did not seem at all distressed.

"I think not, Richard." Maggie stared at him quite soberly, but the twinkle in her eyes gave her away. "As you know, I am twenty-four years of age and the daughter of a vicar. Unless I were to gain a great amount of experience in a very short time, I fear that I should be quite unqualified for the position."

CHAPTER FIVE

Lady Helen, the reigning Marchioness of Larchmont, lowered her teacup to its saucer with a decided clink and stared at her sister in shock. "Richard asked you to introduce him to a particular young lady?"

"Yes." Eustace nodded quickly. "I am certain it was quite harmless, dear Helen. The young lady appeared most charming to me, but he had met her in dubious circumstances, you see. As a proper gentleman, Richard was required to rectify that situation immediately."

"*What* dubious circumstances?" The marchioness's eyes hardened perceptively.

"The ones under which they initially met, of course. Richard could not just leave it at that, not if he desired to see her again. And he did desire to reacquaint himself with her. That was quite apparent to me."

Helen sighed in exasperation. There were times when she wondered whether her younger sister had been dropped on her head as a babe, for Eustace seemed quite incapable of imparting information in any reasonable sequence. Helen knew that she should succeed in extracting the full tale from her sister in the end, but she should suffer many frustrating moments before that task was accomplished.

"Start at the beginning, dear." Lady Larchmont cautioned herself to patience and reached out to pat her sister's hand. "How did Richard first encounter this young lady?"

"Through Alicia's cat. He got out, you see, and Richard followed him to her home, or rather, to her aunt's home. But that was not a proper introduction so he begged me to do it properly the very next day."

Helen nodded. The tale seemed fairly straightforward thus far, an unusual feat for Eustace. "And you paid a call on this young lady with Richard in tow, to introduce them?"

"Yes, indeed." Eustace beamed. "It was quite proper, Helen, so you needn't be anxious. I am well acquainted with the young lady's aunt."

"And her aunt would be whom?" Helen raised her brows and waited for Eustace to provide an answer.

"Lady Worth, of course. She holds such marvelous soirees. I have heard it said that Parliament could not remain in session without her assistance to several well-known politicians. Do you think she might advise Lord Castleton? Some claim he is rather dim-witted, you know. Or perhaps young Whitmore?"

"I am sure I do not know, Eustace. Let us return to our subject, shall we?"

"Of course. It is just that it is so intriguing to think of a female in a position of such influence. Why, I've even heard tell that Prinny, himself, once had occasion to rely upon dear Lenora's advice. Of course that could not possibly be true, could it, Helen?"

"I have not heard anything of the kind, sister."

"Oh." Eustace frowned slightly. "Then perhaps it was just a rumor. You do remember Lady Worth, do you not, Helen?"

"Indeed I do." Helen nodded, beginning to frown. Lady Lenora Worth had once attended a dinner party at Larchmont House. Not only had she monopolized the conversa-

tion at table quite shamelessly, offering her opinion on
several measures that were being considered in the House
of Lords, she had also informed Helen that the Constable
painting she had recently acquired was a forgery.

"Oh, dear. I completely forgot that you do not care for
Lady Worth." Eustace sighed deeply. "But you must not
be anxious, Helen. Miss Pendleton does not resemble her
aunt in the slightest. She is quite charming and her manners are very pretty, indeed. It is only a pity that she is so
unsuitable for Richard."

Helen's lips tightened. "Unsuitable, Eustace?"

"Yes. She quite freely admitted that she is twenty-four
years of age and has not been presented. I suspect the
reason is financial, as she is the daughter of a country vicar
and his purse cannot be deep. But you must not fret,
Helen, for she desires only friendship with dear Richard.
She told me so herself."

Helen sighed. For someone who had lived in London
for most of her adult life, Eustace was amazingly naïve.
"Then Miss Pendleton does not aspire to attend any ton
affairs with Richard?"

"No, indeed! She knows full well that she can never gain
acceptance in our circles, and she seems quite concerned
about doing the proper thing. Miss Pendleton knows her
place, Helen."

Helen nodded. "Good. I shall make certain that she
remains in it. What is it that Richard finds so attractive
about her?"

"I am not certain. Perhaps it is because she is different
from all the other young ladies who have thrown themselves at his feet. Miss Pendleton does not seem at all
impressed by his title or his wealth, and I suspect that this
is the reason they have formed a friendship. Richard told
me that he merely wishes to show her the sights as this is
her first trip to Town."

"Let us hope that it is her last." Helen frowned deeply.
She was convinced there was more to this friendship than
Eustace had realized. How could any miss, even one so
advanced in years as Miss Pendleton, fail to be impressed

by her son's title and wealth? Richard was a prime catch, and it was inconceivable that Miss Pendleton did not entertain hopes of bringing him up to scratch.

"They do make a most charming couple, Helen." Eustace smiled wistfully. "If you had but seen the manner in which they greeted Felix and Felicia, it would have gladdened your heart. Indeed, they appeared like proud parents, presenting their dear children to me."

Helen's eyes widened in alarm. Richard was quite partial to children. "Does Miss Pendleton have children who are in her care?"

"No, Helen." Eustace shook her head. "I apologize if I gave you the wrong impression. I was merely speaking poetically."

"Then who are Felicia and Felix?"

"Felicia is a lovely gray tabby. And you are acquainted with Felix, Helen. He is Alicia's cat."

"Oh, yes." Helen nodded, remembering the big orange cat that her daughter had acquired. "And both cats were there while you paid your call?"

"Felicia resides there. She is Lady Worth's tabby, and Miss Pendleton has prepared a large wicker basket for her and the kittens in the library."

"Kittens?" Helen raised her brows.

"Oh, my, yes! Six of them and as darling as ever can be. One is the very image of Felix. There can be no doubt about paternity, Helen."

Helen nodded, not caring whether her daughter's cat had sired a litter or not. "Then Richard brought Alicia's cat with him to pay a call upon Miss Pendleton?"

"Oh, no. Felix arrived much later, by way of the garden wall. Miss Pendleton says he comes to pay a call on his new family every day at precisely two o'clock. The sentiment Felix displays for his kittens is really quite captivating, Helen. I felt privileged to observe such devotion."

Helen sighed, out of patience with her sister. Eustace possessed a proclivity for romanticizing the most unlikely things, and this was yet another example of this failing. "Male cats do not have paternal instincts, Eustace. They are animals and, as such, are not capable of enjoying human sensibilities. If my daughter's cat visits Miss Pendleton every afternoon, I would surmise that she entices him with tidbits of some sort."

"Perhaps you are right." Eustace looked quite disappointed with this assessment. "She does give him tea."

Helen's perfectly shaped brows lifted with surprise. "Tea? Cats do not drink tea, Eustace."

"Milk tea, not real tea. Miss Pendleton fills two bowls with warmed milk for both Felicity and Felix."

"Ah ha!" Helen smiled, gratified that she had been proven correct. "That is it, no doubt. Felix comes to drink his bowl of milk, not to enjoy the company of his kittens."

"But he truly does seem quite devoted to them. I watched him, Helen, as he greeted the kittens and spent a bit of time with each one. And there is no doubt that he regards Felicity with great affection."

"That is merely a baser instinct, Eustace." Helen sighed again, her patience rapidly waning. "If male cats did not regard female cats with affection, there should *be* no kittens."

Eustace thought about this for a moment and then the color rose to her cheeks. "You are quite right, Helen."

"Of course I am. Now let us turn our thoughts to Richard. I want you to consider this carefully, Eustace. Does he seem quite taken with Miss Pendleton?"

"Oh, my, yes!" Eustace nodded. "I have never seen him so eager to escort any other young lady before."

Helen's eyes narrowed at her sister's choice of word. *"Escort,* Eustace? You did not mention that before. Just where did my son wish to escort her?"

"He told me he desired to take her for a ride through the park. And he could not do so until they had been properly introduced."

Helen nodded, fearing the worst. She was beginning to suspect that Richard's interest in Miss Pendleton ran far deeper than Eustace had led her to believe. "And did Richard carry her through the park?"

"Yes, indeed. And a lovely time they had, too! Lady

Turner could not wait to tell me that Richard was forced to pull over to the berm on Rotten Row because they were laughing so uproariously. She said that she had never seen Richard enjoy himself so very much before.''

Helen frowned. She had observed her son with scores of young debutantes and the most he had given any of them was a polite smile. "Do you know the cause of his laughter, Eustace?''

"No, but Lady Turner reported that their hilarity was undeniably infectious. Several carriages passed them by, and all who heard them could not help but break into laughter of their own.''

Helen sighed with displeasure. It appeared that her son had made a spectacle of himself with Miss Pendleton and it was her duty to nip this unlikely friendship in the bud. "You say that Miss Pendleton is aware that she is not a suitable match for my son?''

"I do believe she is. As I mentioned before, Miss Pendleton is fully aware of her situation.''

"Good. Come closer, Eustace, so that none shall hear us. I have a plan to make certain that Miss Pendleton does not aspire to more than friendship with my son.'' As Helen whispered the plan to Eustace, she noted that her sister's eyes widened perceptively. When she had finished, she leaned back and regarded her with a smile. "What think you, Sister?''

Eustace sighed and then she nodded. "Your plan will succeed, Helen. I cannot imagine that Miss Pendleton would stand in Richard's way if she truly thought that he was truly enamored of another.''

"What is it, Eustace?'' Helen noticed the tears that were threatening to overflow her sister's eyes.

"Nothing to signify, I am sure.'' Eustace gave a forlorn sigh. "It is silly of me, I know, but it is just that Richard and Miss Pendleton are so happy together. And I cannot help but think that they should have made such a lovely match.''

CHAPTER SIX

"Hello, Felix. You must be chilled to the bone." Maggie closed the garden door behind the huge orange cat and scooped him up in her arms. Then she turned to Richard with a frown. "Why did you not bring him with you? You could have carried him under your coat."

Richard laughed. "He's not cold, Maggie, and he has no need of my coat. He has his own and I'd wager to say it's far warmer than mine."

"Just so!" Maggie conceded the point with a smile. "I had forgotten that Felix is wearing his own fur coat. But what is this? Someone has hung a small box on a ribbon around his neck."

"They have?"

Richard's expression was perfectly guileless, but Maggie noticed the glint of mischief in his eyes. "Why did you tie this box around his neck, Richard? There is no use in denying it, for I see your fine hand in this."

"Perhaps you should open the box, Maggie. It is obviously intended for you."

Maggie laughed in delight as she slipped the pink ribbon from Felix's neck and retrieved the small box. It was wrapped in a square of pale-pink paper with her name inscribed on the top. "You should not have given me a gift, Richard. I am not certain that it is proper for me to accept it."

"But I did not give you a gift, Maggie. It is clearly from Felix. All I did was wrap it for him."

"Of course." Maggie giggled. "It should have been nearly impossible for him to tie the ribbon into a bow."

Richard nodded solemnly. "The paper also presented a problem. Felix shredded it quite thoroughly on his first two attempts and was forced to beg for my assistance. I believe he has come to a new appreciation of opposable thumbs."

"No doubt he has." Maggie loosened the pink paper and lifted the lid of the small box. What she saw inside made her gasp in shock.

"Felix would like to know whether or not you approve of his choice. He informed me that he spent hours debating the wisdom of blue eyes versus green."

Maggie was so surprised, she could not speak as he drew out the small brooch that nestled inside the box. It was fashioned of gold and shaped like a cat viewed from the side. Its back was curved up in a graceful arch and one large eye sparkled with a gleam of blue light. "It is the loveliest brooch I have ever seen! And the most clever! Is this a . . . a sapphire?"

"I do believe it is. Felix told me that it put him in mind of your lovely blue eyes."

"Oh, Richard!" Maggie was so delighted by this thoughtful gift, she did not stop to think. She acted on impulse, throwing her arms round his neck and kissing him soundly on the cheek. "It is so beautiful! I shall adore it above all things! But is it right to accept such an expensive gift from you?"

Richard grinned, reaching up to touch his cheek where her lips had caressed it. "It is entirely appropriate, Maggie. This gift is from Felix, not from me, and he shall be quite heartbroken if you do not accept it."

"Then I will." Maggie nodded quickly, a delighted smile

spreading across her face. "But you must swear that Felix gave me this gift."

"You do not need to take my word on the subject. We shall quiz Felix about it." Richard snapped his fingers and Felix looked up from his position by Felicity and the kittens. "Would you come here for a moment, boy? Maggie has a question for you. You must keep in mind that she cannot accept this brooch unless you confirm that you have given it to her."

Maggie watched as Felix crossed the room to stand before her. He looked up at her expectantly and she giggled as she reached down to pet him. "You understand every word that Richard spoke, do you not, Felix?"

Felix opened his mouth and yowled. Then he closed it again and waited for her to speak again.

"Very good." Maggie grinned as she held up the lovely golden cat for him to see. "Did Richard give me this lovely brooch?"

Felix opened his mouth, as if to acknowledge her question. Then he closed it again without making a sound.

"I see." Maggie nodded. "Did *you* give me this lovely brooch, Felix?"

Felix opened his mouth, just as he had before, but this time he yowled long and hard. Then he moved forward to rub up against Maggie's legs in an obvious show of affection.

"Thank you, Felix." Maggie patted her chair and Felix leapt gracefully up on her lap. She nuzzled his soft orange fur and gave him several kisses on the top of his head. "I shall think of you with fondness each time that I wear it and I shall wear it often. You may go now, Felix. I know that you are anxious to return to Felicity and your kittens."

Felix purred, reaching out with his rough tongue to lick Maggie's hand. Then he leapt back to the floor and returned to the basket.

"Perhaps I have lost my senses, but I am convinced he knew exactly what I was saying." Maggie turned to Richard with wonder in her eyes.

"He did." Richard nodded. "I have come to agree with

my sister completely on that score. Felix is not just an ordinary cat."

"Do you sometimes suspect that he is actually quite *extraordinary*?" Maggie stopped, the color rising to her cheeks. She did not want Richard to think that she had lost her senses.

"That thought has entered my mind quite frequently of late." Richard reached out to take Maggie's hand. "I confided to him that I had not met any young ladies who intrigued me in London. And the very next day, he led me to you. You do intrigue me, Maggie. I have not laughed so much, or had so much fun in years. Felix has done me a great service."

Maggie dropped her eyes, the color remaining high on her cheeks. "He has also done a service for me. I mentioned to Felix that I longed for a friend in London. I even asked him to bring me a fascinating gentleman caller. And then he brought you."

"That is quite true. He did." Richard slipped his arm round her shoulders. "And just look at how well it turned out."

Maggie's color rose even higher as she nestled against his side. His nearness made her feel heady and she cautioned herself not to seek hidden meaning in his friendly embrace. "We have become fine friends, have we not, Richard?"

"The finest." Richard dropped a light kiss on the top of her head.

They spoke of other things then, and the time passed quite rapidly. When the clock approached the hour of three, Felix let his wishes be known and Richard stood up to take his leave.

"I had planned to invite you to Vauxhall Gardens this evening, but my mother has sent for me to attend her. As much as I should prefer to spend the evening with you, I cannot send my excuses."

"Of course not." Maggie nodded in perfect understanding. A mother's summons was not to be ignored.

"I am free tomorrow evening. Should you care to join me then to attend the concert and view the fireworks display?"

Maggie nodded quickly. "Indeed I would, Richard! I have been longing to see Vauxhall Gardens. But would it be proper for me to spend an evening in your company without a chaperone?"

"No, it would not. I plan to ask Aunt Eustace to accompany us if that is agreeable to you. I know she is a bit of a bother, but her presence shall satisfy the proprieties."

"Please invite her, Richard." Maggie nodded quickly. "I *like* Lady Pierce. I find her candid comments most refreshing, even when they concern me."

Richard rose and took Maggie's hand. "At least one knows where one stands with Aunt Eustace. Though her words may wound occasionally, I find her as unfailingly honest as you are, and that is a quality I admire greatly in the both of you."

"Thank you, Richard." Maggie smiled back at him, grateful that he did not possess the capacity to read her mind. She had been honest when she had called him a friend, for he was certainly that, but she suspected that her affections for him were beginning to run far deeper than mere friendship.

"Until tomorrow, Maggie. I'll call on you and bring you my aunt's answer. You may expect me to arrive shortly before Felix scratches at your door."

Maggie gave a gasp of surprise as Richard pulled her into his arms and held her close. His lips brushed hers in a gesture of friendship and Maggie trembled as she found herself desiring much more than this friendly display. When he released her, she stood there attempting to regain her composure and to slow the rapid fluttering of her heart.

"I'll take Felix with me." Richard crossed the room to scoop up Felix with one well-muscled arm. "He deserves a ride home in return for the service that he has done for me."

Maggie could barely trust herself to speak. Her mind was still reeling at the unaccustomed emotions Richard's embrace had unleashed in her. "You . . . you refer to the lovely brooch?"

"That, and an even greater service. Felix has found you, Maggie. And now that we are together, the world seems very bright, indeed. To think it is all due to the machinations of my sister's cat!"

Once the door had closed behind Richard and Felix, Maggie stood in the center of the room, staring at the bookshelves without actually seeing them. She wore a most bemused expression on her face and not even Felicity's insistent rubbing against her skirt roused her from her musings. Richard had presented her with a lovely brooch and she suspected that it was much more than a simple token of friendship. What emotions had prompted this thoughtful gift? Was it possible that Richard's affections for her were growing as rapidly as hers were for him?

Richard breathed a deep sigh of relief as he climbed the steps to Larchmont House. He had noted several other equipages in the area that had been set aside for guests, and their presence indicated that his mother was entertaining. That was all to the good as far as Richard was concerned. If the dowager marchioness was busy with her other guests, she should not keep him long.

"Lord Larchmont." His mother's butler greeted him with a polite bow. "My lady desires that you wait in the green salon. She has been anticipating your arrival and will join you there directly."

Richard walked down the familiar hall and entered the green salon. As he gazed about him, he noticed that his mother had replaced the furnishings. The new settee and matching chairs were a particularly bilious shade of green, and the windows had been hung with an equally objectionable hue of bright pink. Combined with the carpet, which was patterned to resemble a field of summer flowers, the total effect of the chamber was jarring to the senses.

What would Maggie have done with this room? Richard smiled as he considered it. No doubt it should have been done in shades of soothing blue. She had informed him, only this afternoon, that it was her color of preference. The spindle-legged furniture, though it was quite fashionable, should have been quickly replaced with an eye to comfort. Maggie had told him that she preferred sturdy furniture with soft cushions that conformed to one's body, rather than forcing one to assume an unnatural posture.

Richard could imagine how pleasant this mansion should be if he gave Maggie leave to furnish it as she wished. He had already filled a warehouse with objects that he had purchased with his eye toward someday taking possession of this residence, and he had no doubt that Maggie should be delighted to find the perfect places to display these acquisitions. He had half a notion to give Maggie carte blanche to make improvements, but he had promised his mother that she should be allowed to reside at Larchmont House until such time as he took a wife.

A bemused expression spread across Richard's face as he considered this option. Maggie had all of the qualities he revered in a woman and she possessed them in abundant quantity. She was caring and kind, concerned about the comfort of others, and quick to provide aid when it was needed. Maggie was honest, loyal, charitable, and patient. She had suffered Aunt Eustace with humor and grace, and had even professed to like her. Maggie tended to see only the best in everyone and she could charm even the most jaded individual.

A smiled turned up the corners of his lips as Richard thought of the private conversations they had enjoyed. Maggie had told him of keeping her father's house and of entertaining the members of their congregation. As his wife, she should be the mistress of a much larger and grander dwelling than she had commanded in the past, but Richard was convinced that she was capable of managing his household and his staff quite admirably.

Maggie would excel at motherhood. Richard smiled as he recalled how tenderly she had held the kittens, even little Artemis, who was a born mischief-maker. She would nurture their children with love and devotion; the concern

she exhibited for Felicity and the kittens bore testament
to that fact.

Though beauty was not high on the list of qualities Richard sought in a wife, there was no denying that Maggie
was lovely. Her tall figure was statuesque, her carriage was
proud, and her inner beauty shone forth from her sparkling azure eyes and her ready smile. He should be proud
to stand at her side as they hosted social events and greeted
the friends they should make as a couple.

Perhaps most important of all, their home should be
filled with joy. Maggie would delight every one of their
acquaintances with her keen intelligence and her sense of
fun, and her happy laughter should be music to the ears
of all who heard it.

Richard's thoughts took another turn and his smile grew
even wider. His private moments with Maggie, above the
stairs, should be tender and loving, a pleasure that would
last them for all the days of their lives. He had felt the
passion in Maggie's embrace, the slight trembling of her
body when he had held her, and the sweet manner in
which she had pressed even closer to his warmth. The
intimacies they shared would be most delightful, indeed.
Maggie was a true innocent, but she had been most eager
when he had held her, and he should patiently bring her
to appreciate the joys that awaited her in his bed. All he
must do to ensure that his happy dream became a reality
was to offer for Maggie.

The more Richard thought about it, the more this plan
pleased him. He loved Maggie. It was clear to him now.
And though she had not stated as much, he felt almost
certain that she loved him in return. His mother and sister
had urged him to find a suitable wife, and at last he was
prepared to do what they had asked of him.

It was at this point that Aunt Eustace's words returned
to haunt him and Richard began to frown. Maggie was not
suitable. Though she came from a perfectly respectable
family, she was far beneath him on the social scale. A
marquis did not marry the daughter of a vicar who had
not even been presented. It was simply not done. He might

spend time with her and even escort her to a simple entertainment or two, but a nobleman in his position had an
obligation to marry well.

Richard got up to pace the floor, a fierce scowl on his
face. The ton would not approve of Maggie, but was he
willing to bow to their wishes and permit them to deny
him his choice in a wife?

"The devil take them!" Richard grinned as he made a
decision. "They shall come around in time. And even if
they do not, I shall be happy and so shall Maggie."

There was the sound of approaching footsteps and Richard began to scowl again. It was his mother, and he had
not yet considered her reaction. The dowager marchioness
would disapprove of Maggie and spare no effort to make
her life a misery. It should not be because she took Maggie,
herself, in dislike, but for the simple fact that Maggie had
not been born to noble parents.

Could he bring his mother around to his point of view?
Richard sighed as he considered the question. It was possible, but he would be wise to delay his announcement to
her until he had devised a plan to gain her approval.

"Richard! You are here at last!" Lady Larchmont swept
into the room. She was dressed in a lovely gown of gold
satin and her ebony hair glistened with shining flecks of
gold dust. "I am so delighted to see you, dear!"

Richard raised his brows. His mother was not usually so
effusive. "And I am delighted to see you, Mother. You
mentioned a problem of some magnitude?"

"Yes, dear. It concerns my dear friend Lady Frothingham. You remember her daughter, Charlotte, do you
not?"

Richard nodded, vaguely recalling a freckle-laden young
miss he had met when they were but children. As he
remembered, she had been a good sort and had even
climbed a tree on a dare from her brother. "Yes, Mother,
I believe I do. Is she the girl we called Charlie?"

"Yes, dear. But you must call her Lady Charlotte, now
that she has become a young lady."

Richard nodded. "Never fear, Mother. I shall be perfectly proper if I have cause to meet her again."

"But that is the precise reason I sent for you, Richard. Dear Charlotte's escort for the evening has suffered a broken leg and she lacks a dinner partner. You will escort her, won't you, dear?"

Richard was about to refuse, claiming another engagement, when he realized that it might serve him well to perform this favor for his mother. If he stayed in her good graces, she would be more amenable to accepting a daughter-in-law who was not of her choosing. "Yes, Mother. I should be delighted to renew my acquaintance with Lady Charlotte."

"I knew I could count on you, Richard." His mother beamed her approval. "Come along, then. We are gathered in the gold drawing room. And after dinner is concluded, there will be dancing. I do hope you will lead Charlotte out in the first set, Richard. I should be most grateful."

"Of course, Mother." Richard bit back a sharp retort. His mother had not told him that there would be dancing until after he had agreed to act as Charlie's dinner partner. "Does she dance, Mother?"

"She dances divinely. And don't look so distressed, Richard. You needn't remain for the entire evening. All you must do is make certain that dear Charlotte is introduced to enough young gentlemen to keep her amused."

A smile played over Richard's lips as he followed in his mother's wake. Wellington could have learned much from her, as she was a master strategist. If she had but mentioned in her note that he should be required to spend the evening dining and dancing with a childhood acquaintance, he would have spared no effort to devise some clever means of escape.

CHAPTER SEVEN

The gold drawing room was filled with guests and Richard smiled politely as his mother performed the introductions. He was acquainted with Lord and Lady Carter from other dinners he had attended at the mansion, and he had also met Lady Carter's cousin, Lady Wainwright. Richard offered his greetings to Lord Willowby and Lady Ansley, the elderly couple who had been engaged for as long as anyone could remember, and made the acquaintance of several other noblemen and their wives.

"Charlotte shall return in just a moment, dear Richard." Lady Frothingham greeted him with a smile. "You are so kind to agree to escort her. Lord Frothingham and I thought we should have to stuff the poor dear into a sack and force her to attend your mother's entertainment."

Richard had all he could do not to burst into laughter at the visual image her statement conjured. "But it seems that you managed to convince her, Lady Frothingham."

"No, indeed. You must accept full credit for that. Your mother sent round a note promising Charlotte that you should escort her and she agreed to come quite willingly.

She told me that she remembered you with fondness when you played together as children."

"I also remember her with fondness." Even as he paid the compliment, Richard's eyes narrowed. It was clear that his mother had promised his cooperation long before he had given it, causing him to question what other aspects of their conversation had been false. "I shall await her return with great pleasure, Lady Frothingham."

As Richard walked away, he permitted a small frown to cross his face. He had no doubt that his mother's tale of a broken leg had been nothing but a fabrication to gain his sympathy, and he wondered what she should have done if he had refused to do her bidding. She would have scrambled to make some excuse, most likely, and poor Charlie should have been forced to be the odd one out at the dinner table.

"Lord Larchmont?"

A soft feminine voice spoke close behind him and Richard turned toward the source of the sound. What he saw caused a delighted smile to spread across his countenance. "Charlie? I mean . . . Lady Charlotte?"

"Charlie." The lovely young blonde in deep green satin greeted him with a smile. "Let us not stand on ceremony, Richard. I cannot be formal with the one who witnessed my fall from a sycamore branch. You caught me, after all, and saved me from coshing my head."

Richard found himself quite at a loss for words. In the years that had passed since he had last seen Charlie, she had been transformed into an exceedingly attractive young lady.

Charlie gave a tinkling laugh and placed one slim hand on his arm. "I am so delighted to see you again, after all these years. Let us be seated, Richard, so that you can tell me all that has happened to you."

Richard led her over to the nearest settee and grinned as he waited for her to take her place. Then he sat down next to her, on what had to be his mother's most uncomfortable piece of furniture. Charlie's hand was still resting on his arm and Richard gave a fleeting thought to Maggie.

Would she be jealous if she saw him with such a lovely creature?

"You have grown exceedingly handsome, Richard." Charlie favored him with a lovely smile. "Not only have you saved me from the embarrassment of dining without a partner, you have made me the envy of every lady here tonight."

"You have turned into a rare beauty, Charlie." Richard smiled back. Not only was Charlie well spoken, he suspected that she was also a consummate flirt. His thoughts turned to Maggie once again and he cautioned himself to be on his guard. No doubt his mother had arranged this meeting for her own ends, not suspecting that his heart was already engaged.

Charlie moved a bit closer and her delightful perfume drifted up to tease his senses. "You must tell me the news of your dear sister and her husband. I understand that they are traveling the Continent?"

"Yes. He is a diplomat and Alicia often accompanies him on his travels." Richard gave one last thought to Maggie. He must remember to assure her that his mother had arranged this meeting and that he had merely obliged her. Then he turned his full attention to the lovely Lady Charlotte and began to tell her all that had occurred in the years that they had been apart.

It was well past eight in the evening and Maggie was relaxing with one of her uncle's books. The thick volume concerned the peoples of the Orient, a subject which had fascinated her in the past. Tonight she found that she could not focus her attentions on the printed page, as thoughts of Richard filled her mind.

"What shall I do if he offers for me?" Maggie addressed Felicity, who had taken up a position next to her on the leather covered chaise longue.

Felicity stared up at her, her eyes gleaming with reflected firelight from the hearth. She gave no response whatsoever, and Maggie grinned. Felix was the only feline who truly talked to her.

"Lady Pierce was entirely correct when she called me unsuitable." Maggie continued with her one-sided conversation. "The daughter of a vicar is not a match for a wealthy marquis. But I am almost certain that Richard loves me, Felicity, and there is no doubt that I love him."

Maggie shivered in pleasure as she thought of Richard's kiss. Though it had been merely a friendly gesture, the sort of display one might offer to a fond acquaintance of the opposite sex, it had affected her deeply. She had been kissed once before, by a classmate of her brother's who had come to visit one summer, but she had not experienced the passion she had felt when Richard had taken her in his arms. She had not trembled with delight, or grown faint as Stephen's classmate had held her. Maggie would not deny that it had been pleasant, but his embrace had not caused her heart to beat in an irregular rhythm or her breath to catch in her throat. There had been no desire to press her body closer to his or run her fingers through his hair. She had not even considered what should occur in private between them if she were to allow him further liberties. But now, with Richard, she could think of little else, and Maggie's color rose as she imagined the bliss that she should enjoy in his arms.

Maggie wondered again what she should do if Richard defied convention and offered for her. Quite naturally, she desired to accept him. Richard was her perfect match. But though the poets claimed that love conquered all, would it be fair to force Richard to endure the censure of his family and the ton by agreeing to become his wife?

It was at this point that Maggie heard a familiar scratching at the garden door. She rushed over to open it and Felix slipped past her into the chamber.

"Felix!" Maggie closed the door behind him to keep out the cold night air. "You have never paid an evening call before. What are you doing here at this hour?"

Felix did not answer her. He just stood there shivering

and Maggie bent down to pick him up. "What is it, dearest? Did something frighten you?"

Maggie pulled off her shawl and wrapped it around Felix, as he was still shivering. Then she took a chair that was close to the fire and held him in her arms. It took several minutes for Felix to stop shaking, but when he did, he licked her hand. Maggie gave a huge sigh of relief and freed him from the folds of the shawl, so he could leap down if he desired.

"You must try to tell me what has happened, Felix." Maggie stared into his yellow eyes. "Would it help if I asked questions?"

Felix sighed deeply, gazing at Maggie with unblinking eyes. Then he bobbed his head up and down in a nod.

"All right then." Maggie accepted his gesture as speech. "Does this matter concern dear Richard?"

Felix nodded once again. And then he looked up at her expectantly, awaiting her next question.

"Richard informed me that his mother had sent for him. Does this also concern Lady Larchmont?"

Felix gave a quick nod and licked her hand, almost as if he were complimenting her on an excellent question. Then he moved forward to paw at the brooch that she had secured to her dress.

"I see." Maggie smiled at him. "The matter concerns Richard, his mother, and this lovely brooch. Perhaps I am mistaken, Felix, but I received the decided impression that Richard desired more than my friendship when he gifted me with this brooch. Am I correct in my assumption?"

Felix yowled, almost before the words left her lips. Then the huge orange cat moved forward to stare directly into her eyes, causing Maggie to giggle.

"Yes, I love him." Maggie felt the color rise to her cheeks. "Am I correct in assuming that he loves me in return?"

Felix yowled again, long and hard, sending Maggie off into a bout of delighted laughter. She could imagine her father's and stepmama's shock if she informed them that she had received this type of joyous confirmation from her gentleman's sister's cat!

"Does Richard intend to declare for me?" Maggie held her breath and only released it when Felix nodded again. Then another line of questioning struck her with the force of a blow, and she shivered slightly. "You said that this matter also concerns Richard's mother. She will not approve of me, will she, Felix?"

Felix yowled, shaking his head from side to side. His rough tongue emerged to lick Maggie's hand, almost as if he were attempting to console her.

"Did you come here to warn me that Richard's mother shall do everything in her power to keep him from me?"

Felix bristled and the fur began to stand up on his back. This action made him appear to be twice as large as he actually was, and Maggie's eyes widened at the sight. Aunt Lenora had mentioned that a cat who was badly frightened or confronted by an enemy could use this tactic to appear more formidable. It was quite obvious that Felix regarded Lady Larchmont as an enemy.

"You are telling me that Lady Larchmont is a formidable opponent, but you must not fret, Felix. If Richard loves me as much as I love him, his mother shall not succeed in defeating us."

Maggie reached out to smooth down his fur and Felix licked her hand again. But the glint of worry did not leave his eyes and that made Maggie wonder exactly what tricks Lady Larchmont might have in her arsenal to keep Richard from declaring for her.

CHAPTER EIGHT

"I'm sorry, Maggie. You know that I'd much rather spend the evening with you, do you not?"

Maggie nodded, not trusting herself to speak. They had planned to attend the opera this evening, in the company of Lady Pierce, but Richard's aunt had suddenly remembered a previous engagement that had made her unavailable. This was the third such occurrence in the past sennight, and Maggie could not help but suspect that orders from Richard's mother had kept Lady Pierce from acting as her chaperone.

Though she had been sorely tempted, Maggie had not told Richard of Felix's evening visit or of the questions he had answered for her. It had not seemed proper to regard Richard's mother as an enemy before she had even made her acquaintance. But every time that Richard mentioned his childhood friend, Lady Charlotte, Maggie could not help but wonder whether she was a part of Lady Larchmont's strategy to keep Richard from declaring his love for her.

Lady Charlotte had been present at every ton function that Richard had attended of late. It was no secret that he had escorted her to several, for he had told Maggie so himself. She was almost certain that he had not hidden anything from her, but Maggie often wished she were a small mouse in the corner at one of the ton functions so that she could observe Lady Charlotte's manner toward Richard with her own eyes. There was no evidence to prove it yea or nay, but Maggie suspected that Lady Larchmont was placing them together in an attempt to effect a coupling of which she approved.

When Maggie had learned that Richard's aunt could not attend the opera with them, she had invited Richard to enjoy a light supper in Aunt Lenora's library at a table set up in front of the hearth. They had planned to spend the evening perusing the maps that Maggie's uncle had collected, but now it seemed even that simple pleasure should be denied them. Richard's mother had sent round an urgent message, begging her son to escort her to a ton function.

"Will Lady Charlotte be there?" Maggie kept her tone deliberately light. Though Richard had told her all about his childhood acquaintance and taken special pains to make clear to her that their bond was one of simple friendship and nothing more, Maggie found that she still suffered from an occasional bout of jealousy.

"I suppose so." Richard gave a casual shrug, and Maggie bit back a smile. He really did not seem at all interested in Lady Charlotte's plans. "I do wish that your aunt would return soon, Maggie."

"As do I." Maggie nodded in total agreement. If Aunt Lenora were here, she could act as their chaperone and they should not have to rely on the recently unreliable Lady Pierce.

"Perhaps your aunt should agree to sponsor you so that you could be formally presented. I should like to escort you to the ton functions."

Maggie felt her heart leap with pleasure. Richard wanted her beside him at these glittering affairs. "But I thought that you were bored by routs and balls."

"I should not be bored if I were with you, Maggie. Just

think of the asides that we should share! I could tell you all I know of the couples we met, and you could give me your impressions of them. I always enjoy myself in your company, Maggie.''

"Do you truly, Richard?'' Maggie held her breath as she waited for his answer.

"Indeed.'' Richard reached out to take her hand. "It is not fair that you are restricted from attending ton affairs with me.''

Maggie nodded her agreement. It was unfair, but there was naught she could do about it.

"If Alicia returns before your aunt does, perhaps she could sponsor you.'' Richard's eyes began to gleam with excitement. "Our family history goes back for hundreds of years, and I am certain that if we all put our minds to it, we should be able to find some distant relative we have in common. It should require only one such connection and Alicia would be allowed to present you.''

"Perhaps.'' Maggie smiled, her hand held warmly in his. Richard truly appeared to want her to become a part of his world, and it was possible that she could be if his mother did not throw a spoke in his wheel.

"I must go.'' Richard rose and pulled her to her feet. "Good-bye, my sweet Maggie. I shall see you tomorrow at the usual time?''

Maggie nodded, her eyes shining. "Good night, Richard. Think of me at the ball tonight, especially if you are required to dance with Lady Charlotte.''

The moment the words left Maggie's lips, a blush rose to stain her cheeks. She had not meant to say that! She lowered her eyes in acute embarrassment and wished that the floor would open up beneath her and drop her down to the depths.

Richard laughed, highly amused at her comment. "I will, Maggie. I always do. You never leave my mind for a single moment, *especially* when I am dancing with Charlie. I keep hoping that she will magically transform herself into you.''

"You do?" Maggie raised her eyes to his, the blush still upon her cheeks.

"I do." Richard pulled her into his arms. And then, in lieu of the polite and friendly kiss he normally gave her when he departed, his lips took full possession of hers.

The sensation was exquisite, delightful in the extreme, and Maggie gave no thought to what a perfectly proper young miss should do in this situation. Her reaction came from her heart, not her mind. She wrapped her arms around Richard's neck and her lips parted in a sigh of pure pleasure.

Maggie shivered as their kiss grew deeper. Never before had she experienced the emotions that swept through her like a tide, rushing and then ebbing to return again with even more fervor. She had no sense of time passing. She felt weightless and timeless, connected to the world by only the pressure of Richard's beloved lips and his arms wrapped around her, holding her tightly.

She heard him groan, deep in his throat, and she pressed herself even more closely against him. Her slight form molded to his until it seemed as if they were one body, one soul, and one heart. She felt his hands smooth over her back sending shivers of delight down her spine. And then he was touching her waist and her hips, strong fingers soothing and gentling her as he would a skittish filly not yet broken to saddle.

Maggie gave back to him in full measure, granting him whatever he desired. She had the sensation of floating in a delightfully warm pool, her body bobbing gently with the current. And all the while, his lips were moving, drinking in her essence and giving his as a gift to her.

Time passed. It must have, for dimly Maggie heard the chime of her uncle's standing clock. Richard was caressing her softly, touching her bodice, his warm fingers stroking the curves of silky softness in a way that caused her very bones to dissolve.

Maggie's breath caught in her throat and then escaped

in a sigh of wondrous passion as her hands found the warmth of his skin. Her fingers explored the muscles of his arms, his chest, and his narrow but powerful waist.

"Maggie." He drew back, his face a study in contrasts. His eyes blazed with raw passion but his words were soft. "You are so very dear to me. Tell me that you love me as I love you."

"Oh, I do!"

Maggie's impassioned declaration was no more than a whisper, but she knew he had heard. His lips found hers in another searching kiss and then he lifted her up, into his arms and carried her over to the leather-covered chaise longue.

"Think of me, Maggie. This evening will be long and dreary without you." He settled her very gently on the cushions. "Tomorrow, when our heads have returned from the clouds, we must speak of this."

"Yes, Richard." Maggie's smile was radiant.

"Until tomorrow, my dearest Maggie."

Maggie sighed in bliss as he strode out the door, and then she gave way to the tears of joy that fell like rain from her eyes. Richard loved her. Her happiness was so all-encompassing that she even gazed at little Artemis with fond indulgence, as the mischievous kitten emerged from her workbasket with the chair cover that Maggie had painstakingly embroidered, raveled and chewed beyond repair.

Richard sighed as he escorted Charlie to the dance floor and led her through the figures of the waltz. He thought of Maggie's warning to him and he grinned as he glanced down into Charlie's green eyes. He did wish that she were Maggie. If he could hold Maggie in his arms, the members of the ton smiling at them in the way that they were smiling now, he should be the happiest gentleman in all of England.

"What is it, Richard? You seemed deep in a brown study

a moment ago." Charlie's generous lips smiled up at him. "Were you remembering the time that my pesky brother sat on your pet frog?"

"Lud, Charlie! I had forgot all about that!" Richard laughed. Charlie always managed to recall something from their childhood days to chase his blue devils away. But then he caught sight of several tabbies of the ton, glancing at them and whispering behind their fans.

"What is it, Richard?" Charlie caught his sudden change of mood.

"Lady Predford and her cousin, Lady Variel, are staring at us and whispering behind their fans."

"And why not?" Charlie giggled as she smiled up at him. "You are wealthy and handsome, and I am rich and beautiful. We are the pattern card of the perfect match. I have heard it said that they are already placing wagers at White's as to when you will offer for me."

Richard's eyes widened with shock. "Are you certain, Charlie?"

"Of course I am." Charlie moved a bit closer into the circle of his arms. "Our marriage is a foregone conclusion, dear Richard. Only the date is in question. Surely you must be aware that our mothers have already begun to plan our wedding."

"No, Charlie. I was not aware." The music concluded at that point and Richard took Charlie's arm. Though he felt like scowling, he forced himself to smile down at her politely as he did not wish to cause tongues to wag any more than they already were. "Will you join me on the veranda where we can discuss this matter with some privacy?"

Charlie looked a bit anxious as they made their way to the French doors and out onto the deserted veranda. "Perhaps I should not have told you, Richard."

"No, indeed. I am grateful that you did." Richard sighed deeply. "It seems that I have been quite oblivious of late. Tell me, Charlie . . . were you, along with our respective mothers, expecting me to declare for you?"

Charlie nodded quickly. "Of course, Richard. Do you doubt that I am your perfect match?"

"You are perfection itself." Richard searched for a way out of this difficulty without riding roughshod over Charlie's tender feelings. "I am sorry if my mother has misled you, but I do not love you, Charlie."

Charlie stared at him for a moment and then she began to laugh. "You are teasing me, Richard, and perhaps I deserve it for speaking out of turn. But you know full well that love has nothing to do with marriage. Can you deny that you are fond of me?"

"No, I cannot." Richard searched for the words to extricate himself from this dilemma. "But surely you do not wish marry me when I love another."

Charlie smiled, seemingly quite unconcerned. "You are speaking of the vicar's daughter, no doubt. I am aware that you have developed a *tendre* for her. Your dear aunt Eustace told me all about it."

"I see." Richard breathed a deep sigh of relief and silently thanked his aunt. At least he should not have to explain his love for Maggie. "Then you do understand why I cannot marry you?"

"No, Richard. I do not understand that at all. You cannot marry the vicar's daughter, as she is not a suitable match for you. But you can marry me, because I am."

Richard stared at her in shock. "You would marry me, Charlie, knowing full well that I love another?"

"Yes, indeed." Charlie nodded quickly. "Many couples have similar arrangements in civilized society, especially among the peerage. It does not matter to me in the slightest, so long as appearances are maintained."

Richard felt his mind spin in shocked circles. Charlie was telling him that it was perfectly acceptable to her if his affections belonged to another. "But, Charlie! What kind of marriage should that be?"

"A good one." Charlie smiled up at him. "After all, you must marry eventually. It is your duty to provide an heir and I shall make an excellent wife and mother. And you have already said that you are fond of me."

Richard nodded. "Yes, Charlie. You know that I am. But—"

"Then there is no reason for us *not* to marry." Charlie interrupted him. "Everyone who is anyone expects us to do so, and you cannot deny the entire ton."

CHAPTER NINE

Felix had no sooner taken his leave when there was a tentative tap upon the library door. Maggie hurried to open it, and her eyes widened in surprise as she saw her aunt's housekeeper, Mrs. Greavy, standing in the hall, her hand raised to rap a second time. "Yes, Mrs. Greavy?"

"Excuse me, Miss Pendleton, but I must speak to you."

"Of course." Maggie nodded and motioned her into the room. She could not help but notice that the housekeeper was twisting her hands together in anxiety. "Has something happened in the kitchens?"

"No, Miss Pendleton. There is nothing amiss in the house. I . . . that is . . . Mr. Spencer . . . in fact, *several* of the staff asked me to speak with you on a matter of . . . of extreme importance. Oh, I do wish that Lady Worth were here! Someone has to tell you, but I am not at all accomplished at this sort of thing!"

"Please sit down, Mrs. Greavy." Maggie motioned toward a chair. It was quite apparent that Mrs. Greavy had been recruited by the staff, against her wishes, to deliver some sort of distressing news. "Is my father well?"

Mrs. Greavy nodded. "I assume so, miss."

"My aunt?"

The housekeeper nodded again. "Oh yes, miss. This does not concern an illness or an accident. It is of a more . . . more *personal* nature."

"Perhaps a glass of sherry might help?"

"Oh, yes, miss. That is exceedingly kind of you. It is just that I am not usually placed in this uncomfortably sensitive position. Perhaps I could suggest that you . . . you take one as well?"

Maggie crossed to the tray at the far corner of the room and poured two glasses of sherry. She handed one to Mrs. Greavy and kept the other for herself, taking a seat quite close to the distressed housekeeper. "You must try to relax, Mrs. Greavy. I am certain that whatever news you bring cannot be so bad as all that."

"Yes, miss." Mrs. Greavy nodded, but she did not look convinced.

Maggie waited for a moment while Mrs. Greavy took a sip of her sherry. When no further words were forthcoming, she urged the housekeeper gently. "Go on, Mrs. Greavy. The hour grows late."

"My cousin's youngest daughter is in Lady Larchmont's employ and she heard a most distressing conversation this very afternoon. Polly came to tell me just as soon as her mistress had left for the ball and we all decided that you must be informed immediately."

Maggie exhaled with great relief, surprised to find that she had been holding her breath. "Servants' gossip, Mrs. Greavy?"

"Much more than that, miss. What Polly told me has not been passed from ear to ear like other tales. She was stationed in Lady Larchmont's private sitting room at the time, and she heard every word herself. It is perfectly true, I assure you."

"And what did Polly hear, Mrs. Greavy?" Maggie bit back a smile. The conveyers of gossip were always quick to assure their listeners that the news they imparted was perfectly true.

"Lady Larchmont had two guests, Lady Frothingham,

and her daughter, Lady Charlotte. They were discussing their preferences regarding Lady Charlotte's wedding gown.''

Maggie greeted this news with a relieved smile. If Richard had but mentioned that Lady Charlotte was to be married, she should not have been at all jealous of the time that he had spent with her. "Go on, Mrs. Greavy."

"Lady Forthingham declared that the gown must be perfect, for it was not every day that the daughter of an earl married a marquis."

"A . . . a marquis?" Maggie's heart jumped into her throat as Mrs. Greavy nodded, but she quickly recovered her composure. Richard was not the only marquis in England.

"That was when they mentioned you, miss." Mrs. Greavy frowned in distress. "At least, we *suspect* that Lady Larchmont was referring to you. She said she was relieved that the vicar's daughter should soon be forced to break off with her son."

Maggie felt her hands begin to tremble and she took another sip of her sherry to control her distress. "Then Lord Larchmont has . . . has declared for Lady Charlotte?"

"No, miss. But all expect him to do so in short order. Lady Larchmont has already instructed the servants to begin preparations for the wedding."

Maggie's fingers tightened around the crystal goblet so tightly she feared that it should shatter in her hand. She set it down carefully and clasped her trembling hands together to keep them still. How could Richard marry Lady Charlotte when he had told her that he loved her only a few short hours ago? "Did they say anything else about me, Mrs. Greavy?"

"Lady Larchmont asked Lady Charlotte if she had reached an understanding with Richard on the matter of his friendship with you."

"And how did Lady Charlotte reply?" Maggie held her breath as she waited for the answer.

"She said that she was aware that Richard had developed a *tendre* for you and that she should . . ." Mrs. Greavy faltered, her full cheeks turning an alarming shade of red. "It is not seemly for me to tell you, miss."

"But I insist, Mrs. Greavy. You have gone this far and now you must finish the tale."

"Yes, miss." Mrs. Greavy hesitated and then she nodded, gaining some courage from Maggie's resolve. "Lady Charlotte said that if Richard preferred your charms to hers, she should let him continue to have you so long as he did his duty by her."

Maggie's eyes hardened and she began to tremble with rage. How dare Lady Charlotte say any such thing! "Is there more, Mrs. Greavy?"

"Yes, miss. Lady Charlotte said that she would prepare a small cottage on their estate for you, where she could keep you under her watchful eye. And once they had returned from their bridal journey, she would give Richard leave to visit you there whenever he so desired!"

Richard wore a scowl as he took the steps two at a time and effected a hasty exit from White's. He had demanded to see the betting book and he had found that Charlie's story was made up of whole cloth. After ordering his driver to carry him to Parkhurst Square at the greatest possible speed, Richard leaned back against the squabs with a sigh. He must see Maggie immediately, to explain the tangle in which he had found himself. Though she had no acquaintances among the ranking members of the ton, he had no doubt that she should hear about his pending engagement before many more hours had passed. The servants had their own means of passing news of this nature from house to house, and their method was known to be even more effective than the speediest post.

What should he say to Maggie? Richard sighed deeply. There was nothing for it but to admit what a fool he had been and to beg Maggie's forgiveness. Once she had given it, he should drop on his knees and offer for her straightaway, for Maggie was the one he loved. Now that he had learned of the plans that his mother had made for him, without his approval or even his knowledge, he should spare no further consideration for her feelings.

"Miss Pendleton?" Spencer knocked softly on the library door. "I am sorry to disturb you, but there is a gentleman here, demanding to see you."

Maggie sighed, looking up from the volume she had been attempting to read. It was of little use to continue her study of the peoples of the Orient. She had been staring at the very same sentence ever since Mrs. Greavy had taken her leave.

Perhaps the reason she could not concentrate was that thoughts of Richard had filled Maggie's mind. She had mentally reviewed each moment of his visit and she had been unable to come to a positive conclusion. Was it possible that she had misinterpreted his intentions when he had professed to love her? She had assumed that he had meant to ask for her hand, but perhaps he had planned to marry Lady Charlotte all along, and merely wished to ask her to be his mistress!

"Miss?"

Spencer prompted her gently, and Maggie shook her head to clear it. He had mentioned a gentleman caller. "Is it Lord Larchmont?"

"No, miss." Spencer shook his head.

"Then send him away, Spencer. I do not wish to receive anyone at this late hour."

"But he claims to be your brother, miss. Captain Stephen Pendleton?"

"Stephen is here?" Maggie jumped up, her book dropping unheeded to the floor. "Oh, Spencer! Why did you not say so before? I have not seen my dear brother in two long years!"

Her aunt's butler broke into an uncharacteristic smile. "I should not have admitted him at this hour, but the family resemblance is quite apparent. I placed him in the gold drawing room to await you."

"Thank you, Spencer." Maggie smiled, her brown study

disappearing completely. "Do you think that you could convince Cook to prepare a light meal for my brother? There is no need for anything fancy. A bit of bread and cheese will suffice."

Spencer nodded. "She has already been informed and is doing so as we speak. And Mrs. Greavy is seeing to it that the best guest chamber is made ready for him."

"Stephen is staying then?" Maggie's eyes began to sparkle.

"Yes, miss. The captain informed me that he has secured a three-day leave."

Maggie's smile grew even wider at this news. "What fun we shall have, Spencer! Stephen is such a dear brother, and he has arrived at exactly the right time!"

Spencer nodded and then he permitted himself the luxury of a small chuckle as his mistress's niece picked up her skirts in a most unladylike fashion and fairly flew down the hallway to greet her brother.

Richard frowned as his driver stopped in front of Lady Worth's townhouse. The door was open and he could hear the sound of happy voices inside. Had Maggie's aunt returned earlier than expected? He leapt from his carriage and strode up the walkway, a polite smile of greeting upon his face. He would pay his respects to Lady Worth and then he would ask for a private word with Maggie. He would not rest until he had gained her promise that she should be his wife.

There was no need to engage the knocker as the door was already ajar. Richard rapped once, just to observe the formalities, and then he slipped through the portal and began to walk down the hallway toward the sound of the voices. There seemed to be quite a commotion and he thought he could hear Maggie's laughter amidst the din.

One of the housemaids moved to rush past him, but she stopped to gaze at him curiously. "Evening, sir. Miss Pendleton is in the gold drawing room."

Richard nodded and approached the chamber. The

door was open and he was about to enter when he realized that Maggie was entertaining a gentleman.

"Maggie?" Richard stopped on the threshold, staring in shock at the sight inside. Maggie was standing on the tips of her toes, enfolded in the arms of a tall and dashing military officer who Richard had never set eyes on before!

As Richard saw the expression on Maggie's face, he staggered slightly, reaching out to steady himself against the wall. Her lips were parted in a joyful smile and love shone forth from her sparkling eyes as she gazed up into the captain's face.

Richard gasped as if he had been dealt a blow much fiercer than any that might conceivably be delivered by an enemy's hand. It took him some time to recover, but when he did, he whirled on his heel and retraced his steps, leaving his driver to follow along behind him as he walked through the darkness toward the sanctuary of his sister's home. Maggie loved this captain and he loved her. There was no doubt in Richard's mind. Not only had he been duped by his mother, he had been duped by Maggie as well.

CHAPTER TEN

"Would you care for anything else, miss?" The footman frowned as he came to collect the untouched contents of the tea tray.

"No thank you, James." Maggie shook her head. "You may take it away."

The footman hesitated for a moment, but then he picked up the tray and quickly left the room. When he had gone, Maggie sighed deeply and stared out at the fog in the garden. She had been able to maintain her high spirits while Stephen was here, but now that he had left, all she could think of was Richard and how he had deserted her.

A tear rolled down Maggie's cheek and she wiped it away with the back of her sleeve. There had been even more gossip that Mrs. Greavy had related to her. Richard had escorted Lady Charlotte to several parties since she had seen him last, and everyone expected him to declare for her at the gala ball that was to be held at Larchmont House tonight.

How could he have left her without a word? Tears formed in Maggie's eyes once again. Though Felix still came for his tea each afternoon, she had not seen Richard since the day he had told her that he loved her.

Maggie choked back a sob of grief. She was certain that Richard had thought better of asking her to be his mistress, knowing full well that she should never agree. No doubt he wished that he had never mentioned the subject of love, but avoiding her company would not render the words he had spoken unsaid. She had believed him when he had told her that he loved her, but she had come to doubt this as well. Richard could not love her and stay away for so long.

Once Stephen had taken his leave, Maggie had prepared herself for her next meeting with Richard. She had intended to tell him that she understood why he must marry Lady Charlotte. She had even thought to congratulate him on his upcoming nuptials, and assure him that she should always remember the friendship they had shared. But Richard had made her brave little speech quite impossible, as he had not seen fit to call upon her. This neglect was tantamount to an insult, and Maggie did not know what she had done to deserve such callous treatment at his hands.

The standing clock began to strike, and Maggie walked sadly to the garden door. Felix should arrive at any moment and there was comfort in that thought. Though Richard had forsaken her, Felix had not, and Maggie was grateful that the huge orange cat was still her friend.

"Good afternoon, Felix." Maggie did her best to smile as Felix appeared at the top of the garden wall. "Please join us. I have prepared your tea."

Felix bounded through the door and took a moment to rub up against her skirts. Maggie reached down to pet him and sighed deeply.

"You are so fortunate, Felix." Maggie blinked back tears. "You are permitted to enjoy Richard's company every day, and I . . . I do not think I shall ever see him again!"

Felix looked up at her with questioning eyes, and Maggie sighed again. He seemed to be asking why this had happened.

"I do not know, Felix. Richard told me that he loved me and then he . . . he disappeared. I know that he can't marry me. The ton should never allow such a match. But I did think that he would come to say good-bye!"

Felix nodded his head and yowled once, whether in sympathy or in confirmation, Maggie was not certain. But he sounded so very forlorn that Maggie scooped him up, buried her face in his soft fur, and let the tears of grief fall from her eyes.

"I shall survive, Felix. You must not be anxious on that score. But my life shall never be the same now that I have found my true love and lost him to another." Felix's rough tongue flicked out to lick her cheek and Maggie sighed again. "Oh, Felix! If I could only speak to dear Richard again, just once!"

Felix's eyes gleamed as he stared up into her face. Then he nodded his head, and before Maggie could react, he twisted out of her arms and leapt to the floor. He yowled once, and then he hurried straight to the basket. But instead of stepping aside so that Felicity could emerge, Felix did something most unusual. He stepped into the basket and curled up next to Felicity, rubbing her smaller head with his huge one.

"Ah. You wish for a private moment with your lady love." Maggie smiled and backed up a few paces. It did appear that Felix was communicating with Felicity, for she turned to regard him with a most startled expression.

Maggie's eyes widened as the hair began to stand up on Felicity's back. Her aunt's cat was bristling, and as Maggie watched, Felicity gave a low grumble of displeasure.

"What was *that* about?" Maggie frowned slightly. She could almost believe that Felix had suggested something of which Felicity did not approve. But Felix nuzzled her fondly until she had calmed, and then Felicity began to purr once again.

Maggie watched as Felix and Felicity exchanged what seemed to be speaking glances, and then Felix moved on to examine his kittens. He nuzzled each one, apparently searching for something, and then he went back to stand over Artemis.

Artemis looked up at her father in some confusion as he gently moved the other kittens from her side and settled down next to her. His head close to hers, he nuzzled and licked, almost as if he were trying to impart some type of information to her.

Maggie found she was fascinated with this unusual behavior. Felix had always paid equal attention to each tiny member of his family. Now it appeared that he had singled Artemis out for some reason, and was in the process of telling her exactly why.

A moment passed and then Felicity joined them, taking up a position on the kitten's other side. Both mother and father nuzzled her and then Artemis gave a soft mew of compliance.

Maggie frowned slightly as she watched them. Was she reading too much into their actions? But nothing like this had ever occurred before and Maggie was enthralled with this unusual exhibit of feline parenting.

The small kitten yawned and snuggled closer to her parents. Both licked her once again, almost as if they were telling her that she was a good child, and then they jumped out of the basket and headed straight for their bowls of milk tea.

Felix did not even take a taste of the treat he had enjoyed so much in the past. He just leaned down and gave the bowl a strong bump with his head that caused the milk to splash out upon the carpet. Before Maggie could react to this startling event, Felicity placed one paw on the rim of her bowl and flipped it over to add to the mess.

"Oh, dear!" Maggie stared down at her aunt's lovely carpet with dismay. She must clean it immediately before a stain could set in.

Maggie turned on her heel and rushed for the doors, opening them quickly and hurrying down the hall. She managed to locate Mrs. Greavy in the kitchens and helped her to gather the necessary items to clean Aunt Lenora's beautiful rug.

It took three of them, Maggie, Mrs. Greavy, and Betsy, to restore the carpet to its original splendor. Once the task was accomplished, Maggie dismissed them with gratitude for their efforts, and sank down upon the chaise longue with a weary sigh.

"I must remember to serve your tea in a less dangerous spot from now on." Maggie turned to the basket to address Felix, and her eyes widened with alarm. Though Felicity and the kittens were curled in the basket quite contentedly, Felix was nowhere in sight.

"Felix? I am not angry with you, dear. Please come out." Maggie rose to her feet and searched the corners of the room. She was beginning to despair of ever finding him when she heard a familiar yowl outside the closed library door.

"Here he is, miss." Spencer opened the door and stepped in with Felix in his arms.

"Felix!" Maggie relieved her aunt's butler of his burden. "However did he escape, Spencer?"

"He must have wandered out while you were engaged in cleaning the carpet, miss. Though I explained that it was curiosity that killed the cat, he did not appear in the least regretful."

After Spencer had left, closing the door securely behind him, Maggie set Felix down on the carpet. "I am greatly relieved that Spencer found you, Felix. I should have felt dreadful if anything had happened to you. It seems that you are my only remaining friend in London so you must take very good care of yourself."

Felix nodded as if he understood, and then he approached the basket to take leave of his little family. He spent more time with Felicity than was usual, but at last he took up a position at the garden door and yowled for Maggie to open it.

"Good-bye, Felix. We shall expect you tomorrow at the usual time." Maggie opened the door, but Felix turned back for one last look, closing one eye in what seemed like a wink.

Maggie watched as he padded through the garden and

bounded over the wall. Then she walked back into the chamber, closed the door, and a tear slipped down her cheek. What she had said was true. Felix was her only friend. And now that Felix was gone, so was her tenuous connection to the man she loved.

Richard sighed as he prepared for yet another evening with Charlie. It should be an evening like any other, pleasant, comfortable, and mildly enjoyable. The esteemed members of the ton were correct. Lady Charlotte was his perfect match. There was only one thing missing in their coupling, and Richard doubted that he should ever find it again. It was spontaneity, that delicious feeling of not knowing precisely what his partner should do. He had enjoyed such an emotion with Maggie and it had filled his world with wondrous surprise and turned every moment into an exciting adventure. But Maggie was lost to him now, and he could not dwell on the past. Perhaps it was fortunate that Charlie had opened his eyes to his duty.

In the past few days, Richard had come to accept the inevitable. If he could not have the one he loved, Charlie should do very nicely. A part of him still felt lost without Maggie, but there was hope that this feeling would fade in time. Maggie had made it clear that she did not want him. On the very same day that he had professed his love for her, he had found her in the arms of the handsome captain.

Perhaps he had not really known Maggie at all. Richard attempted to comfort himself with this notion. If someone had told him that she should behave improperly, he should have called that person out as a liar. But Maggie *had* behaved improperly. Richard had it on good authority that Maggie had allowed the handsome captain to stay under her aunt's roof. Perhaps no actual impropriety had occurred, but the mere *appearance* of impropriety was more than enough to ruin the reputation of a single miss.

"Hello, Felix. What are *you* doing here?" Richard

glanced down with surprise at his sister's cat. Felix did not ordinarily join him in his bedchamber.

Felix sat back on his haunches to regard Richard quite soberly. Then he straightened up again to howl mournfully.

"Whatever is the matter?" Richard began to frown as Felix moved closer and pawed at his leg. "What do you want, boy?"

Felix yowled again and turned his back, flicking his tail impatiently. He took several steps toward the doorway and looked back with what seemed to be a questioning look.

"You want me to follow you?" Richard smiled at the notion, but he shrugged into his coat, picked up his gloves and his hat, and followed Felix down the staircase. When they reached the bottom, Felix led the way to the outer door and yowled again.

"I cannot go with you now, Felix." Richard shook his head. "I am already late and Lady Charlotte is waiting for me to escort her to the ball."

Felix yowled once more and sat back on his haunches to stare at Richard curiously. Then he streaked for the door and sat in front of it, staunchly refusing to let Richard pass by.

"Stop this, Felix." Richard frowned at him. "I plan to offer for Lady Charlotte tonight, and it will not do for me to keep her waiting. Ladies do not like to wait, you know."

Felix bobbed his head up and down as if he understood the words that Richard had spoken. Then he moved to the side quite nicely so that Richard could pass.

"Thank you, Felix. You stay at home and be a good boy until I return." Richard smiled at him and waited for the door to be opened. But before he could step over the threshold, Felix streaked past him and bounded down the steps of the townhouse.

"Come back here, Felix." Richard hurried after his sister's cat. It was chilly this evening and the fog was dense. He could not, in all conscience, leave Felix outside in the elements.

Felix moved down the street at a smart pace, just out of

Richard's reach. He turned back every few steps to yowl piteously and to make certain that Richard was still behind him.

Richard stepped up his pace and Felix moved a bit faster, eluding him quite handily. They went on this way for several moments until Richard realized that Felix was leading him to Maggie's door. "You must go on without me, Felix. I am certain that Miss Pendleton shall let you in."

Felix stopped and yowled so piteously that Richard's blood ran cold. Could it be that Felix had come to him for help? Was Maggie in some sort of trouble and in desperate need of his assistance?

"All right, boy. I'll take a look." Richard frowned as he set off behind Felix. "I will not go in, though. There are very few calamities so great that I would chance being bewitched by Miss Pendleton twice in one lifetime!"

"Artemis? Where are you, Artemis?" Maggie held her torch up high as she peered under a bush.

"We searched the house, miss." Spencer relieved her of the torch so that Maggie could more easily part the branches. "There is no sign of the little mite."

Maggie shivered and pulled her cloak more tightly around her shoulders. "Then she is outside and we must find her quickly."

"How did she get out, miss?" Spencer looked every bit as worried as Maggie.

"I do not know. Perhaps she wandered into the hall when we were removing the stain from the carpet."

Spencer nodded. "It is possible that she followed Felix out, miss, and hid in another chamber. The door to the street has not been opened, but Cook told me that she made several trips to the gardens."

"No doubt that is how it occurred." Maggie gave a worried sigh. "I do believe that Artemis knows her name and will come when called. Let us gather the staff end attempt to coax her out of hiding."

Spencer gave a nod, but there was a worried frown upon his face. "What if we do not find her, miss?"

"We *must* find her." Maggie turned to him with tears in her eyes. "The night is cold and she is far too young to survive until morning in such inclement weather."

Richard drew in his breath sharply as he glanced over the gate and saw torches bobbing in the fog. They were in the garden, for he could hear several voices calling out in the darkness.

Felix turned around abruptly and streaked toward Richard, leaping up into his arms. His rough tongue reached out to lick Richard's hand and he shivered violently.

"Whatever is the matter, Felix?" Richard stopped short as he heard Maggie's voice. He listened for a moment and then he turned to Felix with alarm. "She is calling for Artemis. Is one of your kittens missing, Felix?"

Felix licked frantically at his face, and Richard came to a sudden decision. Felix was clearly overset, and from the sound of Maggie's agitated voice, she was in no better shape. He could not leave Felix and Maggie at a time like this. They needed his assistance to find little Artemis and that was much more important than escorting Charlie to the ball.

"All right, boy. I will find her, never fear." Richard strode up to the front door. It was not locked and he let himself in, hurrying to the library and out the French doors into the garden.

"Artemis? Where are you, Artemis? You must make some sound so that we can find you."

Maggie's voice was thick with tears and Richard strode quickly to her side. "When did you see her last, Maggie?"

"Richard!" Maggie whirled to face him, rushing into his arms. "Oh, please help us, Richard! Artemis was in her basket this afternoon, but now she is missing. And the night is so dreadfully cold!"

Richard nodded, holding Maggie close and lending her the warmth of his body. After a moment, he released her and gave her a gentle shove toward the house. "Go fetch a warmer cloak, Maggie. You are chilled to the bone. And bring Felicity back with you. If Artemis is hiding because she is frightened, the sight of her mother may entice her out."

"I shall do it immediately!" Maggie favored him with a blinding smile. "Thank you, Richard! I should never have thought of that!"

Richard found he was trembling a bit as he turned to the butler. Holding Maggie in his arms once again had served to remind him of the joy he had lost. "Has the house been searched, Spencer?"

"Yes, Lord Larchmont." Spencer nodded.

"Every closet and chamber?"

Spencer nodded again. "All but the best guest chamber, my lord. It has been closed up ever since Miss Pendleton's brother took his leave."

"Miss Pendleton's *brother?*" Richard's mouth dropped open in shock.

"Yes, my lord. Miss Pendleton was so delighted to see him. She told me that she had not laid eyes on the captain for over two years."

Richard nodded, his mind spinning with a complex mix of emotions. The man he had seen Maggie embracing was her brother!

"I fear our cause is lost, sir." Spencer wore a worried frown. "It grows colder by the moment and the poor little kitten has surely expired by now. But Miss Pendleton refuses to call off the search."

Richard's face set in tense lines. "Pluck up, man. We shall search the entire night if that is what Miss Pendleton wishes. I have heard it said that mother cats go to great lengths to rescue their young from danger. Can we, in good conscience, do less?"

"No, my lord." Spencer had the grace to look slightly embarrassed. "But I cannot help but think that there is something havey-cavey about this. If you doubt me, just look to your cat."

Richard's eyes narrowed as he spotted Felix near the

library door, grooming himself quite contentedly. All traces of his earlier desperation had disappeared and, as Richard listened, a deep purr rumbled from his throat.

"I have Felicity!" Maggie rushed out the door with Felicity in her arms. "She must not realize that Artemis is missing, for I found her sleeping quite contentedly in her basket. Where should I put her, Richard?"

Richard gestured toward the spot where Felix was sitting. "Next to Felix. Perhaps they will search for Artemis together."

Maggie placed Felicity next to Felix and the two cats nuzzled each other. They seemed disinclined to go anywhere at all and Maggie stared at them in concern. "They are not at all overset, Richard. Does this mean that Artemis is . . . is dead?"

"No, dearest Maggie. It does not." Richard began to grin as he pulled her into his arms. "It simply means that they have achieved their purpose by bringing us together. Spencer was entirely correct. There is something havey-cavey about the kitten's disappearance."

"But . . . but Artemis *is* missing. We must not lose sight of that." Maggie snuggled into Richard's embrace despite her worried protests. "Oh, Richard. I . . . I thought that I should never see you again!"

Richard sighed, holding the woman he loved once again in his arms. "We must take care that such a misunderstanding does not ever occur again. I do believe the only way to achieve that is to never let you out of my sight."

"But . . . how shall you do that?" Maggie pulled back to gaze up into his face. "I will not consent to become your mistress, Richard. I love you with all my heart, but I should rather give you up than cheapen the affection that I hold for you."

"My mistress?" Richard stared at her in utter shock. "Wherever did you get such a notion, Maggie? I have no intention of asking you to become my mistress!"

"You do not? But Polly was privy to the conversation

that Lady Charlotte had with your mother when they were discussing your wedding plans. The marchioness asked her what she should do about me, and Lady Charlotte said that she should give you leave to set me up in a cottage on your estate and . . . and—''

"I have not declared for Lady Charlotte and I never shall!" Richard interrupted her quickly, the anger blazing fiercely in his eyes. But one glance at Maggie's trembling lips caused him to put it from his mind to deal with at another time and kiss her instead. "You are all that matters to me, Maggie. Will you agree to become my wife?"

"But . . . but but what about your mother? And the ton. They will surely disapprove."

"They shall come around once they see that they cannot control our destiny. I am offering for you quite publicly, Maggie, in front of your aunt's entire staff. Will you marry me?"

"I . . . I . . . yes!"

Maggie's smile was a ray of golden sunshine and Richard kissed her again. It was several moments before he released her and then it was only to step back and give Felix a stern glance. "Does this satisfy you, Felix? Maggie has agreed to become my wife."

Felix stared up at the happy couple for a moment, and then he quite clearly nodded his head. He nudged Felicity and, after a moment, she also nodded.

"Our match has met with their approval." Richard turned to Maggie with a smile. "I must apologize for thinking that your brother was much more than a brother."

Maggie frowned slightly and then her eyes widened in sudden understanding. "So that is why you stayed away! You saw me with Stephen, and you thought that he was . . ."

Richard cut off her comment with another kiss and then he wrapped his arm around her shoulders. "We shall discuss this later, Maggie. Now let us adjourn to the library to celebrate our engagement. I am certain your aunt must keep a bottle or two of excellent champagne in her cellars."

"I shall fetch it immediately, my lord." Spencer bowed and rushed off, the rest of the staff following his lead.

"But . . . but what shall we do about Artemis?" Maggie turned to Richard in some confusion.

"Felix shall take care of that particular problem since he is the one who caused it in the first place." Richard turned to his sister's cat to favor him with a stern glance. "Lead us to her, boy. Maggie cannot fully enjoy our celebration until Artemis is returned to her basket."

Maggie blinked in astonishment as Felix padded into the library, Felicity following at his heels. He escorted the gray tabby to her basket and then he led them up the staircase. He walked down the hall with great dignity and stopped to scratch at the closed door to the largest guest chamber.

"But Artemis cannot possibly be in there." Maggie turned to Richard in surprise. "The door has been closed since Stephen left."

Richard grinned, stilling Maggie's hand as she reached for the latch. "No, Maggie. Watch, and Felix shall open it."

Felix yowled once, as if in protest, but then he reached up with his front paws to work the latch. The door creaked open and Maggie's eyes widened as she spotted a small mound under the rose-patterned coverlet.

"Artemis?" Maggie raised startled eyes to Richard.

"Yes, indeed, or I miss my guess. Retrieve her, Felix."

Felix stalked into the chamber with great dignity and pulled back the coverlet with his paw. Then he moved forward to nuzzle tiny Artemis, who was curled up into a ball, fast asleep.

"Do you suppose that Felix actually planned this to bring us together?" Maggie's voice was awed.

"Perhaps." Richard embraced her tightly, smiling down into her dear face. "It truly does not matter how this remarkable event came about. It has served its purpose very well indeed."

Maggie returned his smile in full measure and then she laughed softly. "If we dare to speak of this, all will think we have lost our senses. Is it truly possible that we owe our future happiness to your sister's matchmaking pet?"

"Most assuredly." Richard chuckled as he held his love tightly in his arms. "After all, my dear sister has always claimed that Felix is a most remarkable cat!"

RESCUING ROSEBUD

JUDITH A. LANSDOWNE

CHAPTER ONE

Miss Winifred Bittle gazed about the attic in frustration. Portmanteaux and band boxes littered the floor. A profusion of trunks and the most unusual shapes hiding beneath Holland covers stood temptingly about. "Rosebud? Dearest? Where are you? Are you up here? I cannot think she would come up here, Aunt Jess. She is such a tiny thing. What a monumental task it would be for her to follow John and Thomas up so very many stairs."

"Up here she came nevertheless," Miss Jessamine Bittle responded. "I saw her myself. Though if she has got back down again I cannot know."

"Well, she is not here now, Aunt Jess. She would answer me else. She is very good at making a reply when I call."

"She is very good at scampering about where she is not wanted and getting into every sort of scrape imaginable, is what you ought to say, Freddie. Goodness, someone has left the window open. That will not do. I expect John and Thomas could not bear the odor. What a smell of camphor!"

Winifred stared at the tiny hexagonal window tilted inward on its hinges and her heart skipped a beat. "Aunt

Jess, you do not think that Rosebud would— No, she would not."

"I do hope not," Jessamine Bittle replied. "But she is such a rascal and she does attempt the most extraordinary things."

"Yes, but she cannot have gone out through here," Winifred insisted hopefully, crossing to the offending window and peering through the opening to discover that the roof tilted only slightly beneath it and would most certainly allow a kitten safe purchase. "Rosebud?" she called, the chilly air blowing in at her. But there was not the tiniest "meow" in reply, so she closed the window up tight and led the way back down out of the attic. "Well, we have already looked everywhere upon the second and third floors, Aunt Jess. Perhaps John and Thomas have had better luck. I cannot be at ease until I know that my precious is safe. You know I cannot."

Unfortunately, Miss Jessamine Bittle's coachman and groom had not had any better luck at all. They had searched the entire first floor, the ground floor, and even the tiny cellar, drawing the rest of the staff into the search along the way, but had not discovered the kitten's hiding place.

"Gone out that attic window," Miss Bittle declared knowingly. "We shall likely never see the scamp again."

Winifred could feel tears gather in her eyes. Really, it was the most annoying thing. She attempted to blink them away, but one rolled silently down her cheek and she was forced to acknowledge it by wiping it away with the back of her hand.

"Oh, do not cry, Freddie," Miss Bittle pleaded. "You know I cannot bear to see you cry, nor can anyone at all who has a heart." And with a wave of her hand, she sent John and Thomas scurrying out into the street to search for the kitten. "Knock on every neighbor's kitchen door and ask the servants if they have seen our Rosebud, John. And Thomas, search through the stable. Perhaps she has settled down amongst the hay."

Winifred felt a perfect nodcock, crying over a kitten.

But Rosebud had been a gift from her youngest brother, Lionel, who had only two weeks before gone off to fight the French in a coat of red, looking every bit the grandest of all the cavalrymen on board the *Swallow*. Winifred loved both of her brothers with all of her heart but Lionel especially, because he was much closer to her in age and they had grown up together in Aunt Jess's charge while Ethan had been away at school. Because she loved Lionel so, she loved the kitten he had given her equally as well.

And Freddie believes in omens, thought Miss Bittle, gazing at her niece with a deal of understanding and sympathy. *If Rosebud is lost or injured or—heaven forbid—killed, she will think it some sign that Lionel is about to suffer a similar fate. I know she will.*

Austin Hobart Holt, Lord Carrington, paced his study, his spurs jangling with each step. He ran his fingers distractedly from time to time through his neatly cropped golden-brown curls. Once or twice he muttered under his breath. For a moment he paused before the leaded windows to stare out at the winter-ravaged group of rosebushes that stood between his townhouse and Garvey's. Then he grumbled and began to pace again.

The Garveys had gone to winter at their estate in the West Riding where Miss Mercy Garvey had, in December, repeated her vows to Whitfield. Damnation! How could she have picked Whitfield over him? He had been so sure of her, so certain that all he need do was offer and Mercy would accept without the least hesitation.

Well, there it was then, was it not? Women were not to be depended upon. How often had his own father warned him of it? Too often. Over and over again. But had he listened? No. Likely his father was turning over in his grave at this very moment. No, more likely his father had already risen up out of his grave and was even now striking out along the road, bones grating and rattling, in the direction of London to wrap his fleshless fingers around his son's neck and squeeze tightly.

"Yes, and you would do it, too, you old tartan," Carrington muttered. "And I should deserve it. I have lost Jezebel."

"I thought it was Miss Garvey what he lost," whispered James, the first footman, his ear firmly pressed against the closed study door a good six inches above the butler's ear and just to the right of it.

"Lost Jezebel as well," Congreve replied quietly. "Wagered Miss Garvey would accept his suit and marry him. Wagered his Jezebel against Lord St. Martin's Blaze."

"Devil take it, no wonder he has been in such foul humor of late," James grumbled. "His lordship did love that horse. He truly did."

"Took his papa twenty years to breed a horse as perfect as Jezebel and this very morning his lordship had to deliver her up into Lord St. Martin's hands," Congreve sighed.

"Women! They are none of them to be depended upon," Carrington growled. He lifted a glass paperweight from his desk and hefted it thoughtfully, but he decided not to throw the thing and set it down again. "Women! Phah! I shall be happy never to see another female again as long as I live!"

The memory of St. Martin leading Jezebel away through the cold January morning less than an hour ago made Carrington cringe. He had been a fool to wager Jez, even upon such a sure thing as Mercy's choosing to honor his suit. Every gentleman who saw her coveted that horse. And now she belonged to St. Martin. Zeus, but he was angry! He had thought to have gotten over it three weeks after he had learned of Mercy's betrayal, but St. Martin had not come to collect Jez until this morning and the wound had torn open again to bleed afresh.

Carrington tugged an enormous volume on ancient history from one of the bookshelves, opened it in the middle, stared down at it a moment, then snapped it closed, hefted it upon one palm and threw the blessed thing across the entire width of the chamber, slamming it against the paneling above the mantel with a tremendous whack—which was followed by a most curious series of clattering, hissing, sputtering, and thunking.

Carrington blinked in wonder. Soot and cinders were puffing down the chimney into the fireplace. "What the devil?" he breathed. And then a most hideous "RRRRRROWWWW!" and a "Spt-Spt-Spt!" met his ears and a tremendous clump of broken brick fell in one great gawoosh into the fire, causing the flames to leap up hungrily. Concluding that something was about to make an unexpected appearance, something alive, and not wishing to have it instantly roasted, Carrington rushed across the room, dove for the fire and stuck his hands between the flames and the flue. Into them dropped the most improbable creature. Carrington pulled away from the flames immediately, of course, with the creature secure in his grip, but not quickly enough to keep the hairs on his hands from getting singed, and his cuffs as well.

"What the devil are you?" he asked, having expected, perhaps, a chimney sweep and instead staring down at a sputtering piece of soot-covered fur from the depths of which two incredibly blue eyes blinked up at him.

"Mrrrow?"

"Oh, devil take it, a cat! Congreve! Congreve!"

"Mrrr-spt-spt-spt!" the creature sputtered.

"Haaaaa-chooo!" Carrington responded. "Congreve!"

At first Carrington did think that he ought to wash his hands and change his jacket, but then he rather thought not. After all, he would be all sooty again the instant he took the kitten back from Congreve. No, much better just to carry the little creature next door, be rid of it, and then take care of his hands and his wardrobe. Garvey had informed him that Lady Garvey's sister and her niece were coming to London sometime after Christmas to visit the shops and the museums, but he had dismissed it from his mind. A good thing Miss Bittle had sent her man around to inquire about the kitten earlier, he thought, and that Congreve remembered, or he should have tossed this catlet out into the cold.

"Give it here then, Congreve," he growled, extending a hand.

"Are you certain, my lord? I should be more than happy to deliver it into Mr. Blather's hands for you."

"Yes, well, I think not. I think I shall make the delivery myself and take the opportunity to introduce myself to the Misses Bittle. Lady Garvey's relatives, you know. Two old maids. Make my bows; welcome them to the neighborhood and all that." *And warn them to keep this animal in their own house and out of mine,* Carrington added in silence as he took the kitten from Congreve and strolled out the door, down the stoop, around the rosebushes and up onto the Garveys' front stoop. He raised the knocker and let it fall.

It was devilish cold upon that stoop. The north wind was whipping down the street at a dreadful pace. Carrington raised the knocker and let it fall again, wishing that he had taken the time to don his greatcoat, hat, and gloves. But he was just next door to his own home—a step away—and the Garveys' butler, Blather, did not generally allow people to lanquish upon the stoop. Nevertheless, the door remained unanswered and Carrington shivered. The kitten attempted to free itself from his grip and squiggle up close against him, but he would not allow it. He held it in one soot-covered hand out and away from him as though its merest touch were poison. The kitten wiggled and waved all four feet anxiously in the air, mewing piteously.

"Stifle it," grumbled Carrington. "You are not dying, you know. It is merely a bit chilly out here."

"Mrrr-phft!" the kitten protested, taking a slap at his wrist with one tiny paw.

Carrington gave the thing a bit of a shake, raised the knocker again and let it fall.

The door veritably flew open, but it was not the Garveys' butler who stood in the doorway. Carrington's eyes widened considerably.

"Yes?"

The young woman's cheeks were pink—from running to answer the door, Carrington guessed, because she was quite breathless—and her hair, once captured neatly in a low bun on the back of her neck, was coming loose and wandering in silky ashen strands about her shoulders. Her eyes looked up at him, deep brown and shining. This certainly was a new addition to Garvey's staff, though he could not for a moment guess what her position might be. And then it occurred to him, as he stared at her, that perhaps she had accompanied the Garveys' relatives.

"What is it that you want?" she asked, with a tinge of asperity. "We are all quite busy at the moment. Rosebud has disappeared and we cannot find her anywhere."

"Rosebud?"

"Yes. None of the neighbors have seen her and so everyone is searching the house again from top to bottom."

"Mrrph," the black little creature in Carrington's hand mumbled, causing him to cease looking at the lovely face and remember his mission.

"Good heavens, what is that?" Winifred asked, her gaze immediately drawn to the kitten.

"Rosebud, I presume."

"That? Most certainly not. Rosebud is all white except for one black ear. Are you even certain that that is a kitten?"

"Mfflewurts!" the kitten declared with some vehemence, squirming in Carrington's hand. "Mrrrow!"

"Definitely a kitten," Carrington drawled, "and it belongs to one of the Misses Bittle, my butler tells me. Allow me entrance, my dear, and we shall see what they think. It may be white under all the soot. Little wretch tumbled down my chimney."

"D-down your chimney?"

"Yes, and deuced lucky it is that I did not let it burn. Go. Fetch Blather if you fear to let me in. He knows me. I am your next-door neighbor. Damnation, it is cold out here."

"Mrrrrr," the kitten agreed, blinking wide blue eyes at Winifred, very familiar wide blue eyes.

"Rosebud?" Winifred asked, considering those eyes. "Is it truly you?"

"Mrft. Mffle."

"Oh! Oh, dear! It is you! Do not hold her like that, so

far away from you, sir. You are frightening her. She is quite accustomed to being cuddled against one's—against one's—"

"Breast?" Carrington offered.

"Y-yes."

"Fine. You cuddle her then," he growled, extending the kitten toward her. "I am not getting soot all over my jacket. It is bad enough I have got it all over my hands and my cuffs."

"Lord Carrington!" Blather exclaimed, trotting hurriedly into the vestibule and coming to a halt behind Winifred.

"You know this gentleman, Mr. Blather?"

"Indeed, miss. I am so sorry not to have been at the door, my lord. Come in, do. You will catch your death of cold."

"Haaa-chooo!" Carrington confirmed. "Take this creature, will you, Blather, and lead me to the Misses Bittle? I shall say good morning and then be off." He stepped up into the vestibule with such abruptness that Winifred was forced to almost leap out of his way.

"My lord, *this* is one of the Misses Bittle," Blather offered solemnly, accepting the kitten in one hand and holding it far away from his pristine waistcoat. "Miss Winifred, may I present your neighbor, Lord Carrington?"

"You are one of Garvey's relations?" Carrington asked, an eyebrow cocking.

"Yes, my lord."

"Well, deuce take it. Garvey might have warned me. Thought the Misses Bittle were spinsters. Thought you were their maid."

"You thought I was a maid?"

"Well, you did answer the door. This is not the country, Miss Bittle. In London, ladies do not answer their own doors. Most unacceptable. Never know who will be there."

"You are fortunate that I answered this door at all or you should be standing outside pounding yet!" Winifred exclaimed, her temper—already sorely tried—flaring.

"I was not pounding. I merely raised the knocker and

let it fall. You are fortunate, Miss Bittle, that I decided to deliver that catlet to you and did not send it out to be drowned," Carrington countered. "Made a perfect mess of me and my study. Soot everywhere. I will be much obliged if you will keep the thing in this house from now on and out of mine. I despise cats."

"Apparently you are just the sort of gentleman who would," Winifred declared, quite out of sympathy with anyone who would drown an animal. "Thank you, Lord Carrington, for not giving in to your murderous tendencies," she added, taking the soot-covered kitten from Blather, thinking for a moment, but then cuddling it, regardless of the mess, against her breast, sacrificing her gown to demonstrate to the man that *her* values were not misdirected. "Come, Rosebud dearest, I shall have you clean and warm in a matter of moments." Lifting her affronted little nose into the air, Winifred turned her back upon Carrington and stalked as regally as she could off in the direction of the kitchen.

"Should you like to follow me upstairs, my lord?" Blather offered quietly. "The other Miss Bittle is in the sun room."

"No, no, thank you, Blather. I think one Miss Bittle is quite enough for this morning," Carrington grumbled, turning back out the door that Blather opened for him. He paused for a moment upon the stoop and stared with grim consideration at the butler.

"Yes, my lord?"

"The other Miss Bittle, Blather, she is—older—than this one, is she? I mean to say—"

"The other Miss Bittle is considerably older, I should say, my lord. Miss Jessamine Bittle is Miss Winifred's aunt."

"Ah, just so." Carrington nodded, turning away and starting toward his own house. "At least she and that catlet have a keeper," he added under his breath. "Thank heaven for that!"

CHAPTER TWO

"I cannot think why Uncle Harland did not mention that he had such a crotchety neighbor," Winifred complained, busily drying Rosebud before the fire in the sun room. "He ought to have warned us, you know, Aunt Jess. We must be very careful not to disturb that gentleman, I think."

Jessamine Bittle smiled at the perfect picture her niece made in her forest-green gown, sitting upon a pillow before the hearth and rubbing at the kitten who wiggled about in a warm towel upon her lap. "Is he an elderly gentleman, dearest?"

"Oh, no. I do not think one can consider him elderly—though he is not a young gentleman, either. I should think he is somewhere near thirty. But quite haughty and most outspoken. And he does not like cats at all."

"Most gentlemen do not, Freddie. I have barely known a one in all my life who cared for cats."

"Lionel loves cats."

"No, does he? He has never said such a thing to me."

Winifred considered for a moment. "Perhaps he does not," she amended thoughtfully. "But he does know how to hold them at least. He does not carry them as though they are dead chickens."

Jessamine could not help but laugh.

"Lord Carrington did, Aunt Jess. He held my precious out at arm's length, like this, just as one would a dead chicken, except not by the feet. I thank goodness for that. And he called her a catlet and said he despised cats. 'I will be much obliged, Miss Bittle, if you will keep this thing in your house and out of mine,' he said in the most annoying tone. He was so very peevish, Aunt Jess. I should like to have boxed his ears!"

"Mrrrwow," Rosebud commented, peeking out from inside the towel. "Mrrr-pff."

"Indeed. You are perfectly correct, Rosebud. We shall not speak of the gentleman again. We have come to London to see the sights and not to concern ourselves with crotchety neighbors."

"Exactly so," Jessamine agreed, though the thought of Lord Carrington played about her mind enticingly. If she remembered correctly, Augusta had let slip that the gentleman was a bachelor and quite eligible. Of course, she had not brought her niece to London to catch a husband. Making a match for the girl would become her sister Augusta's responsibility when she and Lord Garvey returned to London for the Season. By then, Winifred would be most familiar with London and its environs and would not appear to be a green girl fresh from the country, staring wide-eyed at every little thing.

She will appear most sophisticated and elegant, and that is our only hope, Jessamine thought. *Augusta was correct when she wrote me so. Though I think my dearest is lovely and a wonderful prize, the gentlemen of London most likely will not, not when there will be so many perfect young ladies from whom to choose.*

And that thought made Jessamine Bittle nibble at her lower lip in frustration. Perfect! Why must a young woman be perfect? Heaven knew not one gentleman was expected to be perfect. Well, that was unfair. Young women did look for gentlemen to perfectly match their imagined ideal. She had done so and had thrown her life away by doing it, too.

She might have been Mrs. Michael Haggerty with a snug cottage of her own and her own children playing upon the parlor floor—except that he had been an Irishman and without a title and short—and therefore he had not matched her ideal of the perfect mate. And so she had refused his offer of marriage and had sent him off into the arms of another.

And now I am no one's wife, no one's mother, a spinster aunt merely, who lives upon the graciousness and generosity of my brother-in-law and my nephew, Ethan. Though, what Lionel and Winifred should have done without me when their mama and papa were killed, I cannot think. They were babies merely. Who would have cared for them? Not Augusta and Harland, and surely not Ethan, who was little more than a boy himself. But I will have better for my Freddie. I will see that she has a husband and family and must not suffer the stigma of an unmarried woman.

"What are you thinking, Aunt Jess?" Winifred asked, having come to sit upon the footstool before her aunt without Jessamine even noticing. "You have such a serious frown upon your face."

"Have I? I should not, for I was merely thinking where we ought to go first on our little tour."

"May we go to the Tower, Aunt Jess? I should dearly love to see the Tower of London."

"Yes, well, there is little to do there in January, I think, but perhaps the old lady who presides over the crown jewels will take us up to see them. Should you like to see the crown jewels?"

"Yes, and I should like to see the Bloody Tower, too. And Wakefield Tower and the Tower Green where all those people were beheaded. But especially I should like to see Wakefield Tower. That is Lionel's favorite, and he has told me time and again of the famous people who have been confined there."

"Then we shall go," Jessamine confirmed with a nod and a smile. "Tomorrow, if it is not such a dismal day as today. And if it is a dismal day, I think we shall visit the British Museum."

"Or the Egyptian Hall," Winifred offered eagerly. "I should dearly love to see the Egyptian Hall. It has only just opened, you know, Aunt Jess, and is likely to become a smashing success. That is what Lionel says—a smashing success."

"Mrrfph!" Rosebud agreed, no longer black, but once again a fluffy white kitten with one black ear, as she climbed up into Winifred's lap in hopes of being petted.

"I am pleased to have you visit, Teddy, but I have not the least urge to go gaming," Carrington drawled late that evening as he leaned negligently against the drawing-room mantel. "We shall think of something else to do for the next week or so, eh? I have had quite enough wagers to last me for the rest of my life."

"Right," nodded the curly-haired gentleman sprawled at his ease before Carrington's fire. "St. Martin came for Jezebel, did he? I had forgotten that. Dreadful. Would not think to place a wager on anything again for at least a month after such a loss. He will not sell the beast back to you, will he, Uncle Austin?"

"Will not even consider it."

"Well, then, she is lost, your Jezebel. Yes, and your Miss Mercy Garvey is lost as well. She is Lady Whitfield now. You have had a wretched time of it lately."

"Not so wretched as it might have been, Ted. At least I did not actually marry Miss Mercy Garvey."

"But I thought you wished to marry her?"

"Yes, so did I. But I have changed my mind, you see. I am, in fact, relieved that I avoided the parson's mousetrap— though I did so by the skin of my teeth this time. I cannot imagine what came over me to offer for the girl. Think of it, Teddy, to be married to Miss Mercy Garvey and forever at her beck and call. She will rule Whitfield with an iron fist, I have no doubt. He will not be with us at the mills this spring. He will not be attending the races, either. And the hells? Whitfield will never see the inside of a gaming hell again, I can assure you of that. Mercy will keep him under her thumb for the rest of his life."

"But you did wish to marry her, Uncle Austin," Theodore insisted. A bare ten years younger than his uncle, he idolized that gentleman and made it his business to know everything that he could about him. "I cannot think why you should wish to marry her one moment and be relieved that you did not the next."

"You will learn," Carrington murmured. "There is a part of a gentleman, Ted, that longs to be married—to have his own establishment with a lovely woman to manage it, to have his own children with a splendid mother to manage them, to have the peace and quiet and comfort of an orderly home in which to settle back and relax from an annoying day. But there is another part of him that knows the truth."

"The truth?"

"Yes, the truth. Women, though they be ever so lovely and splendid, are never, never comfortable. They forever interfere in a man's life and give him advice he don't want and suggestions he don't need. I have had an extremely close call, Ted. Unsettling, to say the least, and I intend it shall not happen again. I have escaped Hades by a hair's breadth this past year, though Jezebel was a hard price to pay for my deliverance. But I shall never again be tempted by a pretty face and the glimpse of a well-turned ankle, let me tell you. I shall remain a bachelor until the day I die and then, my boy, though you cannot inherit the title nor what is entailed, between your father's fortune and mine, you will be perfectly set for the rest of your life."

"Well, but I do not care to be perfectly set for the rest of my life through such means, thank you very much, Uncle Austin. Mother says that you must be in great pain even now because of your loss. She was adamant that I should come to town and actually drag you into the country with me if you would not come willingly, just so she could help you to mend your broken heart."

"There, that is just what I have been saying!" Carrington exclaimed. "Your mother is a lovely, splendid woman, but she must interfere where she is not wanted. All women must. It is their nature. They are not rational beings, Theodore; they are forever dreaming dreams and feeling feelings; they will rule a man and tell him how he must feel and what he must do from morning till night if they can; and they cannot help but make a gentleman's life most uncomfortable! Why, any man with a bit of sense would actually wish to marry one of them," he added with a growl, "I cannot understand. I must have been out of my mind!"

"Mrrrow spff-phft," Rosebud purred thoughtfully the next morning standing upon the windowsill in Winifred's bedchamber and peering out into the bright sunshine. And then she stood up on her two little hind legs and patted at the glass with the tips of her front toes.

"What is it, Rosebud? What do you see?" Winifred asked, allowing her maid, Gracie, to fit the last pin into her dress and then crossing to the window herself. "My, that is a perfectly splendid coach, is it not?" she commented, staring down into the street. "Someone has come to pay a call upon Lord Carrington. No, it must be Lord Carrington's coach, for that is the man himself just climbing into it."

"Mrrrrr," Rosebud replied enigmatically, continuing an attempt to paw her way through the window glass.

"She is longing to go outside, miss," Gracie smiled.

"Yes, I think so. Well, she shall soon. Once we have broken our fast, we shall be off to the Tower."

"You are taking the kitten with you, Miss Winifred?"

"Most certainly. Rosebud will enjoy it immensely. She has developed a fondness for coaches, I think, since our long trip into London. Look, Gracie, how she tries to reach that coach from here. She cannot wait to be off again."

"I do not think it is the coach she tries to reach," Gracie offered shyly.

"You do not?"

"No, miss."

"What, then? Is there a bird?" Winifred peered out the glass with great concentration. "I do not see a bird."

"No, miss. It is that gentleman, I think."

"Lord Carrington? That cannot possibly be. Why, he treated Rosebud like a—like a—diseased hedgehog, Gracie. Honestly, the way he held her and spoke of her, I could barely keep from boxing his ears!"

"Yes, miss. But cats are most peculiar. They often develop a fondness for those who do not like them. And the gentleman did rescue her, you know, from burning to death."

"He did?"

"Oh, yes, miss. I heard the tale direct from Mr. Blather himself, miss, who is quite the best of friends with Mr. Congreve, his lordship's butler. It seems your Rosebud came tumbling down his lordship's chimney and there was a fire already roaring in the fireplace. But his lordship, knowing it must be some poor animal—for what else could it be but a bird or some such—positively dove across the chamber and stretched his poor hands out into the fire to keep the poor thing from falling into the flames. Rescued our Rosebud from a blazing inferno, he did, and burned his hands awfully doing it, too. But he made not the least mention of it until well after he had returned the little minx to you, miss."

"Oh, my goodness!"

"Just so, miss. He is very courageous, I think, this Lord Carrington, and very caring. There is many a man I know would not move from their chairs to help a suffering animal, much less would they stick their hands into a blazing fire."

With a nod and a curtsey, Gracie took her leave and scurried down the hall to assist Miss Jessamine with her hair.

"Well," Winifred murmured to herself as she knelt upon the window seat stroking Rosebud and staring after Lord Carrington's departing coach, "how could I know he had done such a thing? I simply assumed the hearth was cold and the black upon his hands nothing but old soot."

"Brrrr," Rosebud said, arching her little back beneath Winifred's loving touch. "Brrrrrr-pht."

"I ought not to have treated him so badly, Rosebud, my dearest. He spoke in the most crochety fashion, and I took him to be surly and uncaring. And I was quite wrong. It is quite likely he was so very grouchy because his hands were most painful and he did not wish to mention it."

"Mrrrrow," Rosebud agreed, ecstatic with the stroking, and rolling upon her back to offer her stomach for like treatment.

"I shall speak to Aunt Jess about it. Perhaps there is something we may do to demonstrate to Lord Carrington our gratitude. Have him to dinner perhaps and have Cook prepare all his most favorite things. Yes, that is an excellent idea. I shall speak with Aunt Jess about it at once."

Lord Carrington had dressed in his generally natty fashion that morning, but his burgundy morning coat and gray-and-burgundy striped waistcoat and most of his dove-gray pantaloons were well hidden beneath his many-caped greatcoat. His fine beaver hat, of dark gray with a wide black band circling the crown, sat at a jaunty angle upon his crisp brown curls, covering the most of them just as his greatcoat covered his fashionable clothing. A woolen scarf of deep burgundy was wrapped around his neck, doing its best to cover his chin and some of his ears, and fine leather gloves covered his hands, but nothing could cover the glorious green eyes that were the birthright of all the Holt men. Those eyes shone like emeralds in the sunlight and met Theodore's own brown ones with a certain woeful glee.

"I am rather depressed about it, of course, but then again, it will be somewhat of a treat, Teddy. I have never actually bought a horse."

"Never, Uncle Austin?"

"Never. I have always just brought a horse or two with me from the farm at Hagsford Hollow. M'father bred so many of them that we are overrun with the beasts there.

I sold any number of them when he died and still I cannot count them all. And each one a prime one, too."

"But Jezebel was the very finest," Theodore sighed. "She truly was."

"Yes, but now I am to see if I can discover a likely piece of blood and bone on my own. I wonder, you know, if I will prove as good a judge of possibilities as my father was used to be."

"Possibilities?"

"Indeed. Any man may learn to judge horse flesh if he has half a brain, but to judge a horse's possibilities—that takes a deal more knowledge than most have acquired."

Theodore leaned back against the squabs and smiled the most enigmatic smile.

"What? What are you grinning about?"

"I am remembering something Mama told me before she sent me here to fetch you. It involved judging and possibilities."

"It did?"

"Um-hmmm."

"Well, out with it. What did your mama say?"

"That by accepting Lord Whitfield's suit over yours, Miss Garvey had proved herself a poor judge of gentlemen and displayed a woeful lack of knowledge in the area of possibilities."

"Now what the devil did Angela mean by that?"

"I am sure I do not know, Uncle Austin. Mama sometimes says the oddest things."

CHAPTER THREE

"We ought not go any farther, dearest," Jessamine said, staring about her at the dreary interior of Wakefield Tower.

"But, Aunt Jess, the warder said we might. There is no one about and we may take all the time we require and climb all the way to the top if we wish. Lionel will be so envious when I write that I have seen every single chamber of Wakefield! And I shall describe the Tower most accurately so that he will feel everything—the cold and the damp and the ghosts."

"The ghosts?"

"Yes. Cannot you feel them? They are everywhere here."

"All I feel is cold and damp. This is a dreadful place. I cannot think that it will be good for you to continue on."

"Balderdash!"

"But Freddie, there are so many steps and—"

"I have my walking stick, Aunt Jess, and my leg does not ache at all and I do so wish to see the entire place."

"Mrrrow." Rosebud added her voice to Winifred's plea.

"And why you must bring that kitten to such a place as this," Jessamine sighed, though she could not but smile at the little head poking up out of Winifred's reticule.

"Rosebud is not in the least heavy and she loves to snuggle inside my reticule and I feel much—much more confident about—about—Lionel when she is with me. It is silly, I know—".

"Worse than silly. It is ridiculous. Your brother gave you a kitten, but he did not intend for you to think his future and Rosebud's in some way intertwined."

"No, I know he did not, but I cannot help but feel that in some way—"

"Utter nonsense," Jessamine declared. "But if you must see all of this dreadful place, allow me to carry Rosebud and you shall carry my reticule, which is not near as large nor as heavy. I will never forgive myself if you slip and fall, Freddie."

The two ladies made their way cautiously upward, entering each abandoned chamber where prisoners had been kept. Some were larger than others. Some connected to form a set of rooms; others were tiny; all were bleak and dreary and damp even though the sun shone brightly outside. As they reached the topmost chamber, Winifred shivered and sighed.

"How terrible to be confined in such a place as this for even the shortest time," she whispered.

"Mrrr-phft," Rosebud agreed, sticking her head out of the reticule as Jessamine set it down upon the stained and pitted stone floor. "Brrrrr-mwow!"

"Just so, precious," Winifred murmured quietly, staring through the thin slit of a window at the Thames below. "This is a place of despair inhabited by the spirits of the doomed."

"There are dead men's bones at the bottom of that river," a deep voice growled.

Winifred positively jumped and her walking stick went flying across the room; Jessamine gasped, a hand going to her heart; Rosebud leapt clear out of the reticule and dashed into the adjoining chamber.

"Ow! Damnation! Get off of me, you imp! Where the devil did you come from?" roared the voice angrily.

"Oh! Oh!" Winifred cried. "Rosebud! Precious!" She

hurried without her walking stick into the adjoining chamber. "Well, for goodness' sake!" she exclaimed. "Do you have the least idea how you frightened us? We thought you were a doomed spirit!"

"And you still came rushing in?" asked a perfectly dashing young gentleman with honey-blond curls. "How brave you are."

"I might have guessed," grumbled the voice that had sent Winifred's spine to tingling a moment before. "Come, get this catlet off of me at once, Miss Bittle!"

"Mrrrr! Mrrr-phfft-phfffft!" Rosebud exclaimed. Winifred stared at Lord Carrington but could not see the kitten.

"Ouch! If you do not cease to prick me with those dastardly claws, I shall break your furry neck," Carrington muttered, unbuttoning the brass buttons of his greatcoat.

"Ran up Uncle Austin's leg," Theodore chuckled. "Never seen anything like it. Climbed right up under his greatcoat."

"It is not in the least humorous," Carrington growled.

"B-but it was," Theodore laughed. "You should have seen the look upon your face, Uncle. As a matter of fact, you should see the look upon your face at this very moment."

Winifred could not help herself. Her eyes saw the laughter in Theodore's and she was forced to giggle. Truly, the look upon Lord Carrington's face *was* humorous. Though he was attempting to scowl, his lips twitched and his eyebrows wiggled up and down, and that ruined the attempt completely.

"Freddie, do help the gentleman," Jessamine Bittle urged, stepping into the chamber, her heart still aflutter. "Cannot you see that Rosebud is tickling and scratching him all at one time?"

"Mrrow," Rosebud declared as Lord Carrington's coat opened wide. She scurried up onto one of his broad shoulders and stuck a rough little tongue into his ear. "Rrrrr-brrrr-rrrrr."

Winifred went to seize her, but just as her gloved hands came near enough to do so, Rosebud leapt from his lordship's shoulder into the slit of a window.

"Oh, no," Jessamine breathed. "Freddie, do be careful. Do not frighten her or she will leap out to her death."

"Join the dead men's bones at the bottom of the river," observed Theodore with a chuckle.

"It is not humorous," Winifred declared, tears already forming in her eyes. "Rosebud, precious, do come away from that window. Please do."

Carrington, his greatcoat hanging open, his dove-gray pantaloons covered with little pulls from the kitten's claws, and his silk waistcoat and burgundy jacket sporting bits and pieces of soft white kitten fur, noted the lovely brown eyes awash with sudden tears and swallowed the words he was about to say on the instant. The younger Miss Bittle's lower lip quivered, and though he could see very well that she was fighting against them, tears were actually beginning to wander down her lovely pink cheeks. He straightened his coat and offered the young woman his arm. "Allow me to escort you into the next chamber," he said softly. "Theodore, give Miss Bittle—you are the elder Miss Bittle, are you not? Just as I thought—Theodore, give Miss Bittle your arm and follow behind us."

"But I cannot," protested Winifred. "Rosebud—"

"Your kitten will not like to be left behind," Carrington explained patiently, tucking Miss Bittle's hand through the crook of his arm. "She will hop down from that sill and come dashing after us the very moment we are all out of her sight."

"Do you think so?"

"I am positive."

Winifred was not at all certain that she ought to trust him. He did not so much as know how to hold a kitten. But there was something in the tone of his voice and a certain stabilizing assuredness in his eyes. With a last look at Rosebud who was busily swatting at something outside the window, she allowed his lordship to escort her from the chamber.

"Here, now whose is this?" Lord Carrington asked once they had entered the other chamber. He freed himself from Winifred's hold, crossed the room and picked up the silver-headed ebony walking stick from the floor.

"Mine," Winifred replied. "It leapt out of my hand when I heard you speak of dead men's bones. I thought you were a ghost."

"Well, I am not. Here you are, Miss Bittle. No, do not so much as think to go back and peer around the archway. Your kitten will be with us presently, I assure you. May I present my nephew? Miss Bittle, Mr. Theodore Paxton. And this is your aunt—?"

"Jessamine."

"Just so. Teddy and I are honored to make your acquaintance, Miss Bittle," he said, bowing to Jessamine. "I am your neighbor, Carrington."

"Mrrow-brrr-brrrr," announced a tiny voice, and four little white feet came padding into the chamber. "Mrrrrr-phft."

"Rosebud," Winifred sighed, wiping the tears from her cheeks with the back of one warmly gloved hand.

"Mrrr-ophf?" the kitten queried, sitting down and blinking its wide blue eyes innocently up at her. "Mrrr-ophf-wurrgle?"

"You see, my dear Miss Bittle. It is just as I said. This imp of yours cannot bear to be ignored. Teddy, scoop the thing up, eh, and carry it back down for the ladies."

"Oh, no, you need not do that," Winifred said, bending forward and lifting Rosebud up into her arms. "Naughty kitten," she murmured, rubbing her cheek against the soft fur and setting the kitten to purring. "You must never do such a thing again. If you will be so very kind as to fetch that large reticule, Lord Carrington, I shall just put her away."

"You keep her in a reticule?" Theodore asked, bemused.

"Oh, yes. She loves to be carried about in one, and most generally she behaves with great discretion."

Carrington refrained from making the least comment as he brought the reticule Winifred required and watched her set the kitten into it. "Have you seen enough of Wakefield, ladies?" he asked then. "May Ted and I escort you back down?"

"Yes," Jessamine nodded. "You do not mind, Mr. Paxton, if I lean upon your arm for the length of the way to the bottom?"

"My pleasure, ma'am." Theodore smiled.

"I will carry the kitten then, Freddie dearest, since I have Mr. Paxton to support me and you may carry my reticule."

"No," Carrington protested. "I shall carry the reticule with the kitten until we reach the ground, Miss Bittle. You must simply carry your own, and Miss Freddie—?"

"Winifred," she offered somewhat shyly.

"And Miss Winifred need merely concentrate on getting down safely upon my arm. You have injured your leg, Miss Winifred?" he asked as they began their descent.

"Long ago," she replied. "I was in a carriage accident and it was broken. It did not mend as it should. How do you come to be in Wakefield Tower, my lord? The warder told us that no one at all had come today."

"Yes, he would. Harry generally considers me no one at all I think, because I come so often. There is something about the history of the place draws me to it."

"Mrrrow," Rosebud mumbled from inside the reticule.

"Mrrrow, yourself," Carrington replied. "No one was addressing you, imp." From the corner of his eye he noticed Miss Winifred Bittle smile and he thought, not for the first time, how lovely she looked.

"Lord Carrington is not so crotchety as he pretends," Winifred declared, busily untying her bonnet. "He did not grumble once when I said I wished to see the Tower Green."

"So I noticed," nodded Jessamine. "I also noticed that he carried your reticule all the way to the green and back."

"Did you note Lord Carrington's horse, Aunt Jess? He purchased it just this morning, Mr. Paxton said. Did you not think it a most ordinary horse and had it not the longest ears?"

"A common, ordinary horse with enormous ears."

"Precisely. I should not expect Lord Carrington to ride a common, ordinary horse. But Mr. Paxton explained to me that his uncle thought it was a horse with possibilities."

Miss Jessamine Bittle's blue eyes lit at once. Possibilities? Lord Carrington thought the horse had *possibilities*? "I do think we ought to ask his lordship to dinner," she declared abruptly.

"But Aunt Jessamine, when I suggested as much this morning, you said—"

"I know what I said, dearest, but I was quite wrong. And now Lord Carrington has rescued your Rosebud not once, but twice. Certainly he is deserving of our thanks. We shall include Mr. Theodore Paxton in our invitation as well, and we shall not have them to the house, but order up a private parlor at Grillon's. I know just the thing! We shall attend the theater first and then go on to dinner. Your uncle Harland keeps his own box at Drury Lane. We shall make use of it to thank Lord Carrington for his able assistance."

The gentleman believes in possibilities, thought Jessamine Bittle, hope rising within her. Only think if he should see the possibilities present in my dearest Freddie!

"I cannot believe that you walked all around the Tower grounds carrying a reticule." Theodore grinned as he strolled with his uncle from the mews toward the rear of Carrington house. "I never expected it of you, Uncle Austin."

"Well, it was heavy with that kitten inside it. And it kept unbalancing itself, you know, as the creature padded from one end to the other. I could hardly allow a young woman with a bad leg to carry it to the Tower Green and back."

"No, but you might have talked me into carrying it."

"I might? Now you tell me."

"She is—quite pretty, Miss Winifred Bittle."

"I had not noticed."

"You had not? I thought you to have noticed that right off."

"No. I am no longer taking notice of whether or not women are pretty. Leads men to make complete fools of themselves."

"It does? Just noticing that a young lady is pretty?"

"Take my word for it. First you note that a woman is pretty, then you fall in love with her, then you toss away every ounce of pride you ever possessed. Best not to notice in the first place."

They reached the kitchen door and stepped inside, the heat from the ovens warming their wind-reddened cheeks. Carrington was just unwrapping the burgundy scarf from around his neck when he heard the ringing of the front bell. "Now what the devil?" he mumbled, strolling through the kitchen and into the corridor, Theodore directly upon his heels.

Congreve was just explaining that Lord Carrington was not at home when the two reached the foyer.

"St. Martin? Come in," Carrington urged. "Just stepped in from the mews this minute. Here, Congreve, take his things. Ted and I will see to our own. Then fetch us something to go with a bit of brandy, eh, Congreve? I am near frozen, and ravenous as well," he called over his shoulder as he hung his greatcoat in the closet beneath the stairs, tossed his beaver onto the hat rack, and deposited his scarf and gloves upon the long mahogany table. "So, what brings you to my door, St. Martin? You are not wishing to sell Jezebel back to me?"

"Not exactly."

"You know Ted?"

"Yes. Afternoon, Paxton. I have not come to sell the horse back to you, Carrington, but there is a problem with her."

"A problem? With Jezebel? Come upstairs and we will share a drink and discuss it." Carrington wondered what the devil could be wrong with the finest mare his father had ever bred.

"She is lost," St. Martin sighed as he eased himself down upon the settee and accepted a glass of brandy from Theodore's hand while Carrington filled two more glasses with the golden liquid. "Broke out of her stall about an hour ago, my grooms say, and bolted off down the street. Not a one of them could stop her. Furious about something she was. Thought she may have come here."

Carrington handed a glass to Theodore and stared down at St. Martin. "You lost her? She was furious and broke free from your stables and your men have lost her?"

"She ain't come back here then, eh?" St. Martin asked in disappointment. "Damnation, I have been praying all the way from my house to yours that she had."

The evening grew dark and the wind rose and clouds covered the stars. Carrington tugged the collar of his greatcoat closer about his ears and walked on. Little Bridge Street lay before him with nary a person in sight. The lamps had been lit, but they shed meager light and already the fog was rising from the river. He considered for a moment turning toward home, but only for a moment. Jezebel was running free on the streets of London and there was no telling what might happen to her. "Be sold to some farmer to pull his lorry for tuppence and a drink of gin," Carrington grumbled, crossing the cobbles to the opposite flagway to peer down a narrow alley. "Be led off and hidden in some stables and sold to some Irish earl. Jezebel!" he called into the growing roar of the wind. "Jez! Come to me!" He attempted to whistle—she always had come to his whistle since she had been a mere bit of a thing—but his lips were far too cold and not a sound came out. "Jezebel!" he called again into the alleyway, and then he continued on down Little Bridge Street shivering, despite a resolve not to, beneath layers and layers of wool.

He had been a perfect lunatic to wager Jezebel upon anything. Anything! And now he was well paid for it, too. Not only did he no longer own the mare, but St. Martin's grooms had lost her. *Damnation,* he thought, *I ought to be horse-whipped. I ought to be gibbeted. What could I have been thinking?*

But he knew perfectly well what he had been thinking—that he would have had Miss Mercy Garvey and Jezebel and St. Martin's Blaze, too. "Greedy son of a seagull," he muttered to himself. "Serves me right to have lost all. But it don't serve Jez right to be lost in London on a night like this. She will be petrified if I do not find her soon."

CHAPTER FOUR

Winifred woke to a quiet mewing. She rubbed sleepily at her eyes and whispered into the darkness. "Rosebud, sweetest, what is wrong?" The mewing continued and Winifred sat up in the bed, turned up the lamp, and peered about the room.

"Rosebud? What is it?" she called, hastily putting on her slippers and robe. Lamp in hand, Winifred searched the chamber. Finding no sign of the kitten, not even behind the draperies, she made her way out into the corridor. The mewing sounded louder here. Listening carefully, Winifred made her way to the very end of the corridor and turned into the smallest of the guest chambers. There on the windowsill stood Rosebud, peering out into the night and mewing with all her might.

"What is it?" Winifred whispered, lifting the kitten into her arms and peering out into the darkness. She could see nothing, but she heard horseshoes upon cobbles. She set the lamp behind her and went again to the window and peered out. Below her a horse lifted its head and whinnied. Then it shook, sending its mane shivering in the wind. Winifred stared. In the vague bit of light from the flambeaux that flared at the gate to the rear courtyard the horse looked otherworldly.

"Well, but it is not from another world," she told herself softly. "It is likely one of Uncle Harland's that has wandered out somehow and cannot get back in because the wind has blown the stable doors shut." She thought about arousing Mr. Blather and sending him out to arouse John and Samuel, but that seemed like a great many people to disturb just for one horse. "I will just go and lead the poor animal inside myself," she determined, picking up the lamp and carrying Rosebud back to her bedchamber, where she donned a pair of pink wool stockings and her riding boots.

"Mrrr," Rosebud observed as Winifred stood and made her way from the chamber, and then the kitten dashed out right behind her. With the lamp in one hand and holding the long, wide hems of her nightrail well out of her way with the other, Winifred limped cautiously down the staircase. *It is because of all the walking that I have done today that I am limping so,* she thought. *Otherwise my leg would not bother me at all.*

When she reached the closet beneath the stairs, she opened it and took her uncle's old greatcoat from a peg and his ancient beaver from the shelf above, and a pair of his gloves as well. "I shall not be cold at all in these," she murmured, buttoning the coat and pulling the hat down over her brow and slipping the large gloves over her thin, delicate fingers. "I shall be warm as toast. See if I am not."

She went to the kitchen door, opened the latch and walked around the side of the house to the rear courtyard. The horse was still there, pawing at the cobbles and nickering.

"Here now, my pretty," Winifred cooed. "Do not fuss so. I shall open the door for you and you will be warm in an instant."

She reached up to grab hold of the horse's halter and discovered that it had not got one on. "Well, of all things," she murmured. "And how am I to lead you with nothing to hold on to?"

"Mrrrr-burrrrb," said a little voice beside her.

"Rosebud! How did you get out? Oh, I was not watching. You must go right back inside, you scamp."

"Mrrrrow-ow-burrrrr," declared the kitten and scooted between the horse's forelegs. She rubbed against them one at a time, purring all the while, and then she scurried to Winifred's side. The horse followed the kitten docilely.

"Well, of all things," Winifred whispered again, her voice covered by the roar of the wind. "Come along then, Rosebud. Bring your friend," and she struck out across the yard to the stable doors and opened them wide. Kitten and horse followed her inside.

If he had not looked up at just that moment, Carrington would not have seen the lamp at all. He was just crossing behind Garvey House to his own mews when he noticed a tiny bit of light making its way into Garvey's stable. He came to an abrupt halt and squinted through the darkness. Was that a horse following the light? By gawd, it was! Who would be leading a horse into Garvey's stable at this hour? Something havey-cavey going on there, he thought, and immediately changed direction.

He approached the stable as quietly as possible. He might have stomped directly up to it and not been heard because the wind was making a dreadful racket, but he did not know this. His poor ears were absolutely frozen from his long search for Jezebel. Carefully he opened the stable door a bit and peeked inside. "Devil take it!" he shouted, and flung the doors wide. "Jezebel! Here, lad, what do you think to do with that horse?"

"Wh-what?" Winifred gasped, turning abruptly in his direction and losing her balance. She sat down with a great ooomph upon the straw-covered planking of the stable floor.

"I said," bellowed Carrington, pulling the doors closed behind him, "what do you think to do with that horse? She is not yours. Devil it!" he added as the lamp Winifred had dropped on her way to the floor set fire to the straw beside her and Jezebel dodged away while a number of other horses began to whinny in fear. Carrington hurried to Winifred, doffed his greatcoat and smothered the fire with it. "There. Better," he said breathlessly. "No, do not make a fuss, Jez," he added, slipping the coat back on. "You are quite safe. Come here, my girl."

The horse came to him at once, and in the darkness, Winifred could hear it snuffling and nuzzling at him. "Good girl, Jez," he said. "Very good girl, but that is quite enough for the moment. Now then, there must be a lantern around here somewhere."

Winifred listened to the gentleman fumble about in the darkness, then she heard him mutter, "Just so," and then she heard the striking of flints. "There," he said, lifting a lantern. "You are not burned, are you, lad?"

"N-no," Winifred murmured.

"Mrro," Rosebud murmured as well.

"Great goslings! Miss Bittle?" Carrington stood above her, the lantern light shining down to reveal poor Winifred all tangled in nightclothes and greatcoat and pink stockings and riding boots, with her uncle's beaver far down over her brow and over her ears as well. "By Jove, Miss Bittle, it is you!"

"Yes."

"Whatever are you doing out here in the middle of the night dressed like—like— Deuce take it, I cannot think of one thing to compare you to."

"I am—I was—" Winifred began softly, and then she groaned just the tiniest bit as she shifted about on the floor in an attempt to gain her feet.

"You are injured. Here, let me help you, Miss Bittle." Carrington set the lantern upon the floor and scooped her up into his arms. "Now, if I bend, can you catch the lantern handle?"

"Yes, but you need not carry me, my lord. I am capable—"

"Nothing of the sort. You took quite a fall. I shall simply carry you into your house. It is nothing to be ashamed of, to be carried into one's own house after an accident. Now, seize the lantern. Good girl! And off we go."

He kicked open the stable doors and kicked them shut again, then carried her to the kitchen door, fumbled for the latch and carried her inside where he set her upon a high stool. Then he closed the door, took the lantern and set it upon a counter. "In just a moment we will have a fire," he announced quietly, going to prod at the banked coals in the oven.

She smiled to see him so industrious on her behalf, and while his back was to her, slipped off the stool, lit a taper at the lantern and went about lighting candles to brighten the kitchen.

"You ought not be walking about," he said when he noticed.

"Balderdash, I am fit as a fiddle. Well, perhaps I have bruised my—my—but that is of no account. I shall not die from it. Your ears are red with the cold, my lord! Let me fix you a cup of tea. Have you been out long?"

"All night."

"You poor gentleman! You must be frozen solid!"

His lips parted to acknowledge that indeed he was, but just then the firelight glinted off strands of her long ashen hair and lit the deep brown pools of her eyes and showed him a face in flame and shadow that set his heart to pounding. She smiled up at him from beneath Garvey's old beaver and he thought how thoroughly adorable she looked and then he came to his senses. "No, no tea," he stuttered in a rush. "It is very late, Miss Bittle, and we ought not be— You will tell me how you came to be leading Jezebel into your stable tomorrow, will you not? It is all right that she stays the night there?"

"Well, of course she may stay the night, but— Rosebud!" Winifred exclaimed. "Oh, my goodness, Rosebud. Did she come inside with us, my lord? Look about do. I cannot think that I saw her come inside." Winifred limped hurriedly to the kitchen door and threw it open. "Rosebud," she called in a hushed voice so as not to awaken the entire household. "Precious, where are you?"

"Mrrrrow," came the forlorn reply. "Mrrrrow."

"I can hear the rapscallion," Carrington murmured, close beside Winifred. "Why does she not come in?"

"Perhaps she is locked in the stable?"

"She sounds a good deal closer than that." Carrington went to fetch the lantern and shone the light out into the night.

"Mrrrrrow-pft!" the kitten cried as loudly as it could.

"I cannot see her at all," Winifred murmured. "Not even the glow of her eyes. But I hear her quite plainly all the same."

"By Jove, she is in that tree," Carrington observed, raising the lantern higher to gaze up into the branches of a small elm beside the kitchen window.

"Oh no," Winifred groaned. "Rosebud, you naughty kitten, come down at once. But that is a useless thing to say. She will not come down. She is not at all good at climbing down."

"She climbed up," Carrington offered hopefully.

"Yes, I know. She is a very good climber-upper. But she is extraordinarily bad at climbing down. You do not think that you could—no, it is unconscionable of me to ask it— but it will take her forever to gather the courage to come down and she will catch her death on such a very cold night."

Carrington stared down into those oh so beautiful eyes and noticed tears of worry gathering in them. *No*, he thought. *I am not going to climb up into that flimsy little tree and fetch a kitten! I do not care if the tears come rolling down her cheeks in torrents. I am frozen and tired and I ache everywhere and I am I not going to*—but then he thought of Jezebel safe in this young lady's stables and knew she had come down all on her own dressed in the most unreasonable fashion simply to take his horse in from the cold and he felt the most ungrateful wretch. And that was why he stepped past her, strolled to the bottom of the tree and set down the lantern, doffed his greatcoat, then swung himself up onto the lowest limb.

"Mrrrrr," the kitten commented as a branch brushed

against Carrington's hat and sent it falling to the ground. "Mrrrr," she said again, as he struggled up onto the next highest limb.

"Mrrrr, yourself," Carrington grumbled. "What a poor excuse for a cat. Climbs up; cannot climb down. Whatever possessed you to climb so very high, catlet?" he growled as he swung himself up onto the next limb. "You must be short a sheet."

"Murffle," Rosebud responded, moving tentatively toward him. "Murffle-wurts!" And she sprang onto his shoulder, surprising him no end and almost sending them both crashing to the ground.

The kitten clung to him with all four sets of claws and would not be dislodged until he had carried her all the way back into the kitchen, collecting his hat, his greatcoat, and the lantern along the way.

"Oh, my precious," Winifred sighed, closing the door quickly after them and lifting the kitten from his shoulder. "I cannot thank you enough, my lord."

"Yes, yes, you can. By going upstairs to bed where you belong and taking that—that—catlet with you!" Carrington exclaimed in a hushed but agitated tone. Dead leaves were clinging to his crisp brown curls and some had fallen down the back of his jacket and were scratching his neck. His face smarted from a number of assaults by twigs and he was out of breath to say the least.

"But what about your tea?"

"Tea? No, no tea. I thought I said at first no tea. I ought not to be here alone with you at all, Miss Bittle. It is most unacceptable. I will—I shall—call upon you tomorrow to collect Jez," he added, hurriedly sliding into his greatcoat and jamming his hat upon his head. "Lock the door behind me. Do not forget. You are in London now. There are—are—burglars and things." And with that he was out of the house and off behind the stable, almost at a run.

"Well, and what do you think of that?" Winifred asked the kitten purring in her arms. "He must be very tired, I think, and that is all. Come, Rosebud, we will have a cup of tea for ourselves and then go upstairs to bed. Would you rather have a saucer of cream instead?"

"Mrrow," Rosebud answered, and licked at Winifred's cheek with a rough little tongue. "Rrrrrrrrrrrrrrrr."

Carrington could not calm himself. He slowed his steps as he came around the far side of his own establishment and up the front stoop. He willed his hands not to shake as he slipped his key into the front lock. He tossed his coat and hat and gloves all into a pile in the vestibule and picked up the lighted lamp that Congreve had left for him. And all the while he muttered under his breath that he was not at all upset. Not at all. There was not the least thing to be upset about. He continued this mantra up two flights of stairs and all the way down the corridor to his chambers. He repeated it a bit louder as he set the lamp down and poured himself a brandy. And then he lowered himself into the wing chair that stood before a still blazing fire and discovered among the flames the vision of an adorable woman in her uncle's clothes, pink wool stockings and riding boots, and he began to perspire despite the chill that clung to him.

It was all complete nonsense, of course. Miss Winifred Bittle was not even pretty. Well, perhaps she was pretty, but she was old. Of course, she was not so very old, not at all a spinster like her aunt. But she definitely limped.

"That is not fair at all," he muttered to himself. "What has a limp to do with anything? It is certainly not Winifred's fault that her leg was broken and was not set competently."

Those words sent his mind spinning. What was he doing? He had no business to be making excuses for the young woman—not when his whole being was set upon discovering reasons why he ought not to be thinking about her at all. And he ought not, because the most overwhelming sensations had come upon him in that kitchen. Had he not learned his lesson with Miss Garvey? Had he not explained to Teddy about women and how he never intended to become involved with one of them again? And certainly he did not wish to become involved with this young woman. Why, she had forced him up into a tree in the middle of the night to rescue a cat! How could any gentleman in his right mind think to become involved with a woman like that?

CHAPTER FIVE

"He was truly wonderful, Aunt Jessamine," Winifred proclaimed over breakfast the following day. "There he was, practically frozen to death, but he climbed right up into the elm and rescued Rosebud."

"Yes, well, that was very kind of him to be sure. But you ought not to have gone outside at all, Freddie. You know you ought not. Though I am pleased that you did because Lord Carrington might well have lost his horse forever if you had not led the beast inside. Do you think it heard Rosebud and that is why it came here? Well, nevertheless, you ought not to have invited his lordship to have tea with you in the middle of the night. That part was perfectly outrageous."

"It was? I thought it was merely the polite thing to do. If you had seen how red and cold his ears were and how he shivered, you would have offered him tea on the spot, Aunt Jess."

"Yes, but I am a deal older than you, my girl. There are any number of high-sticklers who would consider you compromised just for having been alone with the fellow in the stable."

"Balderdash!"

"Yes, it is balderdash, but it is *so* nevertheless. You must never do anything like it again. Freddie, how can you possibly eat three coddled eggs *and* a rasher of bacon at this hour?"

"I am very hungry. I do not believe that I have ever been so hungry in all my life. I expect it is because of all the exercise I had yesterday walking about the Tower."

"Perhaps we ought to spend today at home?"

"Oh, no, I am not ill, Aunt Jess. I am not even tired. I am merely hungry. Where are we bound this morning?"

"I did think that we might take in the British Museum. But you may not bring Rosebud with us. If she should climb out of your reticule in the museum and break a Ming vase or scratch upon some ancient tapestry and shred it to bits, we shall never live it down. No, and we shall never be allowed inside the place again, and quite likely the gentleman in charge will die of an apoplexy on the spot and we will be accused of his murder. You must leave her home. Mr. Blather will be pleased to assign someone of the staff to look after her."

"Mrrow," Rosebud offered, hearing her name. "Mrrrr." And she jumped most gracefully up into Winifred's lap and began to sniff at the bacon. With a grin, Winifred broke off a tiny piece and gave it to her.

"Oh, Freddie, do not feed that animal at the table. Of all the things to do!"

"You are not hungry, Uncle Austin?" asked Theodore as he watched Carrington push his beefsteak about on his plate without taking one bite.

"Huh? Oh, no, not very. I have found Jezebel."

"Where? How? Is she all right? Have you taken her back to St. Martin?"

"No. I will send Arthur around to St. Martin's later and tell him to come fetch her. She will not wish to go with him, of course. She is my horse. Always has been. I was there when she was born, you know. Stood right beside my father and helped to tug her into this world."

"That is why you are not eating. You cannot bear to part with her a second time."

"But I must. Won her fair and square, St. Martin did. Ought to teach you a lesson, Teddy. Never wager anything you cannot bear to part with—not even on what appears to be a sure thing."

Theodore did not quite know what to say. His uncle looked positively grim, almost despairing. "Perhaps if you were to offer to buy Jezebel back from him—"

"No. Offered. Wants Jez."

"Well, but perhaps he will change his mind now that she has run away from him. Where did you discover her?"

"Next door. On her way to our stable, I expect. Something gained her attention and so she went in next door."

"At the Garveys'?"

"Yes, at Garvey's. I do not wish to discuss it, Teddy. If you must hold a conversation at this hour of the morning, think of something a deal more palatable upon which to converse."

Theodore sat back in his chair and stared at his uncle with considerable thought. "Might we converse upon Miss Bittle?"

"Miss Bittle?"

"Miss Winifred Bittle. I find her perfectly delightful, do not you? Will she remain in town for the Season?"

"Too old for you. Twenty-three at least. A spinster."

"Oh, no, Uncle."

"Yes. You will suffer immeasurably do you get mixed up with that one. She will rule you in everything."

"Never," laughed Theodore.

"She will. You will not be able to stand up to her. Believe me, I know."

"Miss Bittle is not the sort to rule over anyone, Uncle. She is sweet and quiet and quite lovely."

"And adorable," Carrington mumbled.

Paxton nodded to himself. *I knew I had seen possibilities there*, he thought.

"Miss Bittle is just the sort to wrap a gentleman around her little finger for the rest of his natural life," Carrington sighed then. "One tear in those magnificent eyes of hers and a man will do anything she wishes."

"Did Miss Mercy Garvey's tears have a like effect?"

"Great heavens, no! Miss Garvey never cried. What had she to cry about? Every bachelor in London wished to marry the girl."

"Oh. Well, I expect every remaining bachelor will wish to marry Miss Bittle this Season."

"Never. She is not near the beauty Miss Garvey was. And she is a good deal older, too. And she— Her leg, you know. That will keep any number of gentlemen away."

"It will? But why?"

"Great goslings, Teddy, do you know nothing at all? London gentlemen expect to marry perfect young ladies, not ladies who limp and are a breath away from spinsterhood. She will need some help to make a decent match, our Miss Bittle. I expect that is why the elder Miss Bittle brought her to London so very early, that she might gain some town bronze to make her more appealing."

"I think she is most appealing right now, Uncle Austin."

"So do I," Carrington muttered, sipping at his coffee, long since grown cold. "So do I."

Winifred stared at the Rosetta Stone but could not discover herself to be at all impressed. It was merely a large black rock with scribbling upon it. Not nearly as interesting as Lord Carrington's entrancing emerald eyes. Entrancing? Yes, she decided. They had put her into somewhat of a trance last evening. Why, she had not been the least bit embarrassed by the way she was dressed once she had looked into those incredible eyes, when normally, she would have blushed to the roots of her hair to have been discovered in such disarray.

And, she thought as she wandered around the stone, gazing down at it with feigned interest, *his shoulders are a deal broader than any I have ever seen and he whisked me up*

*into his arms as though I weighed but a feather. He does make a
terrible first impression,* she mused, remembering their conversation at the front door and how he had stood glowering
at her with a soot-covered Rosebud squirming in his grip,
*but many people do. I shall not hold that against him. I shall
not hold anything against him. He is every inch a gentleman and
most handsome besides. I wonder why Cousin Mercy would not
have him?*

"Aunt Jess?" she whispered, catching at that lady's
sleeve. "Why did Mercy choose Lord Whitfield over Lord
Carrington?"

"Mercy, phoo," Jessamine muttered. "As spoiled a miss
as any I have ever met."

"No, she is not."

"Yes, she is, and she will give Lord Whitfield a grim time
of it, too, if ever he should oppose her in anything. She
is much too accustomed to being treated like a princess
by her papa to accept being treated as anything less by her
husband."

"But why did she turn down Lord Carrington?"

"Because she discovered that he had had the audacity
to place a wager with a friend that he would win her hand."

"He d-did?"

"Yes. Her mama told me all about it. Mercy led the poor
man on mercilessly and then turned right around and
accepted Lord Whitfield."

Winifred digested this bit of news in silence as the two
wandered on amongst the museum's treasures, stopping
here and there to gaze at this and that.

"Well, I expect that was a terrible thing for him to do."

"What?"

"To place a wager on his winning Mercy's hand."

"Indeed. It was a dreadful thing for him to do."

"Just so." Winifred nibbled thoughtfully at her lower
lip. "Aunt Jess? Why would he do such a thing?"

"Well, for goodness' sakes! Winifred, we have come to
the British Museum to gaze upon the treasures of the
world, not to discuss our next-door neighbor! Just look at
these sculptures. Are they not marvelous?"

"I suppose so."

"I do not know why he placed such a wager," Jessamine said with laughing exasperation. "However, I would guess that he did so because he truly believed he would have Mercy and he truly wished to have whatever the other gentleman had wagered against him. He longed to have all, dearest, and seized what looked to him like a fine opportunity."

"There is nothing so very wrong in that."

"You would not think so had you been the object of his wager."

"Yes, I would."

"You would?"

"Indeed. If a gentleman loved me so very much as to wish to marry me and then saw a means to gain something he longed for by doing just that—well, I should tell him to go ahead and place the wager myself. He did love Mercy and wish to marry her. She told me as much herself. But she did not love him. She would not have allowed a mere wager to keep them apart else."

Carrington was disappointed not to find the Misses Bittle at home when he and St. Martin called. "We will just go around to the stables then, Blather," he said with a bit of a scowl. "St. Martin has come to reclaim Jezebel."

"Your Jezebel is in our stable, my lord?"

"No, Blather, she is not *my* Jezebel any longer. She is St. Martin's Jezebel. And yes, she is in your stable. Ran off from St. Martin yesterday afternoon. Miss Winifred found her last evening and took her in, so to speak."

"Mrrrrrr," drawled a familiar little voice just then. "Mrrpstpft!" And before any of the three men could think to do one thing, Rosebud dashed between Blather's legs and scrambled madly up Carrington, from the toe of his boot all the way to his shoulder, where she balanced nicely and began to lick his ear.

"Ow," Carrington muttered. "My leg is going to be

nothing but a pincushion full of tiny claw marks if this thing does not cease and desist."

"I am sorry, my lord. Miss Winifred could not take the imp to the museum with her and so—"

"She actually wished to take this catlet to the museum?"

"Yes, my lord. But Miss Jessamine would not allow it."

"No, I should think not," St. Martin murmured. "Why would any sane person think to take a cat near the British Museum?"

Blather reached out to lift Rosebud from Carrington's shoulder, but the kitten spat at him and gave a mighty swipe with her claws. It was such a mighty swipe that she tumbled backward off his lordship's shoulder and was forced to grab hold with her claws to one of the greatcoat capes and climb back up.

"Never mind, Blather," Carrington sighed. "I shall take her with me to the stable. Apparently, she is determined to go. I will return her to you at the kitchen door in five minutes or so when we have got Jez haltered and are ready to lead her out."

St. Martin could not help but grin at the kitten so perilously perched upon Carrington's shoulder. "Visit the Misses Bittle often, do you?" he asked.

"No. Why do you ask?"

"Because it is obvious, Carrington, that the cat knows you. Thing has developed a distinct fondness for you I should say."

"Only because I got it down from a tree last night."

"Oh? Climbed up after it, did you?"

"Of course I climbed up after it. How else was I to get it down? Whistle for it?"

"Mrrrow," Rosebud commented, riding proudly upon the broad shoulder and gazing about her with confident blue eyes.

Jezebel whinnied as soon as they opened the stable doors and stepped inside.

"Thank gawd she was not injured," St. Martin murmured. "Anything might have happened to her."

"Well, nothing did thanks to Miss Bittle's kindness. She

took her in, you know, not having the least idea to whom she belonged.''

''Brrrrrr,'' Rosebud purred as they came up before the stall and Carrington rested his arms upon the gate. Daintily she walked down from his shoulder and balanced on the wooden structure and gave Jezebel's nose a quick lick. The horse nickered and attempted to lick her back. That sent the kitten tumbling into the straw.

''I have never seen such a thing.'' St. Martin grinned. ''They are immediate friends, I think.''

''Appears so.'' Carrington nodded. ''Go ahead. Get the halter on her. She is waiting for it.''

Jezebel, however, was not waiting for it at the hands of Lord St. Martin. The moment he approached the gate and Carrington stepped back, the gray mare reared, striking out at St. Martin's head with iron-shod hooves.

''Jez! What a thing to do!'' Carrington exclaimed. ''He is your master now, not I, and you had best grow accustomed to it.''

The horse whinnied and snorted and pawed at the rough planking.

''Mrrrpht!'' Rosebud cried and scrambled into the stall through the space between the gate boards. ''Mrrrrrrrrpht!''

''A rebellion, I think,'' St. Martin drawled.

''Mrrr-spt-spt-spt!'' Rosebud cried again, the fur upon her back rising as she stood, a tiny guard before the mare.

''Nonsense,'' Carrington sputtered. He took the halter from St. Martin's hand, opened the gate and slipped the thing on over Jezebel's lowered head. ''And you, you fearsome beast, are going to get a smack on the nose if you do not cease to show your temper,'' he added, scooping the kitten up and tapping its tiny pink nose with his index finger. Then, without any consideration of the matter whatsoever, he set Rosebud up upon Jezebel's back, clipped the lead to the horse's halter and led them both out of the stable as St. Martin followed, chuckling.

''You need to be more firm with her, St. Martin,'' Carrington muttered as that gentleman caught up with him. "Jez will not actually smash your skull in with her hooves."

"Looked like that was exactly what she intended to do to me."

"Yes, but she was merely bluffing. Once she discovers that you will not *be* bluffed, she will settle down quickly enough. Here, Rosebud, far enough," Carrington added, turning the lead over to St. Martin and lifting the kitten from Jezebel's back. He went to knock upon the kitchen door and handed her in to the smiling cook who answered. Then he turned back to discover Jezebel attempting to tug the lead out of St. Martin's hand.

With a sigh, he hurried to them, took the lead and walked directly up to Jezebel. He rested his head against her nose and rubbed her cheeks with both hands. "I am so very sorry, my girl," he whispered. "I did never mean to lose you. Honestly, I did not. But I *have* lost you, you see, and I cannot get you back. You belong to St. Martin now and you must learn to obey him. He will not treat you badly, Jez. I promise."

And that was the scene that Miss Winifred Bittle witnessed as the Bittle coach drove slowly past the mews in order to pull into Russell Square and up to the front entrance of the house. The oddest feeling came over her to see Lord Carrington so, hugging the little gray mare and murmuring to her. His crisp brown curls sparkled with gold in the sunlight and his tall, lean, broad-shouldered form threw the most impressive shadow, and, all in all, she thought he must be the most magnificent man in all of England and she was thoroughly pleased to think that they were fast becoming friends.

CHAPTER SIX

Miss Jessamine Bittle delivered the invitation herself on Thursday afternoon, escorted into Carrington's presence by Congreve and thoughtfully provided with a cup of tea and a plate of gingersnaps by that same personage.

"I have come, Lord Carrington, to request that you and your nephew join my niece and myself for an evening at Drury Lane," she said once Congreve had departed. "We shall dine afterward at Grillon's. Harland has a box at the theater and I have already sent James to the hotel to reserve a private parlor for us."

"I—I— Most certainly Ted and I would be pleased, but—" Carrington stuttered in surprise.

"You hesitate because you fear that I mean to promote a match between yourself and my Winifred, do you not?"

"N-no, ma'am. I merely—"

"I assure you," interrupted Miss Bittle, "I am not playing the matchmaker. Nothing at all is expected of you except that you have a most enjoyable time. The entire evening is in the nature of a reward."

"A reward?"

"For services rendered. We have thought and thought

how to repay you for being so very brave as to burn your own hands keeping our kitten from the fire—"

"Burned my—? I merely singed—"

"Do not protest, my lord. Both Winifred and I have heard the truth of it. I realize that the theater and dinner are not much of a reward for such courage, but at least they are something."

"It is most kind of you, Miss Bittle."

"Yes." Jessamine nodded. "You will come, will you not?"

"Indeed."

"Good. This very Saturday evening. We shall take Harland's coach, eh? Depart about half-past five? That will get us there when the doors open. I wish to have time to view this new theater. Perhaps it will prove a good thing that the old Drury Lane burnt to the ground."

Carrington did not know quite what to say and so he said thank you very nicely and Miss Bittle smiled at him.

"There is just one more thing that I should like to discuss with you, Lord Carrington," she declared after swallowing a bite of gingersnap.

"And that is?"

"Rescuing Rosebud."

"Rescuing Rosebud?"

"Yes. You have been rescuing Rosebud far too often."

"Too often, Miss Bittle?"

"Indeed. I heard about your climb into the elm tree in the verimost middle of the night."

"Oh."

"Just so. You must not continue in such a fashion, my lord."

"Why must I not?"

"Because if you do, you will cause Winifred to fall head over heels in love with you. You are a very kind sort of gentleman who does his best to be helpful, but Winifred begins to imagine you an heroic figure. She is romantical, my Freddie."

"I would have left the kitten up the tree if Miss Winifred had not looked at me with tears in her eyes."

"Winifred cannot help her tears. The kitten was a gift

from her brother, Lionel, who has recently gone off to war
and—"

"And?"

"Freddie is *superstitious,*" Miss Bittle whispered as
though it were some horrible disease not to be mentioned
in public.

"She is?"

"Impossibly so."

"And you tell me this because?"

"Because Winifred believes that if anything unfortunate
should happen to Rosebud, a similar misfortune will over-
take Lionel. That is why her tears flow so easily whenever
that rascally cat is in danger."

"I see. Then we absolutely cannot let anything dire happen to the catlet, can we?"

"No, but if Rosebud should require rescuing again, Lord
Carrington, you must *not* be the one to do it—your
nephew perhaps, or one of your servants—but not you.
Winifred already sees you as heroic. One more rescue and
she will lose her heart to you and all hope of her making
a suitable match when the Season begins will be gone. She
is crippled, you know, and London gentlemen are not well
pleased by young ladies who limp. There are few enough
of them will even gaze in Winifred's direction once they
note how she hobbles along from time to time. And Freddie cannot afford to turn those few away simply because
she daydreams of marrying you."

That evening, Carrington stared at his mulligatawny as
though it were some mysterious witch's brew. His spoon
poised just above it, his head bowed over it, his gaze riveted
to the bowl in which it sat, he had frozen, like some
mechanical toy that had ceased to function the moment
before it was to have spooned up the soup.

"Well, if you are not going to so much as taste it, Uncle,
do send it away," Theodore complained with a chuckle,
"so that we may proceed to the next course. I am almost
starving and all this consideration of the soup is not helping

me to fill my stomach. Congreve will not give the footmen leave to proceed further without you give him the nod, you know."

"Huh?" Carrington looked up and saw his nephew grinning at him and his two footmen attempting not to look at him and Congreve at the door of the chamber with a pristine white towel over his arm and an uncorked bottle of wine in one hand. "Did you say something, Teddy?" he asked, turning from Congreve to his nephew. "I am afraid I was lost in thought."

"I said, are you going to eat the soup, Uncle, or simply admire it for the remainder of the evening?"

"Oh." Carrington lowered his spoon into the bowl and raised it to his lips. He scowled. "Like ice!"

"Yes, well, it was almost hot a quarter hour ago when it was served," Theodore offered, "but I expect it grew cold from the icy gaze you have been focussing upon it."

"Icy gaze? Me? Nonsense! I was merely thinking. Congreve, Mr. Paxton is starving. Send the soup away, pour us the wine, and have the next course served, eh?"

The next course proved to be fried sole, stewed eels, and lamb chops with several side dishes, all of which found their ways onto the gentlemen's plates by courtesy of the footmen. Mr. Paxton's portions disappeared in rapid time, but all that disappeared from before his lordship was the wine.

"Are you not feeling just the thing, Uncle Austin?" Theodore asked as the third course made its way to the table and Congreve refilled his lordship's wineglass.

"Fine. Feeling fine. Right as a trivet. Eat up, Theodore. Cannot have you starving right before my eyes," Carrington muttered, downing the wine in one long swallow. "Your mother would part my hair with a carving knife should such a thing occur. More wine, Congreve, if you please."

All in all, the dinner came and went and Theodore ate his fill from every course and Carrington sat and stared and tasted nothing that was set before him. He merely pushed his food around upon his plate with the tines of his fork and drank his wine. He drank Sauterne and Bordeaux and Malaga, and when the sweetmeats appeared, he drank sherry. When at last the table was cleared, he petitioned Theodore to join him in a bottle of port.

"I do not think so," Theodore murmured. "I think I have had quite enough wine for one evening, Uncle Austin."

"You have? I have not. Stay and talk, then. Congreve, leave the bottle and close the doors on your way out."

"Yes, my lord," Congreve whispered with an imploring look at Mr. Paxton who nodded with understanding.

It was a most unusual thing for his uncle to drink so very much wine at his own table, Theodore knew, and Mr. Congreve was as worried about it as he was himself. His uncle Austin might overindulge from time to time at one of his clubs and come home chirping merry, but never had Theodore or Congreve seen him so obviously intent upon becoming completely foxed.

"Devil of a thing to say," Carrington grumbled, once he and Theodore were alone.

"What, Uncle? I cannot recall saying anything devilish."

"Not you, that woman."

"What woman?"

"*That* woman! Mrs.—Miss—Buttle—Boodle—Bittle!"

"Miss Winifred Bittle?"

"No, no, t'other one."

"Oh. Miss Jessamine Bittle? What did she say that was so very devilish?"

"Said that I was not to rescue that wretched catlet anymore. Said that if the occasion should arise, I was to let you do it."

"Now why would she say a thing like that?"

"Don't know. Yes, I do. Afraid her chick will fall in love with me. Ridiculous. Ain't a woman in the world will ever fall in love with me. Did all I could to make Mercy do it and lost her all the same. Women. Irrational. And she called Winiferd-fred a cripple! Can you imagine calling that premarkab—renark—remarkably pretty minx a cripple? Ought to have popped the woman on the jaw! No, no, she did not intend it harshly. Attempting to be honest. Will not want Winiferd-fred, most of 'em. Right she is there. Will not so much as glance sidewise at the girl do they f-find she l-limps a bit. Devil of a thing, ain't it?"

"Indeed," Mr. Paxton offered, having quite lost the thread of his uncle's tirade.

"Jest— Just so! Devil of a thing! And I cannot help it if I am her here—her—hero. Accident that. Still it is all my fault, says Miss Jessamine Bettle—Bittle. Pour me another glass, eh, Teddy m'boy? Cannot seem to get the stuff to come out of the bet—bott—bottle right. Spills on the cloth."

Theodore rose and poured his uncle another glass of port, then took his own chair again. He had planned upon meeting his friend Crawford this evening at Watier's, but he had not actually promised he would do so. Well, he could not do so. That much was obvious. He was inordinately fond of his uncle and could not abandon the gentleman at this precise moment. The world might think what it liked about his uncle Austin, but Austin Hobart Holt had always been there whenever Theodore needed a friend, and Theodore was determined to do likewise for his uncle.

"L-lost Mercy; lost Jez; lost Jez again and now I am will—well—on m'way to losing Winiferd-fred. Cursed, I expect."

"Oh, no, Uncle."

"Yes, cursed," Carrington sighed, nodding.

"I was not aware, Uncle, that you—that your interests lay in Miss Winifred Bittle's direction."

"Don't."

"Well, then—"

"But she is a charmer, ain't she?"

"I am sure she is a most pleasant young woman, Uncle. I have told you so, if you remember."

"More'n pleasant. 'Dorable. Should've seen her, Teddy. All dressed up in Garvey's greatcoat with his beaver fallin' down over her ears—an' pink stockings—she had pink stockings an'—an'—ridin' boots. Bewitching she was."

"W-when?" Theodore asked, bewildered. He had never seen Miss Bittle dressed so. He was certain of it.

"Last night. Invited me to tea."

"Tea? In pink stockings and riding boots? Last night, Uncle?" Theodore attempted to make some sense of what he was hearing, but for the life of him he could not. *It is the wine speaking,* he told himself at last. *None of this is at all rational. I shall just stay with Uncle Austin until he drinks himself under the table and then put him to bed. That is the best I can do for now.*

It was something a person of any refinement ought never to do. Winifred had known that. But she had felt her cause to be of such importance that any lapse of good breeding must, in the end, be excused. And so, when her aunt Jessamine had finished her tea and gone upstairs to retire for the night, Winifred had cornered Mr. Blather in his little pantry where he had been putting away the silver and she had ruthlessly pumped the poor man for every bit of gossip he could remember about Lord Carrington and Miss Mercy Garvey and the wretched wager.

And now, as she sat upon the window seat in her bed-chamber dangling yarn before the kitten and watching Rosebud pounce and tussle and jump up in the air, her heart positively overflowed with pity for the gentleman in the townhouse next door. Tears rose to her eyes and she swiped at them distractedly. That poor gentleman. That poor, dear gentleman. He had been so certain that Mercy loved him, that Mercy would marry him, that he had wagered the little gray mare upon it. *His* little gray mare. The mare his own papa had given to him at the very moment of her birth, Mr. Blather had said. No wonder he had been holding that gray head so lovingly this afternoon. He had been parting with her again—for a second time— because he was proud and honorable and he would never think not to pay his gaming debts no matter what.

"I do think it likely that he loves that mare more than he ever loved Cousin Mercy," Winifred murmured to Rose-bud, who ceased to attack the yarn and sat down to look up at her attentively. "Mr. Blather thinks the same. That is the way it is with some gentlemen. They marry women they do not truly love."

"Mrrow?" Rosebud queried, blue eyes blinking thoughtfully.

"Well, I am certain he cared for Mercy and wished to make her happy as his wife, Rosebud, but that is not quite the same thing as love."

"Brrrrrr?"

"Well, perhaps he did love Cousin Mercy. One cannot be certain of such things unless one sees the parties concerned when they are together, and we shall never have that opportunity now that Mercy has married Lord Whitfield. But our Lord Carrington certainly loves that mare. I could tell that. How his heart must have broken to give her over to Lord St. Martin. And she does not like this Lord St. Martin person. Not at all. That is why she ran away and came to us, Rosebud. She was on her way back to Lord Carrington. She wishes only to be with him."

"Mrrrow-brrrrr," Rosebud declared rather emphatically.

"Yes, dearest, we are going to help Lord Carrington. Austin. That is his name. Austin Hobart Holt. What a magnificent name, do not you think?"

Rosebud wet her foot and rubbed it over her one black ear. "Phhtle-mrrr," she commented, unimpressed.

"Well, I think it a magnificent name. And I think he is a magnificent gentleman. And he has the most beautiful eyes I have ever seen. Truly he has. I should very much like to see what they look like when he is smiling with his heart. I will wager you a sardine to a sea bass, Rosebud, that they sparkle like jewels in the sunlight then."

Perhaps this Lord St. Martin can be convinced to sell the mare, Winifred thought as she lowered the kitten to the floor and stood. She wandered to her bed and slipped out of her cherry-striped robe, a plan hatching in her mind. *Perhaps if I purchase Jezebel, I can give her to Lord Carrington and say that she is a—a—token of my appreciation for his rescuing Rosebud.*

Yes, he cannot be so inordinately proud that he will not accept a token of gratitude.

Winifred slipped between the warmed sheets, turned down the lamp wick and closed her eyes. She opened them again as four little feet bounced across her stomach and Rosebud curled into a purring ball next to her left ear.

"This will never do, you scamp," she giggled, and gave the furry ball a poke with one finger.

"Mrrph," Rosebud grumbled, but she stood up and stretched and then squiggled under the quilt all the way to the foot of the bed where she once again curled into a ball and purred contentedly.

Winifred thought of Lionel and wondered where he would be sleeping this night. She sent him a gentle kiss and prayed that he was just as safe and comfortable as the kitten, no matter where the war had taken him. And then she prayed for her brother, Ethan, who was alone in the country now and likely worrying his head over the estate and how he was to make it bring in enough money to pay for the improvements he intended to make. She prayed for Aunt Jess who had come into her life when her own mother and father had left it and who had looked after her and Lionel and Ethan with all the love and protectiveness of a mother wolf. Aunt Jess was something, she was. And finally Winifred prayed for her next-door neighbor. It was a prayer without any words. Just a vision of green eyes that wished to smile—anyone could tell that they wished to smile—and a hope deep in her heart that she would be the one to bring the smile into them.

CHAPTER SEVEN

Winifred, mounted upon one of her uncle Harland's bays, entered St. Martin's stable yard late on Friday afternoon and gazed about her. In a habit of Spanish fly, her curls covered by a low-crowned hat of a like shade, her cheeks glowing and her eyes flashing, she appeared a veritable Diana off upon the hunt. Her groom, Samuel, noted the looks of admiration that the young lady drew from the stable hands and shuddered.

"We ought not be here, Miss Winifred," he murmured, drawing his black up close to her bay. "This is not Hyde Park."

"Well, I know that, Samuel. This is Lord St. Martin's stable. It took forever for us to find someone who actually knew the correct direction."

"Yes, but we ought not be here, miss. You told your auntie we were going to Hyde Park. An' besides, a young lady don't go calling upon an unattached gentleman, Miss Winifred. Not in London. It is most unacceptable."

"Which is why I told Aunt Jess that we were going to the park, Samuel. So that she would not be upset. Besides, I am not actually calling upon Lord St. Martin. I am merely coming to make him an offer on one of his horses. It is purely business. A young woman may do business with an unattached gentleman, may she not?"

"No," Samuel said distinctly.

"Balderdash. If I do not speak with him, who will? There is no one but Aunt Jessamine, and I do not wish her to become involved in it. You, sir," she called down to one of St. Martin's grooms. "Have you a gray mare here with one white stocking?"

"Indeed, ma'am."

"I should like to see her, if you please. And I should like to speak with Lord St. Martin. Might you send someone to fetch him to me?"

"Yes, ma'am." The groom nodded as Samuel dismounted and helped his young charge to the ground. "Harry! Off with ye. Fetch 'is lordship and say as—"

"Say that Miss Winifred Bittle desires to speak with him."

"Aye, say that."

"Mrrrrow," a little voice agreed, and a white head with one black ear poked out from inside Miss Bittle's sleek wool jacket.

"Hush, Rosebud. You shall see your friend shortly, I assure you. It is positively frigid out here," she added with a smile that would urge any groom to folly. "May we not await his lordship inside?"

"Of course, miss. There is a fire burnin' in the stove. That will warm ye up a bit."

"I should find that delightful." Winifred nodded. "We have been riding about forever. We misinterpreted our directions and rode all the way to Grosvenor Square before we discovered our mistake, and I have no doubt that Samuel is postively frozen."

"*We* did not have any directions," Samuel murmured, shivering. "*We* were informed as how we were riding to the park."

"Yes, well, I made a mistake, but we are here now, safe as houses." Winifred smiled, walking into the stables with only the barest limp and looking interestedly about her.

"Mrrrr-phttt!" Rosebud cried, spotting Jezebel at once.

"Exactly so. I see her as well, Rosebud. No, do not scramble out as yet, my precious. We must first ask Mr.—Mr.— I am so very sorry," she said, blinking innocently at the groom, "but I do not know your name."

"Blankenship, miss."

"We must first ask Mr. Blankenship if we may approach her," she concluded, rubbing a warmly gloved fingertip down the kitten's nose. "May we, Mr. Blankenship?"

"Approach who?" the groom asked, thoroughly bemused by the kitten and unable to take his eyes from it.

"Jezebel. I believe that is her name."

"Oh, no, miss. She be a handful. There is no tellin' what the sight of a feline an' a young lady be like ta do ta 'er."

Winifred was about to explain that the sight of herself and Rosebud would likely make the mare behave more properly, but Rosebud could not be bothered with lengthy explanations and squiggled out of her jacket, tumbled to the planking and scurried into Jezebel's stall.

St. Martin's groom stood petrified, expecting all Hades to break loose, but the mare simply lowered her head and snuffled, and a most satisfied purr arose from the stall floor.

"Well, I'll be deviled," Blankenship muttered with a confused glance at Samuel, who shrugged.

"They are friends," Winifred explained. "Took to each other from the very first."

"Who did?" asked a voice, and a gentleman in a many-caped greatcoat strolled into the stable, closing the door behind him.

"Rosebud and Jezebel. You are Lord St. Martin?"

"The same. Miss Bittle?"

"Yes. I am pleased to make your acquaintance, my lord. I have come to purchase Lord Carrington's Jezebel."

St. Martin studied her intently. "You would be the young woman of whom Carrington spoke. The one who took Jezebel in the night she ran away? Lord Garvey's niece?"

"Yes, I am," Winifred responded, lifting her chin the slightest bit as his lordship's eyes roamed over her. She had not known what to expect from this gentleman, but to be studied with such arrogant thoroughness made her angry and she could feel her temper flare. "When you are quite finished staring, my lord, may we proceed with a proper discussion of business?" she said, biting her lower lip to hold her temper in check.

"I do beg your pardon, Miss Bittle," St. Martin drawled. "I merely wonder what possessed you to come here. I do not know one gently bred young woman who would think to disregard the rules of society and ride alone into a bachelor's establishment, much less send for that gentleman to come into her presence."

"How unfortunate for you then," Winifred replied, glaring, "to have lived so many years without having made the acquaintance of even one gently bred woman with backbone."

"I beg your pardon?" St. Martin's eyebrows rose to a considerable height.

"You certainly should," Winifred sputtered. "The nerve of you, to suggest that I am not gently bred simply because I have business to conduct and choose to do so in the most expedient manner. And I have not come alone," she added, her hands fisting upon her hips. "I have brought Samuel, my groom, with me. And if you do not become a deal less audacious and lower your eyebrows *and* your nose to a more reasonable height, Samuel will beat you about the head until you do!"

This small but impressive foray caused poor Samuel— who was not near equal to his lordship's weight, and approaching his sixtieth year besides—to drop his jaw in sheer horror.

St. Martin, seeing this, burst into laughter.

"I fail to see the humor," Winifred declared once his guffaws quieted. "If you are making jest of me, I warn you, you shall regret it!"

"No, no, please, Miss Bittle," St. Martin managed around a new series of chuckles. "Do not threaten me with further violence at the hands of your groom or you will send the poor fellow into an apoplexy. I sincerely apologize for my words and my manner. You are correct. I have never in my life met a gently bred young woman with backbone—until this very moment—and I think I regret that I have not."

"That is a deal better," Winifred mumbled, uncertain if he meant his words or was making sport of her.

"Do not glare at me so, Miss Bittle. I am sincere, I assure you. And I am truly pleased to make your acquaintance, too."

"Good. Then you will tell me, please, for what price may I purchase Lord Carrington's Jezebel."

St. Martin rubbed at the back of his neck. His smile wavered noticeably. "The fact of the matter is, Miss Bittle, that there is no price upon her. I do not wish to sell the mare."

"Not to anyone?"

"No, Miss Bittle, not to anyone. She is by Panderer out of Scarlet Trophy, you see. Well, most likely you do not understand, but she is a true prize, Miss Bittle. A filly bred from two of the finest racehorses in all of Great Britain."

"You intend to race her, my lord?"

"I intend to breed her, Miss Bittle, to my own Prideful Blaze, whose parentage is near equal to her own, and from their issue I intend to convert a farm filled with adequate horses into a farm filled with horses for whom gentlemen from all over England and the Continent would sell their souls."

Winifred's expression lightened considerably. "That I certainly understand." She nodded. "It is a matter of business."

"Yes, just so."

"But how will you go about accomplishing your goal if Jezebel does not cooperate?"

"Does not— Well, of course she will—cooperate."

"I do not agree. I think that she will pummel your Prideful Blaze until he limps from the place in defeat time and again."

"Miss Bittle. It will not happen. Horses—"

"I know about horses, my lord. My eldest brother is Ethan Bittle of Waymaker Farm."

"Good gawd!"

"Just so. And since I have been raised upon that farm, you will allow me to know a bit about mares like Lord Carrington's Jezebel. She will never cooperate, my lord, without Lord Carrington to gentle her into it. From what I have seen, she is his. His entirely."

"Then why, Miss Bittle, do *you* wish to purchase her?"

"Because—because—" Winifred wondered how to explain to this gentleman that it was because she wished to bring joy to Lord Carrington's marvelous emerald eyes, to see him smile with pure exaltation and to watch him rest his head against Jezebel's nose in welcome this time, not in parting.

St. Martin watched the thoughts play across her face. "Miss Bittle," he asked quietly, "have you backbone enough to step into my house and drink tea with me? Your man, Samuel, shall join us, of course, to play chaperone. It grows cold out here and I begin to think that you make a great deal of sense. We shall discuss Jezebel in a more comfortable place than the stable, eh?"

Hyde Park appeared to be deserted. Carrington had encountered only three gentlemen and they had been departing the place by the west gate just as he had been entering it. Taking care to look in every direction, he rode along Rotten Row and across the green and through the gardens. Impatient and growing worried when no one answered his intimidating bellow, he sent his new gelding thundering to the northernmost corner of the park, across the highway and into the adjoining meadow, past there, into the small wood. He did not know Winifred well, but he knew in his heart that she was bold and courageous and would not have ridden sedately along like a milksop of a London lady. She well might have ridden out of the park at the northern tip.

But as the sun descended and the wind rose, he was

forced to admit that she had not. He cursed under his breath, tugged his hat lower over his brow and raised his coat collar higher. He turned the horse that he had just this morning dubbed Failure back toward the park. He would start again from this point and keep to a walk until either Winifred or her groom answered him. His heart pounded like a sledge against his ribs as he peered into the steadily increasing darkness.

Miss Jessamine Bittle had come knocking upon his door more than an hour ago with tears in her eyes and hands palsied with fear. It had taken her fifteen minutes to settle down enough to tell him that Winifred and her groom had gone to ride in Hyde Park three hours before and had not returned. "Something has happened," she had told him tearfully. "One can ride the length and breadth of the park in much less time than three hours."

"Where are you, Winifred?" Carrington whispered as the wind slashed fiercely at his back. "You took that blasted kitten with you. Did you lose the wretched catlet? Are you searching for her in some obscure place and that is why I cannot find you?"

Failure whinnied and pawed at the frozen ground as the wind increased and a stinging combination of rain and snow rushed down out of the blackening sky upon them. "Devil it," Carrington muttered. "This is all we need, eh, my lad? Sleet to blind us even more than the darkness. Winifred!" he bellowed above the wind. "Miss Bittle! Answer me!"

No answer came and Carrington's heart rose up into his throat as he pictured Winifred lying somewhere upon the cold ground, injured, and her old groom, dead, beside her. He urged his horse forward, toward the Serpentine. He had not ridden down along that stream upon his first trip through the park, unable to imagine why any young lady would choose to ride there now that the winter had made it wild and swollen and ready to flood.

But she is not just any young lady, he told himself. *She is Miss Winifred Bittle.* "I ought to have waited for Theodore to return from Jackson's," he declared in an angry voice.

"Lord knows two of us could do a better job of this. If I do not find her, if she is truly injured and does not find shelter, she will surely freeze to death in this. Winifred!" he shouted again, sleet cutting across his cheek. "Winifred! Samuel! Answer me!"

They moved, horse and man, cautiously down the hillside to the place through which the Serpentine cut its way. With a curse at the darkness, Carrington pulled up beneath an oak, dismounted and searched about for a fallen branch. By feel not sight he found one as big around as his fist and as long as his arm. He unwound the scarf from about his neck, doffed his greatcoat and struggled out of his jacket. Shuddering in his shirtsleeves, he hurriedly donned the greatcoat again and buttoned it tightly about him. Then he wrapped his jacket around the top of the branch, bound it there securely with the scarf and soaked all from the little flask of brandy in his greatcoat pocket. Thank goodness his head had ached so badly from his drinking last evening that Congreve had thought to send the brandy with him to stave off the worst of the pain.

Huddled over the branch between Failure and the tree, he struck his flints time and time again over the brandy-soaked jacket. "Hold, Failure," he murmured as the horse danced at the sound. "Easy, my lad. If we have any luck at all, we shall have a light to see by soon." He struck the flints a ninth time and with a whoosh, the fumes of the brandy caught the spark and the torch burst into flame. "Yes!" he shouted as the horse neighed in fear. He let the torch burn upon the ground and went to the gelding's head and spoke softly to him, gentling the shivering animal with his words and his soft stroke. "I will not let the fire harm you, my lad. It is to help us find Winifred," he whispered. "We shall work our way toward home along this dratted stream bed. Slowly. If Winifred and Samuel have come to some harm here, we must find them before they freeze to death. We cannot let her freeze to death, my lad. She is—she is— We must find her."

His toes numb within his boots and his fingers equally as numb inside his gloves, Carrington took hold of the torch and mounted Failure. "Winifred!" he bellowed again, urging the gelding forward, into the wind. "Winifred! Samuel! Winifred!"

He intended to cross the stream at the wooden bridge just above the King's Oak and to search the side of the Serpentine nearest the west gate bit by bit. But the snow and sleet increased and the light of the torch failed to pick out the structure he sought. At last, judging that he had missed it, he urged Failure into the swollen, frigid stream, the rising waters of the Serpentine roiling up as high as his knees and higher. The gelding, equally as numb as his rider, stumbled and went down. Carrington kicked free of the stirrups and, barely finding his own footing, seized the frightened animal's reins and rallied him, at last leading the animal onto the far shore.

The torch was lost, drowned in the stream; ice formed upon Failure and Carrington alike. They struggled up the slippery slope, Carrington in the lead, the reins wound tight in his fist. He encouraged the horse whenever it stumbled and paused to bellow for Winifred again and again. They had about reached level ground when, with an odd, barely audible whooshing, the earth gave way beneath them, sending horse and man careening downward amidst an avalanche of rock and stone and heavy gravel. Carrington cried out once when one of Failure's flailing hooves kicked him in the shoulder and glanced off the side of his head. And then he was silent, sliding to a stop in a heap of wet wool at the very edge of the stream. He did not murmur or move as Failure screamed in fear and struggled to gain his feet, fighting against the reins that Carrington still held tight in his fist.

CHAPTER EIGHT

St. Martin's coach halted before the Garvey residence and St. Martin helped Winifred to step down onto the flagway. Behind the coach, Samuel and Blankenship drew their own horses, and those they led to a halt. Samuel was bringing home the bay that Miss Bittle had ridden, and Blankenship, confused but with goodwill, was leading Carrington's Jezebel.

Holding tightly to his hat and making his way up the stoop to Carrington House, Theodore Paxton paused in the swirling sleet and snow to stare in surprise at the coach and riders next door. He stepped back down the stoop and walked, shivering, over to the coach. "Miss Bittle? St. Martin? Wretched weather, is it not? Came up fast, too. Thought I should not make it from Bond Street to here without taking a fall. I do not mean to keep you out in this, but that is Uncle Austin's Jezebel your groom is leading, is it not, St. Martin?"

"Just so." St. Martin nodded, offering Winifred his arm and stepping toward the house. "Take them around to the stable, John," he shouted to the coachman. "Follow Miss Bittle's groom. I shall remain for a quarter hour."

The coachman nodded and pulled away from the curb, allowing Samuel and Blankenship to ride ahead of him with their charges.

"You are well met, Mr. Paxton!" Winifred exclaimed. "Will you join Lord St. Martin and myself inside for a moment? We stand in need of your advice about Jezebel."

"If there is something wrong with Jezebel, it is Uncle Austin with whom you need to speak."

"No, no, it is you, Paxton!" St. Martin shouted, as the wind increased and roared about his ears. "We have a bargain to strike with Carrington and do not quite know how to— Come, Miss Bittle, we must get inside. You are near frozen."

"Mrrrrrrow!" a muffled little voice agreed emphatically from deep inside Winifred's wool jacket.

Blather opened the door to them at the first knock and his face grew pale in the light of the foyer lamps. "Miss Winifred!"

"Yes." Winifred nodded, eyeing the butler curiously and stepping by him into the vestibule, motioning the gentlemen to follow. "You must close the door and take Lord St. Martin's things, Mr. Blather, and Mr. Paxton's as well," she pointed out quietly as the man stood staring at the three of them, the door still open, his hand still upon the latch.

"What? Oh, yes! Certainly!" Blather cried, slamming the door and moving to take the gentlemen's coats and hats and gloves. "His lordship found you then? And he sent you to us in Lord St. Martin's care? His lordship is stabling the horses then and will join us in a moment?"

"Lord Carrington, have you found her at last?" cried a trembling voice from abovestairs, and in a moment Miss Jessamine Bittle was staring down from the landing at the group gathered in the vestibule below. "Freddie! Oh, thank heaven! I thought surely something dreadful had happened to you or to Samuel. But where is Lord Carrington? Did he not come in with you?"

"Lord Carrington?" asked Winifred, concerned at once over the state of her aunt's nerves and the mention of her neighbor's name in such a tone as her aunt had said it. "Aunt Jess, what has happened? Why should you expect Lord Carrington?"

Her leg ached from the cold and the long ride this afternoon and her limp had grown much more noticeable. Nevertheless, Winifred rushed from the house like a woman possessed. She was out through the kitchen door and into the stable demanding that Jezebel be saddled for herself and that horses be saddled for Mr. Paxton and Lord St. Martin and any of the grooms who would join them in a search for Lord Carrington before Paxton and St. Martin had even redonned their coats. St. Martin's coachman was rehitching his team on her orders by the time Theodore and St. Martin came running into the stables.

"Miss Bittle, you cannot ride out with us," Theodore told her breathlessly. "The weather is far too bad. It will be extremely dangerous."

"Paxton and I and the men shall find him, Miss Bittle. You may count upon that," St. Martin added, pulling his hat down over his brow and tying his scarf around his neck. "But this is not a night for a woman to be out."

Winifred, who had not so much as unbuttoned one button of her riding jacket while she had stood listening to her aunt's tale in the foyer, did not so much as acknowledge one word the gentlemen said now. She ordered Samuel to give her a leg up and turned Jezebel's head toward the stable doors. "Mount if you are coming," she called to the others, and taking the lantern Samuel offered her, she urged Jezebel out into the night. Behind her, gentlemen and grooms alike scrambled to horses' backs and Miss Bittle's coachman joined St. Martin's coachman on the box of St. Martin's coach. As the wind roared and the sleet and snow sizzled around them, the small party set off with lanterns and flambeaux and a coach piled high with blankets to search for Carrington who had set out for Hyde Park near two hours before and not returned.

Fear clutched Winifred's heart so tightly that it made her gasp for breath. Sleet stung her cheeks and chin; wind deafened her ears; Jezebel stumbled and righted herself upon the slick cobbles, almost tossing Winifred from the perilous sidesaddle. Still, the woman and the mare continued determinedly onward, every fiber in Winifred straining to reach the last place that Austin Hobart Holt had been.

Something dire has happened to him, she thought, as her tears mixed with the cold snow and sleet upon her cheeks, *and it is all my fault. I ought not to have fibbed to Aunt Jess. I ought to have asked Lord St. Martin to send one of his footmen with a message so that she would not worry about me. Oh, damnation! I ought to have done any number of things differently!*

"Mrrrr?" a puzzled little voice asked, but the sound of it was quite blown away upon the wind. Rosebud, unanswered, wiggled about and struggled to poke her head out from the top of Winifred's jacket to see what was going on.

"Oh, my word," Winifred murmured, feeling the movement against her and glancing down. "Rosebud! I did not think!"

The little white head, seeing the snow swirl and feeling the bite of the wind, quickly withdrew back inside the Spanish fly wool jacket and mewed mournfully.

It took the group of would-be rescuers an unconscionably long time to reach Hyde Park. The footing for the horses was treacherous. Winifred's leg ached unbearably and stiffened with the cold. Lord St. Martin and Mr. Paxton caught up and rode one to each side of her, silent, fighting to see through the storm, and behind them were the grooms and coachmen were silent as well.

"Easy to miss him in this if he has gone down!" Mr. Paxton shouted as they entered the park.

"Easy for us to lose ourselves as well," St. Martin acknowledged. "Search in groups."

"Threes!" Winifred shouted above the roar of the wind.

Paxton nodded. "I shall go with Miss Bittle and Samuel!" he yelled at St. Martin, beckoning Samuel forward. "North."

"Go!" St. Martin bellowed. "I will divide the others. The coach remains here. If you find him, one of you must come back to the gate for the coach."

Winifred thought to pry Rosebud from the inside of her jacket and bundle her into the blankets inside the coach, but discarded that thought at once. Mr. Paxton and Samuel were already moving forward across the snow-covered ground. She could not spare one minute to ride back to the coach and deposit Rosebud within. One minute might well be the difference between life and death for Lord Carrington—if he were down—if he were down and injured on this most evil night.

Failure, having at last gained his feet and discovered that he was securely tethered by the reins in Carrington's fist, attempted to turn his back to the wind. This required continual shuffling since the wind persisted in changing direction. While he shuffled, he nibbled distractedly at Carrington's curls, uncovered now except by rapidly forming ice crystals. The gelding's breath came in great white swoops of steam over the gentleman's hair, dissolving the crystals as they formed and inadvertently warming Carrington's left ear. From time to time Failure nickered at the man and nuzzled at his shoulder urging him to rise. When Carrington would not, the horse would shiver and snort and return to his shuffling and his nervous nibbling.

After the longest time, the gelding's ears pricked curiously to the right. He lifted his head and stared through the darkness. Beyond the wild howling of the wind, the roar of the now flooding Serpentine, and the enraged sizzling of the sleet, beyond it all, Failure's enormous ears heard them coming.

With a burst of hope within his brute of a heart, the gelding whinnied and snorted and whinnied again, calling through the storm and the darkness. With renewed energy, he lowered his head and nuzzled at Carrington, licked at his cheek, nuzzled him more strongly, and snorted loudly against his ear, and for these efforts he received a sound—

a groan. It was soft to be sure, but nevertheless it was a sound, and Failure raised his great head and whinnied again as though his life and Carrington's depended upon someone hearing him—which indeed was true.

Winifred had given her lantern into Theodore's hands. She found she could no longer hold it and maintain her seat upon the precarious sidesaddle. The bitter wind and frigid sleet made every step that Jezebel took hazardous to both the mare and her rider. But Winifred would not go back. Though Theodore implored her in a shout to let Samuel escort her to the coach, she declined with a stiff shake of her head. She was not such a poor thing that she would run off to huddle in warmth and safety when the gentleman she loved was in grave danger.

The gentleman I love? she thought in confusion. *No, I did not mean that. He is a gentleman I have come to admire and to respect and to care for as a friend. Yes, and my dear friend has got himself lost in a veritable blizzard in Hyde Park because of me. Because I did not tell Aunt Jess the truth. I must find him and bring him home. Please let us find him,* she prayed then in silence. *Please let us find him safe. Cold and cursing, horseless perhaps, but unharmed.* And then Jezebel halted and pricked her ears forward, and from deep inside Winifred's jacket, Rosebud mewed and struggled upward.

"What?" Winifred asked, peering into the blackness and listening as hard as she could. "What is it?"

"Mrrr-phft!" Rosebud exclaimed, her head popping out between two of the brass buttons on Winifred's jacket. "Mrrr-spt-phft!" The kitten scratched against the wool and hissed and struggled until all at once she was tumbling out and onto Winifred's lap.

"Rosebud!" Winifred cried as the little white kitten with one black ear leapt to the ground and went rushing off into the night. "Rosebud! No!"

Theodore raised the lantern higher at Winifred's cry and caught a glimpse of the kitten as it scampered partway up the hill in front of them and then was blown sideways by the raging wind. He urged his mount after it. "Rosebud!" he called. "Here, Rosebud! Come!" And then he realized that calling a kitten as you would a dog was quite probably a useless exercise and he ceased to do so, dismounting instead and leading his horse so that he might keep the light close to the ground and once finding the kitten, scoop it up and tuck it beneath his greatcoat.

Jezebel stepped forward, stopped, whinnied loudly. She waited a moment and then stepped forward again and stopped again and whinnied again. No kick of heels or shouted words upon Winifred's part could get the mare to keep moving. "What is it?" Winifred cried in frustration. "Rosebud will be lost to us in a matter of moments. Go on, Jezebel! Go on! I can see her now in the light of Mr. Paxton's lantern, just there! Samuel, I cannot get this horse to move. Go and help Mr. Paxton. Hurry!"

No sooner had Samuel gone after Theodore and the kitten than Winifred heard above the wind, or on it perhaps, what she thought to be a horse whinnying. And quite as if she had been waiting for exactly that sound, Jezebel perked her ears toward it and stepped out again and this time kept going—slipping and sliding to be sure, but making her way nevertheless toward the hill that the kitten was attempting to climb. In the light of both Paxton's and Samuel's lanterns Winifred saw Rosebud top the hill and disappear down the other side. Jezebel whinnied loudly and attempted to run, nearly killing herself and Winifred both as she lost her balance midway up that same hill and began to slide backward. Winifred clung tightly while the mare fought for solid footing, found it at last, and struggled on. They passed Mr. Paxton, who was just remounting, and Samuel who had halted, lifting his lantern high to catch sight of the kitten. They crested the hill and Jezebel picked her way, front legs stiff, rear legs slithering, down the opposite side. Winifred gasped in fear. She could see nothing. The sleet and snow blinded her. Mr. Paxton's light was to the rear and Samuel's too far off to her left. She drew on the reins to bring Jezebel to a halt, but the gray ignored her and continued downward.

We are going toward the Serpentine, Winifred thought then. *That is water I hear, not wind. We must be going toward the Serpentine. It runs all through this park. Aunt Jess told me so.*

Never having actually seen the Serpentine, Winifred had no notion of how deep the stream might be or how wild, but she could hear it over the storm and that meant it was not a tiny little dribble of a thing.

Failure shoved at Carrington again and again. He paused a moment, raised his head, pricked his enormous ears forward and whinnied. From out of the darkness a shadow streaked toward him—a small shadow, close to the ground. The big horse shied as it tumbled under his legs and came to a stop—slap! bang!—up beneath Lord Carrington's chin.

Shaken and shivering, Rosebud gazed upward, studying Failure. Then she shook her head, shook her little rear, shook each tiny foot one at a time and climbed up upon Carrington's neck. With great determination Rosebud began to scrub at the gentleman's ear with a tongue like sandpaper. Groaning, Carrington slapped at her. She scrubbed harder then, her tongue going right down inside his ear, which Failure's could not do.

Carrington groaned again and muttered and rolled onto his back. Rosebud tumbled to the ground but leapt up onto his chest and began to scrub urgently at his chin. "Mrrr-spft!" she managed as she scrubbed. "Mrrrrrr-phft-spffft!"

Failure began to back away, gently, tugging easily but persistently at the fist that held the reins. He lowered his head and nibbled at the fingers of Carrington's glove, then at his wrist, then he backed, tugging again. "Wh-what?" Carrington muttered. "Wh-what?"

The very instant that he spoke Failure raised his head and whinnied again into the night as loud and as long as he could, and from just above him and to the right another horse answered, and Jezebel with Winifred upon her back and Mr. Paxton and Samuel both attempting to catch them from behind, tilted and tumbled and slid the rest of the way down the hill, across a portion of the bank, and came to a halt above her master. She lowered her nose and poked him in the stomach; she nibbled at his coat buttons; she took his lapels between her teeth and pulled him upward.

"Austin!" Winifred cried, sliding to the ground, her riding skirts heavy with sleet and rain and snow clinging about her legs, almost tripping her. "Austin, my dear!" She hurried to his head and knelt, catching him as Jezebel released his lapels. She eased his head and shoulders against her breasts and wrapped her arms around him, attempting to share with him what warmth she still possessed. "Austin, darling, can you hear me?"

"Huh?" Carrington mumbled, brushing away a kitten who was no longer there but scrambling up Winifred's shoulder instead.

"Mrrrr-murggle!" Rosebud exclaimed happily, staring down at the gentleman. "Mrrrr-murggle-pfft!"

CHAPTER NINE

For a long time after they had got him home, Carrington was aware of nothing but cold and pain and a great lethargy that turned his limbs to lead. He thought, in fact, when he did think anything at all, that perhaps he had died in the park and that his soul was merely unaware of it as yet. Whenever he attempted to move, he would discover a great weight pinning him down and would abandon the attempt. Once his lips parted and he murmured her name. "Winifred," he whispered hoarsely. "I am so sorry. I cannot save you now. I cannot save myself."

In the ancient four-poster that had been his father's, he lay covered by layer upon layer of quilts. A fire blazed upon his hearth and he was never alone. His valet, Remmington, kept close watch over him. Congreve stepped in whenever he could. Mr. Paxton and Lord St. Martin sat beside his bed in turns and spoke to him of horses and racing and mills and wagers. But his lethargy held, and though from time to time his eyelids fluttered, the fine emerald eyes would not remain open.

It took three entire days before a loud purring and the tickle of cat whiskers upon his ear prodded him into consciousness. "S-stop," he said, and flicked a finger at Rosebud. "It sounds like there are b-bees in my ear."

Winifred and Jessamine both giggled, and Rosebud batted back at the fierce finger with one tiny paw and then wrapped both paws around it and began to give it a thorough scrubbing.

"Wh-what the devil?" Carrington mumbled, blinking in the sunlight of a perfectly pristine Sunday afternoon.

"Rosebud thought that you would never play with her again," Winifred told him, limping to the edge of his bed and smiling down at him.

"Winifred!" Ignoring the fuzziness in his head and the aching all over his body and the throbbing in his bandaged shoulder, Carrington struggled to take her hand and raise himself upon an elbow and stare about him. This movement sent Rosebud tumbling across the counterpane and elicited a loud "Sppppft!", which made a grin tremble upon Carrington's lips. "I am home," he sighed, and then he lay back against the pillows, still holding tight to Winifred's hand. "I am home and you are here with me, Winifred! We did not die!"

"Great heavens no," Winifred declared. "We are all quite alive, thank you. Would you like a glass of water? It is right here. I shall help you to drink some."

He drank gratefully once his head was supported by her shoulder. "I am cold," he murmured then. "I am so very cold."

"You will be warm soon," Miss Jessamine offered. "It does take a while, my lord, to find warmth once you have been frozen to the very bone."

"It was not merely some nightmare then? It did happen?"

"It did happen," Winifred replied, setting the glass aside and boosting herself to the mattress where she sat dangling her feet and holding one of his hands in her own. "It was a true and real nightmare. To be injured and freezing and near drowned all at one and the same time— Oh, Austin, I cannot guess how you must have suffered. And all of it— all of it—my fault."

"No, never your f-fault."

"Yes, because I lied to Aunt Jess. I was not in the park at all, Austin. I was at Lord St. Martin's."

"St. Martin's?"

"Indeed," Lord St. Martin offered from a chair at the foot of the bed, drawing Carrington's attention to his presence and Mr. Paxton's as well. "Came to talk me out of Jezebel, she did. And did a fine job of it too."

"Jez? T-talk you out of Jez?" Carrington's brow wrinkled and his eyes blinked tiredly and a small sigh escaped him.

"It is too much for him to think of at this moment," Miss Jessamine Bittle declared. "You must rest, my lord. We shall come to visit you again tomorrow. But now you must rest. Come, Winifred, you and Rosebud both, and give the man some peace."

Winifred leaned down and placed a chaste kiss upon his chin. "That," she whispered, "is for your courage and for your caring. You are my hero, Austin Hobart Holt." Before he could manage to gather his thoughts into some sort of order, she was standing, and scooping the kitten into her arms and limping from the room.

Limping, he thought. She is limping so badly. What has happened to her? But before he could ask his nephew, who now stood over him, his eyes had closed and he was fast asleep.

It was near a week before all was made clear to Carrington and it took the combined efforts of Theodore and Lord St. Martin and Miss Jessamine Bittle to do it, too. They managed the thing one afternoon after Miss Bittle blithely ordered Winifred to cease lollygagging about and take herself off to Madame Georgette's to begin the fittings for the new wardrobe she was to have for the Season. "John shall take you in the coach," she said. "And Gracie shall accompany you inside."

Winifred did not at all like to miss an afternoon with Lord Carrington and said so, but she went off in the coach to the modiste's shop to please her aunt. And Aunt Jessamine stepped next door immediately the girl was gone from sight.

"You must accept the mare," she told Lord Carrington, dressed this day in shirt and pantaloons and slippers, with a pristine neckcloth tied neatly around his neck, a red robe tied about his waist, and a colorful quilt thrown over his knees and legs. He sat in a wing chair drawn up before the sunniest of the drawing-room windows.

"I cannot. Miss Jessamine, you cannot approve of your niece purchasing Jez from St. Martin to give to me. I cannot think how she did it, but—"

"That is just the thing," Theodore offered, who stood with one arm stretched along the mantel. "Miss Winifred has not actually purchased Jezebel, Uncle Austin."

"She has not?"

"No, she has not," St. Martin concurred. "It is all in the manner of a bargain. You are to have Jezebel and to breed her to Blaze at least twice and I am to have the first of their foals and you the second."

"And what is Miss Bittle to gain from it?"

"Your smile," Miss Jessamine Bittle declared.

"My—smile?"

"Exactly so. Winifred wishes to see you smile a smile that lights your eyes and makes them sparkle with laughter," Miss Jessamine explained without hesitation. "She confessed this to me the very morning after you all came safely home. It is her fondest wish, she says, to see you smile with your heart—all the way up into your eyes. She hopes that restoring Jezebel to you will serve to do the trick."

"Jez will always be your horse alone, Carrington," St. Martin murmured. "That much is perfectly clear. It was Jezebel and that kitten found you. Your gelding called to them through the storm, Miss Bittle said, though none of us heard him. You are surrounded by animals who will not be parted from you and Jezebel is prime among them. You had best take her back."

It was the first Carrington had heard of his rescue and he pressed them for details. "That is why Winifred limps so dreadfully now," he murmured when he had heard the whole of it. "She has injured her leg by riding through that devil of a storm to rescue me!"

The very next afternoon Winifred was most surprised to hear the knocker as she was pinning on her hat in preparation for a visit next door. Mr. Blather had gone off to the kitchen for a moment and so she stepped across the vestibule and opened it. "Lord Carrington! What on earth!"

"I believe this catlet belongs to you," Carrington growled, stepping into the foyer, Rosebud purring in the crook of his arm. "I see you are still opening your own door, Miss Bittle."

"I—"

"No, do not protest. You *are* opening your own door. You have not learned yet that such a thing can prove dangerous in London."

"It is none of your business whether I open a door or not," Winifred protested softly, her heart fluttering up into her throat at the mere sight of him standing there so tall and confident and obviously feeling much more himself. "Wherever did you find Rosebud? She ate breakfast with me only an hour ago," Winifred managed to say as an urgent need to take the gentleman into her arms and keep him there forever overwhelmed her. "I—I left her playing with a ball of yarn in the sun."

"How very odd," Carrington drawled with a cock of an eyebrow. "She came nibbling upon my rasher of bacon a mere twenty minutes ago, then she proceeded to tug the tassel from one of my boots and led Congreve and Theodore a merry chase. She ran in at our kitchen door, Congreve said, just as the pot boy stepped out. Escaped you. Likes my house better than yours."

"Well," Winifred said. "Well, she is fond of you, my lord."

"Is she? Is that why she leapt away from you and came bouncing through a blizzard to find me?"

"Oh! You know!"

"Everything," he said, taking Winifred's hand and leading her into the tiny front parlor just off the vestibule. "Did you truly hear Failure call to them, Miss Bittle? No one else did."

"Yes, yes, I did. Rosebud and Jezebel heard him as well."

"Mrrrr," Rosebud agreed, snuggling close against Carrington and batting her blue eyes teasingly at Winifred.

"I do wish you will not call him Failure," Winifred added, her hand fairly burning in his. "What a thing to name a horse! I realize he is not a prime article, but—"

"He has possibilities," Carrington completed the sentence for her as she sat down upon the puce fainting couch and he sat down beside her.

"Just so." Winifred nodded, wiping her suddenly perspiring hands upon the dove-gray wool of her skirt. "His ears are quite large and he is not flashy, but he has a noble heart."

"Like yours."

"L-like mine?"

Carrington nodded, his own heart catching for a moment in his throat as he noted the slow reddening of Winifred's very pretty cheeks. "A brave and noble heart, and a lovely smile and the most beautiful brown eyes."

"Failure?"

"No, Miss Bittle, yourself. And because you request it of me, I shall not call him Failure. I shall call him—Possible."

"Mrrr-spft!" Rosebud cried approvingly, joyfully taking a swipe at the button on Carrington's cuff as he moved his hand to take hold of Winifred's again.

"Quiet, catlet," his lordship ordered, "or I will change your name from Rosebud to Impossible."

Winifred giggled, and then she looked up to see Carrington's green eyes flashing with laughter, bright and warm and wonderful in the afternoon sunlight, and she sat and stared at those eyes as bewitched as she had known she would be.

He did not move, did not say another word, simply continued to smile that smile that sent Winifred's heart to thundering. When, after a time, Winifred fought free of the enchantment and lowered her gaze, he put a finger under her chin and tickled it upward until her eyes were full upon him again. "I have something to say to you, my dearest Miss Winifred Bittle."

"You have?"

"Yes, and do not interrupt me until I have finished."

"Very well." Winifred nodded.

"I know that we have not been long acquainted and that you know little about me," Carrington began.

"I know a good deal more about you than you think I do, my lord. I am Mercy's cousin after all and—"

"Winifred, you promised!"

"Oh. Yes."

"I know that we have not been long acquainted and that you know little about me," he began again, his collar growing extremely tight and his stomach beginning to flutter. He wondered for an instant if he had been wrong to come here so soon, to attempt to say this now, but he dismissed the thought. "I—I find—that I have grown most fond of you, Winifred."

"Well, and I am fond of you as well, Lord Carrington."

"Winifred, you promised not to interrupt."

"Mrrrf!" Rosebud scolded, leaping into Winifred's lap.

"Now, where was I? Oh, yes. I find that I have grown most fond of you, Winifred, and I should like to—like to—get to know you a great deal better."

Winifred's eyes began to sparkle with laughter and her hands ceased to perspire, and the hand that Lord Carrington did not hold went to pat Rosebud's tummy as the kitten rolled over onto her back and played with a cherry riband upon Winifred's dress.

"No, do not laugh. This is serious, Winifred. I love you," he sputtered in spite of his determination not to say exactly that until she had had more time to come to know him.

"You love me?"

"Deuce take it, Winifred, I had it all worked out how to explain to you that I wished to give you time to meet other gentlemen and—and—to decide if perhaps you might come to— It made perfectly good sense when I wrote it all down this morning."

"You wrote it all down this morning?"

"Rrrrrr," Rosebud confirmed.

"Yes, but you will not cease to distract me and now my mind has gone and spilled it all out and I have said exactly what I should not."

"You meant to tell me that I have an entire Season to look forward to, no doubt. And that there will be any number of beaux vying for my hand," Winifred whispered, her heart soaring into the skies at the thought that he loved her.

"S-something like that. B-because there will be, you know. Once they come to know you, I cannot think of one gentleman who would not wish to make you his wife."

"How odd." Winifred smiled, brushing a lock of hair from his brow with the verimost tip of her index finger. "I can think of several—but they are in the country, so perhaps they do not count. Oh, but there is Lord St. Martin. He is in London and he does not wish to make me his wife, though he does wish an introduction to Ethan, because he wishes to speak to him of breeding horses."

"Winifred! I am not speaking of breeding horses, I am speaking of—of—love—and you promised not to interrupt and you are doing nothing but!"

"Than I shall cease to do so," Winifred replied, staring at the dear, frustrated face before her.

"I cannot think of one gentleman who would not wish to make you his wife," Carrington repeated, running a finger around his collar to loosen it. "I said that. Well, it is true. And I am—I am not the—the best of them. Lord knows Mercy did not want me."

"Because you wagered Jezebel on her," interrupted Winifred with a frown. "I would have married you regardless."

"You would?"

"Yes."

Carrington caught his lower lip between his teeth and then caught Rosebud up with one hand and set her upon the carpeting. He pulled Winifred into his arms, ignoring the pain it caused his shoulder, and kissed her tenderly. Then he kissed her with all the love he felt for her in his very soul. And he was most relieved to have Winifred kiss him back just as heartily.

Winifred could feel his heart beating in rhythm with her own as he held her. *Oh, how I love him! Cousin Mercy could never have married Austin Hobart Holt,* she thought, *because Austin Hobart Holt was intended to be mine from the very first.*

"Mrrrrow!" Rosebud screeched, the sound separating the two.

"Oh, Austin, look! She is balanced upon the very top of the drapery rod," Winifred cried. "She will fall and kill herself!"

"No," Carrington sighed, "not now, you wretched catlet!"

"What is going on in here?" Miss Jessamine Bittle asked a moment later as she entered the chamber upon Mr. Theodore Paxton's arm. "Lord Carrington, do come down. You cannot possibly balance upon the back of that chair without tipping—"

"—Over," finished Theodore as the chair did precisely that and sent his uncle to the floor with a great ka-thump.

"Oh, Austin!" Winifred exclaimed, kneeling down beside him, laughing and crying both. "I am so very sorry."

"Mrrrffle," Rosebud agreed, leaping with considerable agility down onto Lord Carrington's head, then slipping and sliding through his curls to his shoulder where she began to lick at his ear with great sympathy. "Mrrrfle-brrrrrrrr."

FOUR-PENNY CAT

JEANNE SAVERY

In tenth century Britain, the value of a kitten
was a penny . . . and after he captured his first
mouse, two pence. Really good mousers were
priced at four pence.
—*The Stanyan Book of Cats,* p. 17,
edited by Allen James,
Stanyan Books, Random House, 1971.

Mrs. Carolyn Weston bundled herself into the warm
military cape she'd rescued from her dead husband's possessions and set off on her daily walk as she did in all
weathers. This day she chose go through the village and
onto the frosty hills by way of an ancient right of way
through the high pastures of Lord Manningford's estate,
Krilling's Woods.

The widow walked briskly toward the next village where
a kindly vicar had offered to loan her a history of a nearly
forgotten abbey from which she hoped to gain inspiration
for her next book. She had better! In actual fact, she nearly
despaired of ever again coming up with a variation on the
theme of the Gothic novels she had been used to producing
at the rate of two a year.

If she did *not* manage to dream up a new story and very
soon now, it was extremely likely she would be forced to
let go her very helpful Mrs. Williams—which would be too
bad for the both of them. Mrs. Williams had reached that
uncertain age where it would be difficult for her to find
a new position. And Mrs. Weston, herself, had become very

agreeably accustomed to having someone else do much of the cleaning and all of the cooking.

Had she, perhaps, been spoiled by Mrs. Williams's excellent help? It was not that she could *not* do for herself. She had, Carolyn thought rather smugly, become amazingly independent and unbelievably competent in all sorts of odd ways in the years she'd followed the drum with her husband.

Her father, in the first flush of anger, had threatened to disown her because of her foolish elopement with the dashing officer. In the end, he had not, of course. They had written, the letters sent often, moving back and forth, but, thanks to the Army's movements, arriving erratically. It had been a terrible loss when her beloved father had died soon after she lost her husband. But, because of the lieutenent's death, her father had had his beloved only child with him for those last few weeks, something for which they were both thankful.

Carolyn's father's long illness had resulted in the erosion of his small fortune which, so long as he'd earned money as an Oxford tutor, had kept the widowed scholar in relative comfort. Carolyn had not cared that she'd inherited very little, but she was forced to admit it made life a trifle difficult!

And it would be far *more* difficult if she did not come up with a new story!

How her husband would have ranted if he'd lived to discover how little she'd inherited! Carolyn grimaced at the memory of the man she'd married. She had quickly recovered from her infatuation with her officer husband, but she had, as the saying goes, made her bed. She lay in it with what grace she could. She never argued with him, did her best to provide something in the way of a home for the two of them wherever they might be, and was thankful that, at the least, the man did not beat her, which was not true for one or two of her acquaintances who also followed the drum.

All in all, her years with the Army had not been without interest. She had learned an amazing amount about all sorts of things a woman living a normal, more protected, life here in England would never dream existed. She was glad she had the opportunity, even if life had not been particularly comfortable much of the time.

But enough of her dreary past. Carolyn tucked such thoughts back into the corner of her mind where they lived and reverted to thinking of her next novel. She frowned very slightly, her pace slowing and her thoughts preoccupied to such a degree she was almost upon Lord Manningford's cook before she realized anyone was anywhere near.

"Mrs. Jones! Do forgive me for so nearly running you down," Carolyn said, stopping abruptly.

"There now! As if it were your fault I was stomping along with m'head in the clouds!" the woman responded. Wrapped in a bun, graying hair protruded from under the back of the hat she'd crammed on the top of her head.

"We were both preoccupied, then, and either *both* are at fault or—" Carolyn grinned a quick, impish grin. "I like this notion *ever* so much the better, *neither* of us is to blame." She sobered when the cook merely smiled faintly and, sympathy in her voice, added, "Is there ought I may do to relieve your concerns?"

"Now, then, isn't that like your kind heart to inquire! But there's nothing anyone can do, or so *I* think." The cook shook her head a trifle sadly. " 'Tis merely another letter from Lady Mary Violet. Lady *Hethering*, I *should* say," the cook corrected herself.

"Lady Hethering . . . ?" Carolyn repeated.

She'd met the woman at church on an occasion when Sir Hethering and his wife visited Krilling's Wood the previous summer. She'd rather liked what little she'd discovered of the blunt-speaking, square-faced woman, frank to a fault but with an endearing inability to take offense when others responded in kind.

"That would be Lord Manningford's sister, would it not?"

"Lady Mary Violet. His sister, yes."

"*Is* there a problem?" Carolyn asked, repeating her offer of help.

"Just the usual, although what Lady Mary Violet thinks *I* may do I haven't a notion," the cook said.

"Do?" Carolyn probed even as she silently scolded herself for her nosiness. Unfortunately, curiosity had always been her besetting sin and she doubted she'd change much at her age.

Mrs. Jones sighed. "She worries about her brother, you see. And she worries about the succession. But if my lord refuses to meet proper young women and refuses to think of marriage, why, what may *I* do?"

Carolyn chuckled. "I should think the only thing would be to hire the very prettiest of maids so that he may see what he is missing?"

Mrs. Jones blushed. "Now that *would* be just the thing, wouldn't it then? Me to encourage the master to behave like . . . like . . . like . . ." She sputtered for a few more moments, took a big breath and added, "And me responsible for hiring the poor girls!" Mrs. Jones cast a horrified look toward Carolyn. "No. I'll have me no pretty maids at the Woods." Her lips compressed and she shook her head. "And besides that, I'll not take it on myself to go aworrying himself. Lady Hethering will have to think of another way."

"I agree. It is neither your problem nor your duty."

"I don't suppose it is." Mrs. Jones abruptly changed the subject. "That cat I gave you. Tuppence, I think you called it? Did it work out?"

"Ah!" Carolyn smiled a wide bright smile which lit an otherwise uninteresting oval face. "You may tell your master that his one-penny kitten is shaping to become a four-penny cat! I am quite proud of the little devil. She brought me her first mouse just last week and has since brought me a second and unfortunately"—Carolyn made a moue of distaste—"a *bird*."

"Four-penny cat?" Mrs. Jones asked doubtfully.

Carolyn chuckled. "You just tell him. If he knew the bit about a one-penny kitten, he'll understand about a four-penny cat! And, Mrs. Jones, do stop worrying your head about Lord Manningford. If he feels the need for a wife, he himself will take care of the problem. After all, there are any number of young women right here in the parish who would say him yea before he'd managed to voice half the question!''

Carolyn made her good-byes and, chilled by standing still for so long, hurried on. As she climbed higher into the hills, her mind played with the notion Lord Manningford might take a wife. As she'd suggested, he'd have no difficulty finding one. She had noticed the romantic sighs whenever the young girls looked at the scarred man on those rare occasions he limped into church and, for that matter, the way older women's complexions darkened if he were, by some chance, to pay one even the least of polite attentions.

Mrs. Weston had been amused by the situation, actually, but, when alone in her narrow bed in the first-floor front room of her small cottage, she actually found *herself* dreaming a dream or two involving the strangely attractive Lord Manningford. Amusing it might be, the way every other maid and woman in the parish found him intriguing; far less amusing that she did herself!

She, at least, should have learned that attractive is as attractive does . . . to misquote the old saw.

"Four-penny cat? She actually said the kit was shaping into *a four-penny cat*?"

"She said you'd understand," Mrs. Jones said, eyeing her master who never spoke so abruptly. "Can't say *I* did,'' she added a trifle crossly and hoping for enlightenment.

Instead of an explanation, all Mrs. Jones got was his lordship's back, turned on her as he strode toward the side door, the one closest to the stables.

"My lord . . .'' she called.

"Later, Mrs. Jones. Later.''

Now where, wondered Mrs. Jones, *is his lordship going at this time of day? Why, the ducks are about done to perfection and I've that sauce on the stove which will curdle if not served soon!*

The duck dried to the point where it was inedible and the sauce was thrown out to the pigs fattening for winter hams and even now awaiting the first *really* cold day for butchering. Everything else, except for what the cook felt would hold for the master, was served up to the Woods' servants, and far too good a meal for them it was, grumbled Mrs. Jones.

While they ate it, Lord Manningford rode aimlessly along the route he'd already taken once that day. This time he didn't inspect his coverts or the hedges or the animals grazing in the fields. He didn't even bother to check the condition of the bridge which he'd almost decided must be replaced for fear next spring's thaw would bring down tree roots and tumbling rocks to totally wreck what was left of the substructure.

In fact, he didn't once think about his estate.

Instead, he wondered about a woman who knew the wisdom of previous centuries. Where had *she* learned that bit about the value of cats? Few scholars were aware of the precious manuscripts saved from monasteries destined for destruction during Henry VIII's reign and by his decree. Fewer still found where they were stored in college librar-ies, among other places. And only a *very few indeed* studied them, translating the medieval Latin into a more modern tongue.

In fact, he'd thought he himself the only scholar now interested in them. Momentarily the thought he might *not* be nagged at him, that another might be writing a history of abbey life which would be in print before his own was finished. Then it occurred to him that it would be pleasant to have someone with whom he could discuss his interpre-tation of how life went on in a monastery. A smile played around his lips as he thought of how his tutor at Oxford would have scolded him severely for thinking he owned those particular manuscripts, thinking that research mate-rials could or should be hoarded by a single person.

The elderly man with flyaway white hair feathering about his pink skull in wisps had been very like Manningford's childhood notion of a gnome. A benevolent gnome, of course. Even after Manningford left Oxford, he'd kept up a correspondence with his tutor, occasionally asking his advice, often relating his findings concerning the medieval church which was their mutual passion and, when the old man grew ill, making several journeys a year merely to visit with the scholar.

The poor man had developed a wasting illness which he'd borne cheerfully, forbidding that anyone write his only daughter and tell her how sick he'd become. But how could she not have known? Why had she not read between the lines of the old man's letters and guessed her father's need of her? Luke realized he still felt aggrieved by the woman's neglect!

But that, too, was an old irritation which he should put behind him. Instead, he must think of a means by which he could discover, without her knowing he was the least bit curious, how the blasted woman had come to know the value of cats in medieval England!

Come to that, just which woman was it? He thought back to late summer and the day Mrs. Jones had diffidently asked if she might give away one of the kitchen cat's kittens to a lady in the village who wished one. He'd twisted his weak knee that morning and it pained him rather badly so he'd been a trifle testy. He recalled telling Mrs. Jones that, if she didn't give them away, they must be drowned. After all, he remembered saying, they were nothing but one-penny kittens.

His cook had looked confused and asked, "I'm to charge Mrs. . . ."

Manningford frowned at a fox who had the audacity to sit licking its white bib not twenty yards from where he sat his horse. "Mrs. Who?" he asked the fox. "What name did Mrs. Jones supply?"

Why could he not remember who had wanted that cat? Luke grimaced. He supposed it wasn't at all strange he could not remember. He had, after all, deliberately isolated himself from the locals to whatever degree was possible soon after the only woman he'd ever asked to wed him had, shudderingly, told him she would not.

Oh so sweetly the chit had informed him that, although fathers might find him a more than adequate bridegroom, no sensitive woman, properly brought up, could possibly abide his ruined face. The information shocked him. His face had never before bothered him. She also informed him that his limp, which kept him from the dance floor and overly long walks, although there was little else he could not do, only added to the horror.

Luke had bowed, and conscious of his limp for the first time in years, left her presence. He'd returned to the family estate and, now, rarely left it. He *never* went to social occasions where he might, by his very presence, rouse revulsion in the breast of some innocent young maid and, unless his blessed sister forced it on him, rarely did so much as attend services at the village church.

All of which meant he'd no notion where the kitchen cat's offspring now resided. He finally, reluctantly, decided he'd no way of discovering it. Not and keep hidden his interest in a woman who knew what a four-penny cat might be! An interest which would be academic in any case. He could never approach her, even as a possible friend, so why should he waste time wondering about her?

He wouldn't.

Instead, he'd return to Krilling's Woods and his current work, which was translating a copy of the 1024 journal of the then-abbot of the particular monastery he considered his own! Idly, he hoped the destitute scholar he'd hired to make copies of the originals did accurate work. In fact, now it had crossed his mind to wonder, it might be good sense to take a few random pages of the man's copy into Oxford and compare them to the original. It would be a very foolish thing if he spent hours and hours on his translation and then discovered he'd been translating one mistake after another!

"Yes. That is what I will do."

His gelding twitched his ears at the sound of his words. He twitched them again as snow began falling, huge, wet flakes drifting down onto head and shoulders and whitening the horse's mane.

"Don't like the snow, do you, Summer's Son?" The horse nodded in seeming agreement and Luke chuckled. "Well, come to that, neither do I."

Humor faded. Snow meant postponement of any journey into Oxford. Foolish to think of going in the winter anyway. Which was too bad, because now it occurred to him to check the copy, he'd be unable to settle to his translation.

Luke sighed, turned his horse's head, and took the shortest route possible back to the stable, going immediately into the house where, once the warmer inside temperature hit him, he discovered he'd become chilled. He was, therefore, pleased to discover his valet had not only ordered a fire in his room, but had ready a great deal of hot water and the extra-large tub.

A bath would not only warm him, but would soothe his aching knee.

"Ahhh . . ." He sank into the water. "When finished, I'll have a light supper, Rumble. Here in my room, please. I'll make an early night of it."

Perhaps, he thought, the weather would change for the better and he could, after all, set off for Oxford.

The weather changed—but for the worse. The gentle wet snow turned into a three-day storm which covered the hills deeply and left farms and villages isolated. It was the worst blizzard in living memory and, if this first storm of the year was a forewarning of the winter to come, no one wished to know it!

Most of all, Carolyn Weston didn't wish to know it. She knew far too well the suffering bad weather caused, having lived through some harsh winters during her years with the Army when the enlisted men, worn down by a summer's hard campaign, died of winter ailments and even the officers suffered from poor housing and bad food. The poor here at home suffered, too, she thought, and wondered what she might do to ease their situation. At least those here in the village.

When she'd finished her morning's work, which just now consisted of finishing, in poor light, the book she'd borrowed from the neighboring village's vicar, she moved to stare out the small front window. The snow had eased. It was now a steady gentler fall, far better than the wildly blown sleety stuff they'd endured all day yesterday. She should get out before it worsened again. The footing would be bad under the new fallen snow, but didn't she have a patent clog somewhere, designed to keep one from slipping?

She went to the back of the house where Mrs. Williams was elbow deep in bread dough.

"Is it baking day? Have I miscounted?"

"It is only that when a good fire is so necessary to keep us warm, I think it a shame to waste it!"

"An excellent notion, especially since we should, perhaps, make extra for those who cannot bake for themselves?"

"If this keeps up there may be more than a few of those," the cook said, her tone revealing concern.

"I'm thinking of visiting Mrs. Gladbrook to discover how we might help prevent disaster."

Mrs. Williams straightened, holding her doughy hands over the table. "You don't mean *now*, do you? You aren't thinking of walking out in all that snow, are you?"

"Well—" Carolyn cast her cook a look which was half mischief and half apology. "Yes, I am. That is, I am if I can only remember where I put those odd clogs with the studs on the bottom?" She eyed her housekeeper.

"Clogs? Oh! Your pattens. Now where did we put them?" She went back to her kneading, leaning into the dough and folding it, only to lean into it again, turning it, folding it. "Did we hang them in the shed?" she asked.

"Why," Carolyn asked, "would we put them where I could not reach them if I needed them?"

Mrs. Williams grinned, revealing a hole where a lower front tooth should be. "In the hopes," she said, teasing her mistress about her penchant for always hoping for the best, "that you would *not* be needing them, perhaps?"

Carolyn admitted the possibility, hopeless optimist that she was. "Do you truly think they are hanging in the shed?"

she asked, and stooped to pick up the kitchen cat who wound around her ankles, in and out, under her skirts. The creature happily settled into her arms, purring loudly as the spot behind her ears was scratched just as she liked.

"They might be in that cubby under the stairs."

"I'll look there first," Carolyn decided, and, absent-mindedly, carried off the cat.

Tuppence made no objection. As would be obvious to the meanest observer, she liked to be carried.

Vicar Gladbrook himself opened the door to Carolyn. "Come in, come in! Why, look at you! You've become a snowlady, and in only that short walk from Rose cottage. At least"—the vicar, like everyone else, knew of Carolyn's long walks—"I do hope you have not attempted more in such terrible weather as this is?"

Carolyn spoke as she stooped to undo the pattens from her shoes. "I'd not have came out at all, but I am worried about some of the more elderly villagers. I wondered if there was something I could do to help in what is rapidly becoming a very bad situation indeed. There are some who will, I fear, run out of coal and wood and . . . well, frankly, I've no notion what else. Do tell me what you think I might do?"

"Two minds with but a single thought!" The vicar beamed, leading the way into the formal front parlor the Gladbrook family rarely used. "My lord, see who has come with exactly your fears on her mind!"

"*Her* mind?" Lord Manningford straightened from where he stared into a small fire in a tiny hearth. He turned in the practiced way he had which kept the ruined side of his face away from the vicar's newest guest. Silently, he cursed that someone, anyone, had forced themselves out into the cold and snow for any reason whatever.

He'd not have come if it had occurred to him he'd meet someone else at the vicar's! He'd have sent a groom with a letter outlining what he was prepared to do for his tenants and for the poor in and around the village and then have awaited the vicar's word as to what would be needed.

"Mrs. Weston," the vicar asked brightly, "have you had the honor of meeting our Lord Manningford? He rode in from Krilling's Woods for the very reason you have walked up the road from your cottage." He beamed yet again from one to the other.

"I've not had the honor of an introduction, Vicar, but I had the great good luck to adopt one of his kitchen cat's kittens. Do you suppose," she asked, mischief in her eyes, "that that is too tenuous a connection to impose upon his lordship's good nature and ask *him* what I may do to help our village?"

She smiled. Manningford had the odd notion a lamp had been lit, shining from the inside of her skin.

"The good vicar and I have discussed several problems, Mrs. Weston," Manningford said repressively, doing his best to ignore a tightening feeling inside him. "I believe we have things well in hand."

His voice might have contained a certain chill, but, in spite of his better judgment, Luke felt a great deal of interest in this bright-eyed woman who was being helped from a man's snow-wet cape by the vicar. *This* then was the woman who knew a four-penny cat when she saw one!

"There will be much to do," the vicar inserted. "Very much, I fear," he said suggestively.

"I have my cook baking extra bread, Mr. Gladbrook, but to whom should it be delivered? Or would you rather organize a central commissary where . . ." She broke off when Lord Manningford made an odd sound. "My lord?"

"Commissary?" he asked, smiling. "Surely an exceedingly military term for such a lovely young woman!"

Carolyn felt herself blush. "It is my military experience, I fear." She searched her mind. "I don't know what else one would call it." After a moment, she suggested, "A storehouse, perhaps?"

"It is"—His lordship unbent to the point his voice sounded more normal even to himself—"an excellent notion, a central source to whom all in need may apply.

The wagon with coals and wood should be here soon. It was nearly ready to leave when I started out. I left my housekeeper putting together supplies of food which will be brought in later. So where, Vicar, would you suggest we put our stores?"

The vicar, flustered, looked from one to the other. "Well . . . perhaps . . ." He brightened. "The church? Yes, yes. The church, the church. Would that not be the best place?"

"I wonder," Carolyn suggested softly, "if the unused schoolhouse might not be better. It might be difficult to have church services around a pile of wood or with loaves of bread and blankets filling the pews, might it not?"

"The old schoolhouse. The schoolhouse! Now why did I not think of that?" The vicar's familiar beam crossed his face.

"The *unused* school? Do I not pay a teacher's salary?" Lord Manningford asked a trifle sternly.

"The last teacher left some time ago. I have"—the vicar again looked around the room as if inspiration might strike him from one wall or the other—"been dilatory in finding a replacement?"

"Some time ago. You must be overly burdened, Mr. Gladbrook," Manningford said. "I will take this one from your shoulders and will, myself, find a new teacher." He watched his vicar's expression change, suggesting disapproval. "You think, perhaps, that I cannot find a proper teacher?"

Disproval was replaced by the look of a startled rabbit. The vicar waved his hands. "No no, of course you can, of *course* you can . . . Certainly you can do that."

"Perhaps you are one of those who does not approve of providing teachers for the, er, lower orders?" Carolyn inserted the question gently.

The vicar cast a worried look toward Lord Manningford, but then sighed. "That is it exactly. Exactly. I was quite content when the good Lord made it necessary for the last man to leave. You understand, my lord, it was *His* will. His *will*. You see, my lord," he continued in an earnest tone, "an education for the poor can only lead to all sorts of nasty problems. *Nasty* problems. They grow dissatisfied. Dissatisfied, I say. They come to believe they deserve more than they have. They make demands and . . ."

Manningford's expression had been darkening as the vicar ran on, his words spilling out one after another, but at last he nodded. "I recall that you came here from the midlands, did you not? You fear the machine-breakers. But many of those poor men were uneducated, Mr. Gladbrook. It is not *education* which makes them dissatisfied since they are clearly dissatisfied without an education! The ability to read and write and knowing how to figure can only *aid* those who have the least little bit of ambition to better themselves!"

"I saw . . . such horror, such horror . . ." Mr. Gladbrook said sadly.

"Yes, I am sure you did," Mrs. Weston said soothingly and changed the subject. "At the moment, we wish to avoid horror of quite a different sort. The old schoolhouse should, perhaps, be swept out, and we will need someone to dole out the coals and food. *Preferably,"* she added with a smile and an amused glance toward his lordship, "someone who can keep a record of who received what!"

"Yes, of course," his lordship responded, controlling his features admirably, "someone who can write and knows their numbers."

The vicar, who was a jovial man when all went along smoothly, but who had little in the way of true humor, looked suspiciously from one to the other. "My eldest son, with the help and advice of his mother, should be capable of handling that admirably. Admirably, I'm sure," he said, just a touch of a scold in his voice. "Now . . ."

The vicar outlined what he felt would be required by the poorer elements of the village. He spoke of three elderly people who would be unable to come to the schoolhouse and of two others who were ill.

When he finished, Lord Manningford nodded. "I can see our work is cut out for us. This storm is, I fear, only a harbinger of a long and miserable winter. Mrs. Weston, I do not wish to insult you, but I doubt if your budget allows you to help as you'd wish to do. It is clear you will do all you can, so may I suggest, without insulting you, that you allow me to supply you with flour and whatever else is needed for your bread-making and, if you'd be so good, I'll send meat which you may roast at the same time or do whatever one does with it. But a roast could be taken to the school where it may be sliced and shared out. Most homes, even the worst, have soup kettles, and I'll see each has a supply of meal for porridge. What else?"

Carolyn opened her mouth to remind his lordship of the need for warm clothes and covers. She closed it when his lordship snapped his fingers and added, "Bedding. I believe my housekeeper was telling me only last fall that moths had gotten into some of the winter blankets. She was exceedingly apologetic about it. I doubt, however, that she threw them out, saving soul that she is. I will have them brought in. She can sort through the storage rooms where old clothing has been put away for decades. Centuries, perhaps. I do not know why it is, but an old house like Krilling's Woods seems to accumulate possessions as a forest accumulates layers of old leaves! We'll see if we cannot find what is needed."

"Very well, then." Mrs. Weston turned to the vicar. Sir, if your son and your good wife will see to readying the schoolhouse and if, perhaps, you might set the word about that stores will be available for those in need?"

"Yes. We can do that. I must make my pastoral rounds, of course, even in such weather as this and I will do what I can to pass the word while I am out. While I'm out . . ." He did not look at all happy at the thought.

"If you come by way of my house, Vicar, I will loan you my patented winter pattens. I have discovered that their advertiser did not lie and that they are truly quite helpful in avoiding falls. I'd leave them now, but I must return home myself . . . yes, my lord?"

"I will carry you home on my horse, leaving the pattens for our good vicar. If you will have Summer's Son brought around, Vicar, I will lead him to Mrs. Weston's home and you may keep the patent pattens!''

"Will you come in, my lord, and take a cup of hot chocolate to warm you before you return home?''

"Before I make my way to Orcap Hill ..." Luke hesitated. She seemed sincere. Did he dare spend time with her? Dare take the opportunity, perhaps, to discover how she'd come to know about the one-penny kitten? He drew in a deep breath and decided to chance it. "I would like that very much if it would not be too much trouble.''

Luke stared at the woman perched atop his gelding as if she'd sat sidesaddle in a man's saddle every day of the week. There had been no squeamishness when he reached to lift her up and she had looked him in the eye as if his face was not the disaster he knew it to be. Was it possible she did not care?

And now she smiled at him, that glorious smile which changed her face, making it light up from within. He blinked, realized he'd been standing there staring for some time, and reached to lift her down. Again there was not the slightest hint she found him repulsive. Luke felt something deep inside of him warm, something hard and cold which seemed to melt. This woman treated him as she might any man, and it was a new experience for him!

As Luke followed her up the short path to her door it occurred to him that her reaction might be so accepting because of her experience with the military. She must have seen loathsome sights such as most young women would never, thank the good Lord, know.

That is, if she had actually followed the drum and not, as many military wives did, have a house somewhere far behind the lines where her husband, occasionally, found time to visit. In Lisbon, perhaps?

But she'd spoken of the commissary as if it were part of her daily life. Did that not indicate she'd lived in the camps? Perhaps before this winter were over he'd feel comfortable enough he could ask. Which implied he'd see her again, talk to her. Which was nonsense, of course.

But now . . . Luke closed the door which left them enclosed in a short hall, narrow, steep stairs rising to one side and two inner doors leading out of it.

"Oh, dear me, yes." Mrs. Weston exclaimed. She pointed to where the cat had left her latest offering. It lay, nearly centered, on the narrow table set for receiving hats and gloves. "Truly she is a four-penny cat!"

Lord Manningford picked up the dead mouse and threw it into the street which brought fervent thanks from Mrs. Weston.

"That cat is too generous by half," she said, and added, "In here, my lord." Mrs. Weston opened a door which led into a tiny parlor. "Do watch your head. You are overly tall for my small cottage. Take a seat near the hearth while I step into the kitchen to see to the chocolate."

Luke stopped. "No. I will continue on my way. I did not realize you must do for yours . . ."

Startled, he grasped her fingers where they lay gently against his lips and, a trifle roughly, pushed them away. He saw her blush and was sorry for it, but hadn't a notion how he might explain.

"It is not that I haven't a cook, my lord," she said. "It is that I like doing some things for myself. I learned to make my chocolate from a French prisoner, an officer, who was allowed to visit among some of our officers. I like it just so. You see?"

She smiled but did not again attempt to touch him. When she turned he watched her go. That melted bit inside froze up again and he sighed softly. He wished there were some way to tell her it was not that he didn't like her touch. It was that he liked it too well!

Luke stirred the embers, added kindling, and then, when it caught, a few coals. Then he went out to his horse and moved the gelding to a more sheltered spot, covering him with his coat. By the time his hostess returned, he was seated on a bench in the inglenook which closed in the fireplace making an easily warmed corner. His feet were extended toward the fire, but, when she entered, he pulled them in and rose to his feet.

"I heard the door, did I not? Did we forget something?"

"Merely that I wished to put Summer's Son in a more protected place. I hope it is all right that I tied him at the side of the house out of the wind. That smells wonderful, Mrs. Weston," he added when she extended a tray toward him bearing two large white cups. He blew on his, looking through the steam. The woman held her own cup between her two hands as if the heat felt good, and her gaze had a dreamy look to it. Was she thinking of her dead husband?

Or, perhaps that French officer?

Suddenly Carolyn looked up, startled. "Oh! I have gone off into a dream world, have I not? Do be seated." She plopped into the chair when he insisted he preferred the bench.

"You said you must ride to Orcap Hill? Will you be speaking to the vicar there?" she asked.

"As I did here. The village is smaller, but, for reasons I don't understand, healthier. There will be little needed, assuming they've enough fuel, but I fear, industrious as they are, they will *not* have planned for the sort of winter I am assured by my best weather prophet we will suffer in the months ahead!"

"And you? You are enough beforehand with your orders that you can supply half the county as you appear to have promised to do?"

"Do you chide me?"

Carolyn chuckled. "I am merely curious. It is my greatest flaw, curiosity. I cannot control it."

The cat had been curled up on a wide windowsill but now dropped to the floor, slid under a small desk, and padded over to sit at her feet looking up at her. One small white paw patted gently at her leg.

Carolyn looked down. "If you are looking for a handout, Tuppence, you are out of luck. If you merely wish a lap, well . . . ?" Carolyn raised her hands slightly, leaving her lap free.

The cat hopped up, trod on her skirts for a bit, and

then settled into a tight ring. Carolyn dropped a hand to its shoulders, her fingers rubbing behind the perky ears, and soon a rumbling purr sounded overloud in the silence. Carolyn looked up and found Lord Manningford's eyes on her, a bemused look to them.

"Is something wrong? Have I a smut?" She rubbed the end of her nose vigorously.

"Nothing is wrong. It is only that it is years since I saw a woman with a cat. It reminded me of Nurse—" He chuckled. "And you needn't poker up. It is the cat which reminds me. *You* are nothing like her. You must gain a hundred pounds and you must adopt the most outrageously starched apron and an equally stiff white thing to cover your lovely hair. Then you *might* begin to resemble her in other ways than sitting with the cat. Oh ho! You must also rid yourself of that twinkle in your eyes. Nurse was a loving and hardworking woman, but she had little or nothing in the way of humor!"

"You are a palaverer, my lord. You will turn my head with such compliments."

"At least you recognize they are compliments." He admitted to a degree of ruefulness. "I fear I am a trifle out of practice at such things."

"You needn't practice for my benefit, my lord," she responded seriously. "I am far beyond the need for such flummery. Besides, I am much too blunt and practical a woman for nonsense. Instead, do explain to me," she coaxed, "how you can provide so much in the way of coal?"

He threw back his head and laughed as he had not done for years. "Mrs. Weston, I have never known a woman to match you. Coals. You truly wish to know? Yes, of course you do," he answered his own question. "I can see you do. It is quite simple, actually. I own a coal mine! It is not such a large vein as to be profitable commercially, but it will keep me and mine for some few years yet. I've men on the estate who have worked in the big mines. They left mining because they disliked the work and, in one case, feared a cave-in would soon occur. It did, too," he added, and drew in a deep breath. "In any case, they are willing to dig enough coal for our use, and if it becomes necessary, they'll go back into my mine again this winter. It will very likely become necessary, too."

"Thank you."

"For explaining?"

"For explaining what was none of my business." Carolyn sighed. She finished the last of her chocolate and set the cup aside. "May I get you more?" she asked.

He glanced at his own empty cup and wondered when he'd drunk it! "No. I must be on my way." He stood, careful of his head. "I will stop at the farrier's as I ride out of town and have the blacksmith take a look at those pattens the vicar borrowed. Perhaps he can make something similar and yours may be returned to you!"

"You might like a pair for your own use, my lord, They are a truly excellent design."

As they moved toward the front door, Carolyn asked if Luke would return a book to the vicar he was to visit next and he agreed, of course. He was surprised to discover that he disliked the notion of going. As they said their good-byes the feeling grew.

It was, Luke decided, a warning he not become overly familiar with the woman. As he rode down the street toward the blacksmith's, he lectured himself sternly. He had satisfied his curiosity about her and that must be enough. He must, he told himself, avoid the little widow or it was possible he'd fall victim to those smiling eyes. And, if he did, then he'd likely make a fool of himself. Again.

But she didn't cringe, did she? asked a sly voice.

Perhaps she could look upon my ruined face and not recoil, he answered the devil's advocate inside his head, *but she might very well quail from the notion of actually touching me.*

Except, had she not already touched him? She'd placed her fingers ever so softly over his lips, preventing him from speaking.

She did. And was surprised when you pushed her away, said the voice.

Well, thought Luke, scowling, *let us be quite frank then. Let us say exactly what we mean. She'd recoil from making love with me and I must not forget it. Any woman would,* he insisted, drowning out the voice which began another artful comment.

Luke dismounted and went into the smithy. He had to wait while the smith finished beating out a long flat bar with a curve at one end. He could not guess what it might be for, but he'd wasted far too much time with the widow so, after explaining his errand and without discovering what the odd piece might be, he continued his ride through the gently but persistently falling snow to the other village.

Several days passed and the new village routine settled into place. Two elderly women lived alone at Mrs. Weston's end of the village and she and her cook took on the care of them along with the extra cooking.

Early each morning they began the baking. Six loaves, one for their use and five extra to be shared around. At ten the vicar's son would arrive, a sturdy fourteen-year-old being readied at home to enter, in a few years, his father's Cambridge college. He'd bring a bag of the precious coal and take away all but two of the loaves and a roast. When he'd gone, Carolyn dipped out servings of the day's hot stew, which had cooked overnight in a large iron kettle settled deep in well-banked embers.

The coal, the small tightly covered kettles, and two wrapped half-loaves would be settled onto the long sled, an indulgence she'd ordered earlier that fall, thinking she and some of the village children might enjoy themselves in snowy play on the hill behind her house. The village carpenter had outdone himself. The back of the sled had been boxed in by well-smoothed boards a few inches high, the wood painted a bright carmine red. Carolyn had been more than pleased as she'd watched the blacksmith attach his runners, designed to curve up and over the front.

But the sled, ordered as the indulgence of a whim, was now almost a necessity! She might have found another means of making her deliveries, but Carolyn actually enjoyed pulling the long red sled behind her, Tuppence occasionally perched on top of the coal bag. The cat, however, never went beyond the first woman's small three-room cottage where she'd jump down and return home.

Mrs. Greenbottom was appreciative of the coal and food, but, since the delivery enabled her to stay inside in the warmth, she was capable of managing all else for herself, and so she informed Carolyn the first day when asked if there were anything more one could do to ease her way.

The second lady, Miss Sweetbriar, was another kettle of fish entirely. She lived in a larger cottage a little way out of the village. It was up a road which, near the top of the hill, curved back on itself. The cottage actually faced *away* from the village below it. The woman living in it was not only elderly, she was unwell, barely able to move from her bed to a seat by the fire and then back again. Carolyn pitied the uncomplaining woman and did what she could each day to make her life more comfortable.

Lord Manningford made it his habit to come into the village early in the morning, long before Mrs. Weston was likely to be stirring. He could not get the woman from his thoughts, which was seriously upsetting. He was more than ever certain that he must avoid her, and took care to plan his day accordingly.

But the best laid plans, as Walter Scott said, gang oft agley, and one sun-bright day Luke was obliged to inspect a tenant's damaged chimney which had caught fire during the night. Luckily, the fire was discovered quickly and caused minimal damage, but the farmer was exceedingly apologetic, explaining that it was not his lordship's fault at all, but the man's own foolish wife. She admitted she disliked cleaning up after the sweep and had had the man skimp his work, not thinking they'd be using that particular chimney and then, the winter so cold and all, well, the farmer had decided the chill should be taken from the room and all, and . . .

. . . and Lord Manningford finally managed to hush his tenant's rambling explanation by offering to send around the estate's chimney expert. He remounted and, much later than usual, made his way to the village.

Upon reaching it, he saw Mrs. Weston trudging along the far end of the street pulling what looked a very heavy load behind her. Anger welled up in him although he couldn't have said why, and he trotted right on by the schoolhouse where he usually checked to see if ought was needed. He joined his *bête noire* just as she was making her first stop.

Mrs. Weston looked up and smiled a welcome. "My lord! I must thank you for delivering Vicar Simpson's book for me. Given the snow, I don't believe I'd have been able to do so before spring. I enjoy the walk over the hills, but there are limits!"

Lord Manningford dismounted. "A rather odd book for a lady, I thought?"

She smiled again, this time somewhat ruefully. "Yes, and quite useless. I've still to find a . . ." She broke off, looked a trifle conscious and, instead of finishing her thought, said, "but you cannot be interested in my ridiculous predicament. Are you checking on us, seeing if we are making proper use of your generous supplies?"

"Quite unnecessary, since I am certain you do. No, I come each day to see if there is something else I might do. Here," he added when he saw she was lifting a covered iron pot. "That is too heavy for you. Allow me . . ."

"If you would bring out Mrs. Greenbottom's coal hod and fill it, I would appreciate it, but I can manage the stew pot nicely."

"Nevertheless I will carry it." He took the kettle from her and followed her up the path. Mrs. Greenbottom met them at the door with her hod and then, flustered by his lordship's presence, dropped it, stuttered, dropped an awkward curtsey, stuttered some more, and backed away from the door when Carolyn gently suggested she bring in the food.

Finally the elderly woman managed to find her tongue. "Well, I never!" Mrs. Greenbottom exclaimed, staring down the garden path where Luke was filling the hod.

"His lordship running errands! Just like he was the vicar's boy!"

Carolyn chuckled. "I doubt it will harm him, Mrs. Greenbottom. Do you want the bread on the table or the dresser? And thank you very much for scrubbing out the extra pot! I believe we'll have a haricot tomorrow. Will you like that for a change?"

Still talking in a soothing manner, Carolyn saw that the coals, quite half the bag, were placed by the hearth, that the pail was full of fresh water and that all was, in general, quite well and good in the clean little house.

"And where do you take the remainder?" his lordship asked in a rather abrupt tone once they'd returned to the street.

"I walk up to Miss Sweetbriar's cottage."

"Miss . . . Sweetbriar?" He frowned. "Why do I not place the lady?"

"Perhaps you have not met her. She was brought to the village by Vicar Gladbrook late this past autumn. She is, if I correctly remember what was told me, related to his *first* wife." As Carolyn spoke she picked up the rope she'd attached to the front of the sled and prepared to begin her trek up the hill.

Manningford glanced back toward the vicarage. "But surely . . . if not with the vicar, where then does she live?"

Carolyn pointed. "Up there. That pretty little stone cottage in the tiny garden just a little way around the curve." She tipped her head. "Why do you frown?"

"No one has lived there for some time. I had thought it not in the best of condition."

"The roof leaks a trifle, but only to the detriment of the upper floor, which my cook tells me is quite rotten in places and needs attention. Miss Sweetbriar, however, suffers from a chronic illness and cannot climb stairs. The downstairs rooms are snug enough," Mrs. Weston added, uncertain as to the source of his lordship's irritation.

"Ill." He compressed his lips and took the rope from her hand. "I will go today. I wish to check the situation."

He trudged on up the road in the path she'd made the preceding days.

Carolyn, shaking her head at his stubbornness, tied his gelding to Mrs. Greenbottom's fence and then, folding her warm cape tightly around her, trailed along behind. Halfway up the hill he turned, saw she followed the sled and, his irritation still more obvious, waited for her.

"My lord," she asked hesitantly, "what is wrong?"

"I don't know that anything is wrong." He drew in a deep breath. "No, that is not true. There *is*. The house has been empty since the previous occupants succumbed to typhoid. No one, willingly, would now live there, you see. Typhoid, you know. It doesn't always go away."

"Typhoid? Oh, dear."

"I have often wondered if bad water were the culprit where there is typhoid. So often the illness occurs in low-lying areas where the streams are sluggish or there is a shallow pond. But up there?" He nodded up the hill. "Very likely I am wrong."

"The cottage's old well is near the convenience and the water was unpalatable, so perhaps you are not wrong. The vicar had a new one dug."

"A new well." Luke's lips compressed. "I do not own the cottage. There's no reason I should have been consulted. Still, I feel responsible for what happens in the village. I do not like it that you visit a sick woman living in that place."

"The woman is ill, but it is mostly old age, from which all who live long enough will suffer. It is not something I will succumb to because I do what I can to help her."

"You sound as if you would soothe a fractious child," he said bitingly. "Besides, this hill is too steep for you to climb each day. I admit it is easier to pull your sled than I'd have thought, but, still, this isn't work for a *lady.*"

Carolyn felt a warm glow touched off by his concern, but she had, after only a few short months with the Army, concluded that the distinctions society made between ladies and other women were exceedingly artificial. "Nonsense," she said. "In fact, I appreciate the exercise. You will not forbid me to do what I enjoy so much!"

They arrived at the picturesque cottage and Carolyn opened the gate, motioning Lord Manningford, sled and all, into the garden. She walked right up to the door, knocked, and then immediately opened it. Inured by her work in Peninsular hospitals to the smell of illness, she walked into the odd miasma without a thought.

Lord Manningford was *not* immune. He paused in the doorway and then, setting his jaw, forced himself on in. He emptied the coal into the bin beside the fireplace and watched Carolyn talk soothingly to the woman, slicing her a thick slice of bread and toasting it.

Carolyn glanced up and smiled. "My lord? Would you please fill the water bucket for me? I freely admit I find that task a trifle difficult. The winch in the well is sometimes reluctant to turn due to the cold. The new well is to the left. You will see my tracks going to and from it." She nodded toward the bucket standing on a bench near the fireplace.

As she made her request she worked briskly and, as he left with the bucket, she handed the old lady a bowl of broth from the stew and the toast which, he guessed, would be dunked.

As soon as the front door shut behind his lordship, Carolyn picked up the covered pot at the end of the bed. She took it out back before Lord Manningford could return with the water, suspecting, from his previous comments, that he'd object strongly if he found her taking out the slops like the lowliest of tweenie maids!

His lordship wasn't stupid, and he knew where she'd been. He scowled at her but said nothing, only turning to stare at the bent woman who shakily moved hand to broth and then to mouth, mumbling the soaked bread in a rather disgustingly avid manner.

When the woman finished eating, Carolyn asked Luke to leave them for a little. When he returned, she'd put the old lady into a clean gown and was bundling the dirtied one into a bag which she took out and put, with yesterday's stew pot, at the front of the sled.

"The vicar must hire someone to care for his relative. I will tell him so," Lord Manningford said abruptly. "Are you now ready to return to the village?"

Carolyn tightened her lips against a smile and impish lights appeared in her eyes.

He tipped his head, eyeing her. "Why do I have this odd notion you've mischief in mind?"

"Hmmm . . . well, you see, I do mean to return to the village"—her smile grew—"but *not* as you mean."

"Not. I see." He shook his head. "No, I do *not* see. Are you or are you not returning?"

She chuckled. "What I *should* say is that I am not going back by way of the road."

Lord Manningford glanced at the sled. He looked toward the hill and then at Mrs. Weston. A muscle jumped in his jaw. "I believe I've guessed. Is it not dangerous?"

"I've done it three times now. It's"—her face lit up with a joyous light—"glorious!"

"Thrice. And nary a spill?"

"When the notion occurred to me last fall, I explored the hillside. There are several rocks, one tree, and a few bushes, but I know where they are." Impulsively, she added, "Why do you not join me? The sled is quite big enough for two."

"I've never . . ." He bit off his words and glanced away.

Carolyn's eyes widened in amazement. "You have never flown downhill on a sled, my lord? Oh, you *must*. Come now. We go around the back of the cottage. There is a gate there and, at the bottom, we stop just beyond my garden fence in which there is also a convenient gate! Do come," she coaxed, taking his hand and tugging.

"Sledding . . ." He broke off, staring at their joined hands.

"Do you think it will undermine your dignity?" she teased, a rather mischievous sideways look turned his way.

He smiled, his gaze meeting and holding hers. For a

moment. Then remembering the danger, he glanced away. "It is more that I feel I'm too old for such foolishness."

"Now that is truly nonsense! One is never too old to be delighted by an experience."

He looked at her wonderingly. "You have such a happy outlook. Your life must have included much joy that you see only the good and find delight in the"—he searched for words to express his meaning—"the *little things*. Much joy and little pain."

Carolyn sobered instantly. "Little pain? I've known my share, my lord, but I refuse to allow it to ruin the whole of my life. The part of my life which I regret the most—" She bit her lip staring at nothing at all. After a moment she continued. "Well, the person I hurt, although it was the last thing in the world I wanted to do, informed me I was not guilty at all, but forgave me since I asked it and added that if I insisted on the need for atonement, then I should live the rest of my life in such a way he'd be pleased with me."

"That sounds like a loving father's words," Lord Manningford said and, forgetting his vow, he stared deep into her eyes.

She smiled. "They were. Very nearly his last words. After much heart searching, I managed, I think, to learn the lesson he would teach me."

"Perhaps you have. Well . . . lead on, Mrs. Weston. Show me this hill on which we are to endanger life and limb!"

"No! On which we will have the greatest of good fun, arriving at the bottom hale and healthy!"

Their eyes met still again and a chuckle was shared between them before they trudged around the cottage to the back. They went through a gate opening into the hill pasture beyond and Carolyn carefully situated the sled. She pointed to the back. "If you will seat yourself there, my lord, I will sit before you, and we will be off."

It was only as she settled herself and felt his arms come around her, felt his legs alongside her, that it occurred to Carolyn that they were in a rather compromising position.

Well, she thought, *done is done. Therefore it is too late to repine!*

Besides, she *enjoyed* the feeling of what was very nearly an embrace. It had been a long time since strong masculine arms surrounded her. Not since her husband's death had she experienced even the mildest forms of the closeness one found in marriage. Feeling Lord Manningford's arms about her, she concluded she'd like to know those sensations again—if ever she'd the opportunity.

Since that was unlikely . . . well, there was this moment, and moments must be savored when and where they were found!

Carolyn leaned forward, his lordship leaning with her, and pushed off. They started slowly and she felt him relax. And then the sled picked up speed and his arms tightened. It was wonderful. She enjoyed every second of it, her joyous laughter ringing out.

Lord Manningford was somewhat less certain of the delight. That is, he was until they reached the flat area at the bottom and the sled slowed to a stop. Then he wished the ride were not over. Or that they might do it again. He quickly put that notion aside and, his hands at her waist, helped Mrs. Weston to her feet before getting to his own. He stared down into her glowing face.

"Shall we do it again, my lord?" she asked, adding fuel to the dangerous thought he'd already pushed aside. Her white, even teeth showed in a wide smile and her eyes sparkled.

How he was tempted. Not only was there the exhilaration of the speedy ride, but there was the added wonder of holding this special little lady in his arms.

Ah! But that was the true danger, was it not? Not the hill or the speed?

"I must go," he said abruptly. When her smile faded, he added, "I admit I am glad you insisted I must have a ride on your sled." He saw her smile fade further. "Perhaps another day," he said, knowing he must avoid that day, and her, as he would the typhoid . . .

. . . which thought reminded him he must speak to the

vicar about his elderly connection. Mrs. Weston must not be allowed to continue acting as the old woman's servant! Lord Manningford made his good-byes, retrieved his horse from where it patiently awaited him, and then, leading it, strode back toward the schoolhouse where he discovered from the vicar's wife that her husband was at the manse working on Sunday's sermon.

Mrs. Gladbrook, bundled up in enough warm clothing for a regiment, shivered. She awaited one last person who was to come for supplies that day, a rather shiftless man who had no sense of time and very little comprehension that his dilatory ways might be putting others to some trouble. His lordship wondered if the vicar, too, was merely thoughtless that he allow his wife to do this duty or if he was one of those selfish men who believed someone else, anyone but himself, should do the things which led to the least discomfort.

"Mrs. Gladbrook," Manningford ordered, "I will send in extra coal and you are to have a fire in here each morning. You will take a chill if you do not. I'll not worry about any coals you use and you are not to do so, either, do you hear me?" he finished kindly.

Mrs. Gladbrook thanked him shyly and he left the schoolhouse.

After a brief argument with the vicar, his lordship decided the vicar's lack of understanding was based in both answers. The man definitely liked his comforts, but he truly didn't think of how others were faring when occupied with work which was his responsibility.

Manningford had a few pointed words to say.

The vicar appeared to ignore the fact his wife was becoming chilled, but was appalled, actually, to discover what Mrs. Weston did each day for his elderly relative. He'd been aware the woman was ill, of course, since he visited her during his pastoral rounds, but he hadn't thought of what that meant in terms of caring for her, and yes, he responded to his lordship's softly spoken suggestion, he'd see if there were not a village woman who would, for a few shillings a week, go each day to do the necessary! Feeding her and such like.

"And seeing she is washed and her clothes changed?"

"Washed?"

"And her laundry? Cleaning her rooms?"

"Well, yes. Cleaning, you say. Yes," the vicar repeated doubtfully, "perhaps a little cleaning? I do suppose some-one must . . ."

He looked around his own shining office, bewildered, obviously, that such furbishing and polishing didn't simply happen.

"Yes, yes, someone does such things, do they not?" he muttered. "Oh, dear. Oh, dearie me. Who? Who?"

Manningford's mouth twisted. Even in his own home the foolish man hadn't a thought in his head of how the work was accomplished—or by *whom!* "By fairies in the night, perhaps?" Manningford suggested caustically.

Vicar Gladbrook brightened, his eyes widening. "Fairies in the night. Very good, my lord! Very good indeed. Fairies! Oh my, oh my, fairies in the night . . ."

Lord Manningford, wondering if he should not replace the man with someone who had a better understanding of the daily needs of humanity, rode home slowly. But he soon put the good vicar from his mind, the ride down the hill with Mrs. Weston in his arms replacing those troubling thoughts . . . and rousing others which quickly shattered his peace of mind.

He must *not* begin dreaming there could ever be any-thing of any consequence between himself and Mrs. Weston!

"And what"—he spoke to a pert fox who sat atop a stone fence, front feet set neatly together, and grinning a foxy grin—"did she want with that book about the abbey? Which was, she said, *no help!*"

Help? A predicament, she'd said. What sort of predica-ment? What help did the lady require? She had made little of it, but had she not appeared a trifle embarrassed?

Lord Manningford pursed his lips, filled by a wry feeling. It seemed every way he turned he discovered something new to worry about. Something about which he must feel concern. If it wasn't the weather and the problems facing the poor, or the vicar's ailing relative, or *his* competency, it was Mrs. Weston's *predicament!*

But how in heaven's name *might* a history book have been of help, but hadn't? A history of a long forgotten abbey. In modern times, even the *location* of that particular abbey's ruins was difficult to find. The site had been pillaged over and over by locals wishing to use the dressed stone for other purposes. There was nothing left.

Or nearly. When Luke found the place a few summers previously there were no more than a few large stone blocks, nearly covered with wild thyme, which had once paved a room or courtyard. To one side was a sunken place where a ceiling had fallen in, revealing a bit of stone-faced wall of what might have been a storage room.

Lord Manningford shook his head. Mrs. Weston was surely a mystery. He smiled a wry smile. It was truly unfortunate, was it not, that he loved a mystery? It would make it harder to put her from his mind and keep her out. At which point he'd reached his stables and dismounted.

Making the decision he'd not think one more thought about the blessed woman, he entered his home by way of a back door and moved directly to his library. There he turned his steps to the volumes about abbeys. He chose three, one written from a canon law perspective, one about the daily life, and the last a slim leather-bound translation of one abbot's jottings, which he'd made in Latin, of his day's happenings. Manningford set them aside to take to the widow.

Then he realized what he'd done and gritted his teeth so hard he was in danger of breaking one. Would he never rid his mind of the woman? Very gently, forcing himself to take great care of his precious volumes, he replaced each in its own place on the shelves.

He would *not* waste his time mooning about thinking of that woman. Or *any* woman.

* * *

Carolyn shut herself up in the small upstairs room she called her study and seated herself at her desk. Today she would decide upon a plot for her next Gothic novel.

Or else.

She *liked* her life. She liked Mrs. Williams who cooked and cleaned and made life so comfortable. She must not lose her. It would not do at all to stop writing. What she made from it was no fortune, but wasn't to be despised either. It allowed her comforts, such as Mrs. Williams, and indulgences, such as her sled. And she would not give those up.

Instead, she would think up a nice new plot. Her notion of a ruined abbey and a man who pretended to be a monk simply wouldn't come together. What else might she dream up? Could her villain be badly scarred, perhaps . . .

. . . Or no!

Excitement filled Carolyn as a new thought suggested itself to her mind. Her *villain*, bless him, would look like a golden angel. Her *hero* would be scarred—

She paused, staring at the wall over her desk.

—although not too badly, perhaps.

Romantically scarred. Perhaps at the hands of the villain when the two were boys together? And ever since they had been in competition with each other. All their lives, perhaps . . . and the golden one knew the scarred one loved a young and beautiful heiress but believed he could never ever have her and the golden one knew the heiress really loved his rival.

So the golden one would do his best to keep the two apart!

Yes! It would do very well. And it would be a trifle different.

Again Carolyn paused.

Too different? Would her readers accept a romantically scarred hero and hiss a villain who looked perfection itself?

Carolyn chewed on the black enameled end of her steel-nibbed pen and looked right through the wall facing her.

Did she *dare*? Would her *publisher* accept such a variation from the more normal handsome hero and villainous-looking villain?

Oh, dear.

Unfortunately, now she'd thought of the idea, she itched to begin writing. Plot and scenes were streaming into her mind from all directions just as they had at her very first attempt at writing a novel. She felt the excitement which came when she *knew* she would tell a good story.

Yes, it would be good. Carolyn decided she'd write it, and if her publisher did not like it . . . well, she'd have had the enjoyment of doing it!

Several hours later Mrs. Williams opened the door, saw her mistress bent over her desk, the floor littered with discarded sheets of paper, and a slim stack of finished work piling up on the table to the side. Mrs. Weston had not responded when Mrs. Williams called up that a luncheon, if it was wanted, waited in the kitchen. It had happened before when Mrs. Weston was at her scribbling so Mrs. Williams had felt no particular concern.

Now, however, it was time for dinner. Mrs. Weston must be made to come and eat and not to say "in a minute" and then again, fifteen minutes later, say the same thing, and *still* not come, even when called a third time. The cook watched the pen dip into the inkwell, back to the page, run quickly across it, a fine Italianate script appearing and then another dip, more words.

Oh, dear. What to do.

Mrs. Weston was not one to complain, but Mrs. Williams had guessed her mistress was longing to get at her scribbling and, for some reason, had not. Now she was. In fact, Mrs. Williams had never seen her working so quickly.

Would she be able to come back to it if she were truly interrupted? Mrs. Williams softly closed the door and, thinking, stared at it. What should she do? At first she thought she'd do nothing at all. A stew, after all, could bubble gently on the hob for hours and hours and only be improved by it!

A second thought intruded. Perhaps she might make up a plate of good bread and butter and slice a piece or two of that cheese Mrs. Weston liked so well? And put it at Mrs. Weston's elbow? Perhaps she would nibble while she worked? Now there was a notion. And perhaps one might cut up an apple as well? The apples, stored in the underground shed, had been good keepers this year and were crisp and full of moist goodness.

Yes, that was what she'd do.

But still, Mrs. Williams vowed as she tromped down the narrow stairs, *I'll not go to bed this night until Mrs. Weston has, finally, seated herself at the table in the parlor like the good Christian woman she is and has partaken of a large plate of stew!*

Early the next morning Lord Manningford turned over one more time, gave up the notion he'd get any more sleep, and arose. He'd put it off because of the weather, but today he *must* ride into Bath, although he'd decided to postpone, until spring, a journey so long as one into Oxford. A muscle jumping in his jaw, he went to his library where he again removed the three books from his shelves. He asked his butler that they be wrapped carefully, perhaps in a bit of oiled cloth, and that they and Summer's Son be ready when he'd finished with his agent. The man had been on a visit to his lordship's more southerly estate situated in Devon near the Cornish border and been prevented by the storm from returning until now.

"There were a few days when nothing moved, my lord, not even the Royal Mail. But a thaw set in and down out of the hills the roads are passable. Just this last bit that hasn't melted or, where it has, is icy, makes the curves a mite dangerous."

"You should not have come on last night but should have waited for this morning, Denning."

"Yes." The man grinned. "I know I should, but by the

time I realized what I was in for, I was well beyond anywhere I might have stopped! Only the Shevingham estate . . ."

Denning was the only man who knew the story of Luke and the present Lady Shevingham. He grimaced.

Luke sighed softly. "Still, Denning, I believe you should have asked for shelter. They'd not have denied it."

"I wouldn't give the time of day to her ladyship, so why should she shelter me?" the man asked with a blunt disregard for propriety.

Luke had long before forgiven Lady Shevingham for her honest rejection of his suit, but Denning, who was working with the late Lord Manningford upon Luke's return from that terrible visit, had learned all that happened and hated the woman for hurting a sensitive boy so badly.

"Now, my lord," Denning added, "about that situation in Devon . . ."

Luke silently blessed his agent for changing the subject and they discussed the problem. In the end, Luke agreed with Denning's assessment. He didn't like the notion he must remove a tenant from one of his farms, but the fellow simply could not or would not do the work. Not since his wife died.

Perhaps they might find something less demanding for the man to do until he pulled himself together? He suggested the notion.

"He was a good worker." The agent, frowning, spoke slowly. "He's too young to pension off. Don't like to turn him off any more'n you do, my lord. Set his feet on the road to the workhouse that way, we would." His frown deepened, ridges creasing his brow. "But, sir, we can't have another year like this last, neither!" He shook his head. "First the poor man's son was pressed and lost at sea and then his wife died. One sees *why* he's the way he is and you've been more patient than any other man I know. Still, enough is enough, my lord."

"Yes, but do try to come up with an alternative to merely dismissing him. Was there anything other than that which must be dealt with immediately?"

"Nothing but what will wait, my lord."

"Then we will talk again when I return from Bath where I must see my solicitor and mean to see a play if there is a troupe presenting one."

Lord Manningford forgot all about his responsibilities the instant he picked up the package laid on the hall table and tucked it under his arm. Summer's Son awaited him, a groom whipping a blanket from the gelding's back as Manningford strolled down the front steps pulling on his gloves.

The groom took the parcel and stowed it in a commodious saddle bag, checked that the cloak bag was securely fastened behind the saddle, and then backed off and watched Lord Manningford mount. "Never know his lordship couldn't walk atall, oncet," the salt-and-pepper grizzled groom muttered to himself. "Never know it *these* days, that's for sure and all."

Manningford didn't hear the man or he'd have had a few words to say to him. He himself rarely recalled that year of pain and misery when it was believed he'd never leave his bed, a year when, left alone for long hours, he'd secretly worked himself to a thread to prove everyone wrong, especially his brother who enjoyed taunting him.

Luke disliked remembering the look on his brother's face the night when, for the first time, he'd dressed and limped, all by himself, into the dining room to join the family for dinner. That expression proved to him what he'd suspected for some time. His brother hated him. He'd never understood why. Ford was the elder by something just under a year. He was their father's favorite and he'd have inherited everything.

Luke was aware he'd never know what it was which had made his brother wish him dead and had decided it was foolish to waste time on speculation. Ford himself was long gone. He'd died in a dishonorable duel, fought drunk and over a hedge tavern's serving wench who was no better than she should be! The scandal which erupted and flowed hotly throughout the ton's gossip network had resulted in their father's suffering a fit which had left him partially paralyzed.

Luke had had to return from college, had taken on responsibilities for which he'd had no training, and nothing he ever did seemed to please the querulous man his father became. His mother had tried to explain how weakness made a man feel something less than a man and that Luke should forgive his father his megrims.

But that explanation, for a time, only made Luke, with his limp and scarred face, feel less than a man himself! He, after all, suffered from a weakness, did he not? The weakness in leg and knee which were so badly crushed it had been thought they might never heal?

Luke drew in a deep breath of sharp cold air. His college tutor had lectured him up one side and down the other when, depressed, he'd taken himself and his self-pity to Oxford. With only a little encouragement, he'd confessed every confused thought, hope, and pain. Not the least had been his proposal to and the brutal rejection by the woman who became Lady Shevingham, an offer his brother was supposed to have made, an offer his sick father had insisted *he* make, and make instantly, for the sake of the succession.

"Self-pity," his old friend and mentor scolded, "has no place in this world. Waste of time, Luke, my boy. Waste of time."

Especially when one had much to learn and much to do and a petty weakness which must be overcome in order to accomplish it all. And with that bracing thought again in mind, originally insinuated into his head by his beloved tutor, Luke rode into the village.

Lord Manningford stopped at the schoolhouse where he discovered everything was pretty well back to normal. Mrs. Gladbrook thought they could close the emergency station, reopening it only if another storm forced them to do so.

"I'll see supplies are stored here, Mrs. Gladbrook, so they'll be ready, just in case."

"We must pray," the vicar's wife said piously, "that such will be unneeded again this year."

Lord Manningford nodded agreement, although he believed it better to be prepared for the worst even if one hoped for the best. He walked his horse down to the widow's cottage and stared at it for a moment. The bright red sled was missing from where it was usually tilted up by the door. He wondered if Mrs. Weston, despite his attempts to take the burden from her shoulders, had gone on her rounds after all. Then he heard children's voices laughing and squealing and realized the sound came from behind the cottage.

Was Mrs. Weston giving the children a treat as she'd done himself? And why not? He tied Summer's Son to the widow's fence and made his way around the side of the cottage. Several children dotted the hillside, three pulling the sled up the hill and three more at the top jumping up and down and yelling that the others should hurry. Of Mrs. Weston there was no sign.

Luke returned to the front where he retrieved his bundled books and knocked on the widow's door. He heard Mrs. Williams shuffling down the short hall, heard her muttering and scolding softly . . . and smiled when the door opened and the woman's scowl faded into surprise.

"My lord!"

"Just whom did you expect?"

"Another dratted youngster wanting permission to play with that silly sled. *Not* Mrs. Weston's brightest notion, that sled! The nipperkins haven't stopped knocking up our door the whole of the morning."

"Perhaps, instead of complaining, you should be pleased they ask. They might have, hmm, *borrowed* the sled. Without asking, I mean."

Mrs. Williams nodded grimly. "They tried that. Once. Mrs. Weston had words to say to the boy who did it, and she must have scalded him with her tongue because no one has done it since. What may I do for *you*, my lord?"

"I've come to see Mrs. Weston—"

Mrs. Williams glanced up the stairs, a flustered look about her.

"—if she has a moment?"

"Well, that's it, isn't it?" The cook twisted her hands in her apron. "I don't rightly know if she does."

"Might you," Lord Manningford asked gently, "ask?"

"I *might*."

"Well?" Lord Manningford was beginning to feel a touch of irritation.

"I don't know if she'd hear me," Mrs. Williams said, obviously feeling more than a little annoyed herself.

Lord Manningford blinked. "What can she be doing that she wouldn't listen?"

"She's at her scribbling again, that's what. Don't know how it is, but when she's working at her desk the roof might fall down around her ears. *She'd* not notice."

"Her scribbling . . . ?"

Mrs. Williams shrugged. "Don't read, do I? So I don't know, do I?" She glared. "As if I would anyway. I'm not one to poke and pry into what's not my business!"

"No, of course you are not."

Another mystery? Was Mrs. Weston a bluestocking, one interested in his own period? But the study of medieval history required a thorough grounding in Latin, did it not? Had Mrs. Weston, unlike any other woman he'd ever met, been taught that ancient language? And was she, too, writing a history?

Was *that* why she'd wanted the vicar's book?

"I'll just go up and see if she'll see you, my lord," Mrs. Williams said once it had occurred to her Lord Manningford was not going to remove himself from the doorstep.

"What?" Luke asked, her words pulling him from his reverie. "Oh, no. I'll not both—"

But he'd changed his mind too late. Mrs. Williams was already huffing her way up the stairs. Luke stepped on into the hall and closed the door and was rewarded when Mrs. Williams returned and sent him up.

"I'm to bring up coffee," she said, obviously not approving.

"Do so for Mrs. Weston if she wishes it, but I'll only stay a moment."

When Mrs. Williams once again chugged up the stairs, Mrs. Weston sat turned from her desk, three musty-looking volumes on her lap and the wrapping on the floor beside her. His lordship stood with his back to the window.

Mrs. Weston looks, thought Mrs. Williams, *more'n a little at a loss.*

"Thank you," Carolyn said to her housekeeper. "Set it on the table, please."

Shatterbrained is what she looks, the cook decided. *And not atall like herself. Now what's his lordship gone and done to her?*

Mrs. Williams cast a suspicious look toward his lordship, only to discover that he, too, looked more than a trifle confused. *So that's it. No more sense than a chicken, either of them.* Shaking her head at the ridiculous difficulties the gentry managed to make for themselves when indulging in a simple courtship, Mrs. Williams stomped back down to her kitchen.

"Now if those two had a jot of sense," Mrs. Williams muttered to the kitchen cat as she was presented with a mouse, "they'd simply up and get themselves married. Be a very good thing for the both of them, I think."

Tuppence wasn't happy to have her gift promptly tossed out of doors. She sat down and began washing her back leg. The leg extended into the air, she appeared to listened, between licks, to the cook's tirade. Then Tuppence stood, stretched, and wandered out of the kitchen. Well beyond ken of the cook, the cat bounded up the stairs. Tuppence's nose twitched as she looked into the little study, turning her head toward one human and then the other.

The two stared at each other, each trying very hard to think of what to say. The cat, ignored, hopped up on the table and crept toward the tray.

Carolyn was not so utterly bemused that she didn't notice and promptly act. She quickly set the books on the table and picked up the cat. "Tuppence," she scolded, "you are not to get into the cream pitcher!"

"Tuppence?" Lord Manningford relaxed. "That animal looks much too fat and contented to be worth tuppence!"

"She left a mouse on my pillow the other morning. Mrs.

Williams says we no longer have an army of the creatures invading the larder! Tuppence is fat and contented because, young as she is, she's a four-penny cat and she knows it!"

Lord Manningford reached to tickle the cat under her chin. "How do you happen to know that odd bit of information, Mrs. Weston? About the worth of a cat? It is a rather obscure piece of ancient lore and, I'd thought, not known to many."

Mrs. Weston chuckled. "I grew up with the saying. My father was always berating my kittens as lazy creatures and telling me I spoiled them so they'd never grow into four-penny cats." She smiled, rueful. "I fear he was correct, too! I doubt I've ever before had one the worth of this one. And such a beauty, too."

"She is a handsome animal, is she not." *Like you*, thought his lordship, but did not say.

"Will you take coffee, my lord?"

"Perhaps one cupful, but I must not stay long. I mean to ride into Bath where I will check if the mail has arrived from London. I thought that, if you'd any commissions for me, I might run an errand or two for you?"

"Thank you. But you already mean to bring back the village mail, if there is any, and I cannot think of anything—" As Carolyn spoke, her gaze dropped to her manuscript. "Ah! But, *yes*. It would be a great favor if you'd be so kind as to purchase me more paper. I'll have need of a goodly quantity. I'd much appreciate it, my lord."

"If you will send along a sheet I may use as a sample of the quality you require, I'll be glad to bring it—" He accepted the cup she handed him, the cat now draped over her shoulder. "And of course I mean to bring the post for the village."

"Are you certain the weather will hold?" Mrs. Weston asked, keeping her eyes on the cup she'd balanced on her knee.

Had there been a touch of anxiety in that? he wondered . . . and decided she'd be anxious for *anyone* who thought to ride so far at this time of year.

"You'll surely not attempt to return today?" she added, her eyes widening at the thought and rising to meet his.

"No." He smiled. "I've no intention of doing it in one day. I'll stay over at least one night and mean to take in a concert or a play, if there is one. If the weather worsens, I've friends in Bath with whom I may visit. They send me regular invitations, so I know I'll be welcome."

"Then I needn't concern myself. And I'll thank you very much for the paper. I'm rather prodigal with it, as"—she blushed, looking around the floor—"you can see."

"What I see is that you are writing a very great deal."

Carolyn thought she heard the faintest of questions in his tone and gave him a sharp glance. The color which had faded from her face and neck returned two-fold. "My lord . . ." At a loss, she paused. "Oh fiddle-dee-diddle!"

"I am," he said, looking into his cup, "rather hoping your interest in the abbey indicates an interest in the medieval world which is my own passion?"

This time there was no doubting that he asked a question.

"I am no scholar, my lord, although I find those centuries of English history fascinating. When I was very young my father would tell me stories which"—she grinned, a conspiratorial look—"I later learned he freely borrowed from the *Canterbury Tales*. Then, as I grew older, my handwriting proved to be much clearer than his and he allowed me to copy out his papers. I learned a great deal by doing so."

"Your father is a scholar?"

"Hmm . . . *was* . . ."

He saw sadness envelop her and sighed that he'd once again managed to put his foot into his mouth and would have to chew and swallow it. Would he never learn how to speak to a woman? Never learn to avoid personal topics? He stood up.

"My lord? Oh, I must apologize!" She too rose to her feet. "Please do not feel insulted that I"—she hesitated—"rather forgot, for a moment, that you were here?"

"You were thinking of a beloved father. I am not

insulted. I am, however, upset that my prying question brought that sadness on you."

"A very understandable question. He was a scholar and he was the most wonderfully understanding man to ever walk the earth. When I was young, at that age which believes no one can tell it anything new, I did a foolish thing. Later, because of it, I hurt him badly." Again her gaze turned inward, but only for a moment. She smiled. "Now, how did I come to speak of the idiocies of my youth, when what I must do is admit to you that my writings have little to do with the past." She bit her lip, debating. Then, a trifle hesitantly, she said, "My lord, I write Gothic novels. I sold five, but then"—she shrugged—"I could think up no new story. Not to save me. Which—"

She got that mischievous look he'd come to watch for.

"—explains the book I borrowed from the vicar? It didn't help."

He chuckled. "Making a confession to cleanse the soul, Mrs. Weston? Do you fear I'll look down upon you for writing novels? But, my dear, it is my understanding that they give a deal of pleasure to a great many women, especially the old and the ill who can occupy themselves in no other way. I am not one to condemn the books."

Carolyn released a pent-up breath in a theatrical fashion. "Well! Thank you for your generosity and understanding. I feared you would look at me with horror, stomp from the house, and rush directly to the vicar to whom you would denounce me. The vicar," she said, her voice prim, "gave one whole sermon on the evils of novel reading. If he were to discover he had the writer of such books in his own village . . . well, perhaps he'd go off in an apoplexy?"

"Is it possible I heard a hopeful note in that?"

Carolyn blushed again. "I hope not, but . . ." She cast him another sideways look.

He smiled. "I suspect you agree with my feeling he is not the most understanding of men?" Luke's smile faded. "Recently, I had reason to conclude he is not a very wise man, either. As well as the teacher I must hire, I am consid-

ering whether I should not find the village a new vicar?"
He cast her a questioning glance.

Carolyn looked half guilty and half amused. Her eyes
twinkled but her mouth primmed. "My lord," she said,
"what do you know of Vicar Gladbrook's *family*? Or perhaps I mean his, hmm, *connections*?"

"Ah!" His lordship's dark visage lightened with an
understanding smile. "You mean someone who might have
influence. Someone who could get him preferment? I wonder I didn't see him as the sort who would do very well as
a minor secretary to one of our bishops." He smiled one
of his rare smiles. "I will think about it. But that is for the
future and now I really must be on my way. I will leave
you to your scribbling, as your Mrs. Williams called it. And
I will not forget the paper!"

Mrs. Weston followed him down the narrow stairs and,
the cat in her arms, watched him ride off. She spoke to
cat. "He is the nicest man, Tuppence. Why do you suppose
he is not wed? A great love he cannot forget? A disappointment in his youth, perhaps? Or is he shy because of his
scar?"

An arrested look crossed her face. She turned on her
heel, staring upward. Suddenly she dropped the cat who,
after one look of disgust, sat herself down and thoroughly
cleaned a paw.

Mrs. Weston didn't notice. She picked up her skirts so
she'd not trip and rushed up to her study where she stared
at the finished manuscript pages. Seating herself, she
slowly, reluctantly, began to read. When she'd finished the
few dozen pages, she stared off at nothing at all, her lip
between her teeth, frowning and thinking and worrying
and wondering what she should do.

The roads were difficult and it was late afternoon before
Lord Manningford arrived in Bath and, as a result, he went
directly to Jon Blake's house. Luke had met Jonathan when
both were in Oxford. Although they'd grown up within
twenty miles of each other, their families had, until then,

no more than a nodding acquaintance. Jon's family were merely gentry and would have had little in common with an earl in any case and certainly not one such as Luke's father who stood stiffly on his stiffs, tending to look down his nose at those he perceived to be below him.

Luke and Jon discovered they'd a great deal in common not least of which was their scorn of their peers, every one of whom seemed determined to outdo the others in all the milder forms of depravity. Luke and Jon were oddities in that they were far more interested in their studies than was usual among young men of their station.

Jon, a younger son, went into the Church by his own decision even though a sea-faring uncle offered to promote his future with the Navy. His family thought him foolish to turn down such an offer, but Jon knew what he wanted. Due to his obvious intelligence and by his own efforts, he had risen to the right hand of Bishop Moss, Bishop of Bath and Wells, and at a very young age, too.

Some years earlier, while yet a minor secretary, he'd married the daughter of a manufacturer who came to Bath for his health, and to look out a title for his girl. Once Beth met Jon, however, she lost all interest in catching a title or, for that matter, any other man. Jon's father-in-law had never been able to decide whether to laud his chit's perspicacity or whether to wonder at her luck because, at the time of their marriage, Jon, as his father-in-law liked to put it, was no more than a minor cog in the bishop's machinery!

In any case, Jon was Luke's only friend from their college days. And, ever since Jon became firmly settled in his own small but delightful home in a close near the Cathedral, Luke had had a standing invitation to stay there whenever he was in Bath.

But when Luke finally stood outside the house, he wondered if he should not, this time, go elsewhere. The windows were aglow with candlelight and he heard laughter from the room used for dining. Then he recalled a time he *had* gone away, thinking his presence would be a burden since Jon was already entertaining. Jon, discovering what he called Luke's foolishness, had berated him in language better suited to a sergeant major than a man of the cloth!

The memory brought a smile to Luke's lips, and he lifted and dropped the heavy brass door knocker. He heard steps and Mrs. Blake opened the door. A bright smile lit up her slightly round face, starting with her eyes and involving every bit of it, a truly warm welcome.

"Jon," she called. "Come see who has arrived!"

A chair scraped back from a table and soon Luke found himself embraced, his back well slapped and no doubt at all about his welcome. He smiled, his heart full, that there was someone in the world who could and would welcome his presence so unconditionally.

"I fear I've come at a bad time?" He glanced toward the dining room from which he could still hear low voices.

"Merely my cousin who is in Bath with her husband. The poor fellow is recovering too slowly from a saber wound. Actually, the thing refuses to heal properly, becoming easily reinfected, which is rather worrying," Jon said. "Lieutenant Thomas Trent and Mary," he added as he tugged Luke toward the parlor. "Bethie will see to laying you a plate and you will join us and no nonsense about arriving in all your dirt. Better the faint smell of a horse than that our food be overcooked, do you not agree, Mary? Tom?"

The youngish officer began a struggle to rise to his feet and his wife sent him a worried look.

"Sit, sit!" Luke said. "If this ruffian I call friend will not allow me to do the proper thing and change, then you must forget your manners as well. Ah, Beth," he added when his hostess reappeared, "that does smell a delight! Surely the aroma will hide my stink!" He sniffed at the wonderful odors wafting from the platter.

His hostess had carried in a platter of meats carved from both bird and beast. She was followed by a maid who had a large tray on which rested, among side dishes, another place setting. Soon everyone was introduced and all were served mounded plates.

"This is such a treat, you cannot know," the young officer said, a blissful look on his face. "Since we've returned to England, I have discovered my Mary cooks very well. The trouble is, often there is little *to* cook when following the Army as she insists on doing."

"Don't you start that again, Tom. Where would you be if I had *not* insisted I be there in case you needed me. You *did* need me." Mary glared.

"So I did. So I did. Peace, little one. It is just that I feel guilty at the rough way you must live and so I snap about it."

"It is also, I suspect," said Luke, "that you resent feeling as if your body has betrayed you while your wound refuses to heal."

"I noticed your limp," Tom said. "Were you . . ."

"Tom, do you play whist?" Jon asked, not so innocently interrupting.

Luke chuckled. "Peace Jon, I am no longer the sensitive ass I was when you first knew me." He turned back to Trent. "A half-wild horse rolled on me when I was a boy, Lieutenant. For a time it was thought I'd never walk again. I was bed-bound and believed my life over." He looked thoughtful. "You know, it never occurred to me I'd reason to thank my brother for anything, but it was his taunts when he and I were alone in that bedroom which made me decide I'd learn to walk if it killed me."

"And you managed it."

The lieutenant, Luke noticed for the first time, was seated in a wheeled chair. "I did. With much gritting of teeth to say nothing of months of hellish failure and more than a little pain. But I did it."

The implication that Luke dared the lieutenant to believe he, too, could do it was fairly well hidden but the young officer lost just a little of the drawn look about his eyes. "Months?" he asked.

"I was more than a year older before I walked from my bed to a chair by the fireplace. It took another month or two before I trusted myself to dress and join my family for the first time at the evening meal." A reminiscent smile curled Luke's mouth. "I'll never forget my brother's expression! What a victory it was!"

"You have suggested your brother and you were at outs," Mary said, "but surely he didn't dislike seeing you walk into that dining room?"

"Did he not?" Luke looked around the table. He drew in a breath and let it out. "Beth, instead of old history which can interest no one but me, do tell me about my goddaughter's progress. Can *she* walk?"

Elizabeth smiled. "She wants to. She tries. But she has yet to take her first step. Perhaps she will while you are here in honor of her godfather's visit!"

Later that evening, Luke and the lieutenant were speaking together while the women traipsed upstairs to the nursery and Jon dealt with a local vicar sent on to him by his bishop. "I do worry about her," Thomas said, in the midst of a conversation about troop movements.

"She seems a strong young woman. Does she complain?"

"Never. Another officer's wife took Mary under her wing when we first arrived and taught her . . . oh, all sorts of things. Mrs. Weston was wonderful, but that's just it. Mrs. Weston is now a widow and we don't know what happened to her, where she is. We're not the only ones to wonder. I was commissioned by a superior officer to discover where she is and how she's getting on." He grinned. "There is one of the older officers who would wed her in a moment if she'd have him and one or two, far better off than the rest of us, who would give her an allowance if they knew she was in need. I think the whole regiment, from the lowliest camp follower on up, had reason to love the woman!" He sobered, shaking is head. "Since I cannot locate her, I wonder if she is not, perhaps, very much in need!"

"Weston." Feeling more than a trifle grim, Manningford asked, "A Mrs. Carolyn Weston, perhaps?"

"Yes!" The lieutenant swung his chair around so that he faced his new acquaintance. "You know her? You know if she is well and happy?"

"She lives quite comfortably in a village near my estate."

"A wonderful woman!"

"Everything I know substantiates that view," Luke agreed, thinking of how hard Mrs. Weston had worked during the village's recent difficulties and of her cheerful outlook on life.

"How wonderful to have met you, someone who knows her! Do you"—the lieutenant looked hopeful.—"think we might visit her? When I can travel comfortably, that is? Mary will wish to do so. It has been her letter writing which has done all we could do to trace Mrs. Weston."

"You are speaking about my search for Mrs. Weston?" Mary asked, returning just then. "No one in Oxford has a notion where she went."

"Oxford?"

"Her father was a tutor. She meant to go there when she left Portugal."

"A tutor."

"She feared he was ill," Mary confided. "I think she must have been correct because I have discovered he is dead now."

Her words innocently suggested to Luke the sudden notion that Mrs. Weston was the despised daughter of his beloved tutor who died, ill and alone. *Oh,* he thought and not for the first time, *if only my own father hadn't chosen just that time to stick his spoon in the wall. If it hadn't been for his funeral, for all that needed doing as the heir—* Luke felt a muscle jump in his jaw. *If only I could have been there!*

"Mary," Tom was saying to his wife, "Lord Manningford may know our Mrs. Weston. He says there is a widowed Mrs. Carolyn Weston living in a village near his estate."

Mary had seated herself but rose to her feet. "Truly?" Luke nodded. Mary turned quickly, her skirts flaring. "Oh, Tom, may we visit her?"

"Now, we do not *know* this is the correct Mrs. Weston. Do not get your hopes too high, my dear. It is not such an uncommon name, after all."

"I feel it in my bones, Tom. I must see Carolyn again. I must thank her for all she taught me. But even more"— she paused, went on in a rush—"Tom, I do not like it that we misplaced her, as it were. I miss her and would hate to lose her friendship forever."

"Once I may travel without worrying, I'll open up this blasted wound again," her husband soothed, "we will see if this is your Mrs. Weston." Tom held out his hand.

Preoccupied with each other, they didn't notice Luke leave the room. Luke felt . . . well, he didn't know what he felt. If the only woman he'd ever found the least bit interesting turned out to be the selfish woman who would not return to care for her ill and dying father—well, how could he ever reconcile the opposing emotions raging within him?

"It cannot be. Surely it cannot be . . ." he muttered, leaning his forehead against the cold pane of glass beside the front door. *But if it is,* he thought grimly, *then there must be an explanation.*

Luke heard a door toward the back of the house open and straightened. Jon escorted a black-clad man, his white collar gleaming in the dim light, all that was provided by the small candelabra placed on a table by the stairs.

". . . is what I will do, Mr. Blake," said the stranger. "Thank you for your excellent advice. Good evening, my lord," the sprightly little man said, his gray hair sticking out in wisps below the hat he plopped onto his head. "Forgive my intrusion, my lord," he added. "Something which simply would not wait for morning, I fear." Faint frown lines deepened in his broad brow.

"Definitely it wouldn't wait for morning," Jon agreed, winking at Luke. "You sleep on what we discussed, but I think you will find our plan a good one. Good night and do keep me informed . . ." Jon talked soothingly as he eased the older man from the house and, whooshing out a long breath, leaned back against the closed door. "I didn't think I'd ever be rid of him. Poor soul. He worries so, and about things which cannot be helped. Even though we are often made aware of serious problems, it is not always possible to correct a situation." Jon shrugged. "Sometimes it is merely that there is no solution. Sometimes it is that two duties are in conflict." He shrugged again. "In this case, the poor woman who came to him for advice has been forbidden by her husband to do what she believes the right thing to do. The husband has the right, in law, to forbid her, of course." Jon sighed. "Some men are exceedingly selfish, I think. The man thinks only of his own comfort and has no care to ease his wife's guilt, which a visit to her family home might do. Her mother is ill, you see, and not expected to live, and there has been a breach between them the daughter wishes to heal."

Luke opened his mouth to speak and then shut it. Jon didn't know it, but he had just given Luke reason to hope his confused feelings concerning Mrs. Weston might be resolved!

A cat slunk around the newel post and slipped up the stairs with a wary look toward Jon. Watching it, a wry thought entered Luke's mind: His growing feelings for the widow were like the one-penny kitten his cook had given Mrs. Weston. With luck, they might grow to two-penny value. If he were really lucky, and Mrs. Weston actually did like him for himself alone, as she appeared to do, then perhaps she'd someday return his feelings and the whole would grow to be worth four pence!

Luke couldn't restrain a chuckle at the ridiculous analogy which, when he thought about it, didn't even make sense.

Jon, still thinking about the vicar's problem, stared at Luke. His jaw dropped and then his mouth closed with a snap. "You find it *amusing* that a woman is forbidden by her husband to visit her mother who may be dying?"

Luke looked chagrined. "Jon, surely you know me better! No, I laughed at an utterly ridiculous notion which ran through my head just then, which had nothing at all to do with that poor woman." Jon relaxed. "I fear I left your guests to their own devices some minutes ago. Not that they seemed unhappy to see me go. Or perhaps, didn't see me go?" He grinned and winked. "But perhaps they've looked around and have begun to wonder if everyone went off to bed and left them to see themselves out."

Beth tripped down the stairs at that moment and they

all entered the front parlor. "I'll set up the table for the four of you," Beth said. "I should have done so before dinner."

Tom cast his hostess a startled look. "But shouldn't we play something which you may play as well?"

"Pick-up-sticks perhaps?" Beth laughed. "Tom, I am hopeless when it comes to cards, not knowing one from the other. It is worse, I fear. I am, you see, unwilling to learn. No, I will sit beside the fire and add another few stitches to the kneeling pads I am sewing for the Lady's Chapel."

"How many must you do?" Mary asked. She inspected a finished pad while Jon found the cards and set a pair of candelabra and a lamp just so. When Beth told her, Mary's mouth dropped open. "But . . . it will take years!"

Beth chuckled. "I seem to remember, Mary, from something you once wrote, that you are not very adept at your needle. Perhaps you do not enjoy the work? I do, you see, and during long winter evenings I do little else. I'm progressing quite nicely, I assure you. Come summer when it is warmer and the light lingers and we may be out and about? That is an entirely different story, is it not?"

When the party broke up and Luke was able to go to his bed, his mind returned to the conflict Tom and Mary's innocent revelations roused. He had, from the time he realized his tutor's daughter did not mean to return to care for the failing man, felt strongly that the daughter could not be worthy of the least regard.

And yet, if Mrs. Weston did turn out to be that woman, he *knew* she was special in so many ways! *Could* the answer be the sort of thing Jon mentioned concerning his visitor's parishioner? Had Mrs. Weston married a man who had forbidden her to return home? Or perhaps—

Another horrifying thought entered Luke's mind.

—there'd been no money for such journey? Perhaps Mrs. Weston had suffered deprivations even greater than those Tom and Mary jokingly described.

Luke found that although he was tired from the long ride into Bath he could not fall asleep. Finally he rose and, quietly, returned to the ground floor. He built up the fire in Jon's study a bit, lit a pair of tapers and found a book to read. It was much later, the dull low bong of a church bell tolling thrice, before he returned to his bed and slept—in the hourly intervals between the bell's soundings, that is.

Those bells. He wondered how Jon could claim he never heard them!

The next morning, when asked his plans, Luke listed his various errands, most of which would take little time, and added that, since there would be a moon tonight, he meant to set off for home as soon as he finished.

The rush of words from Jon and Beth clashed as each attempted to convince him he must stay longer, that they'd not seen him for months and would very likely not see him again until spring and that, as a special treat, something they knew he loved, he must at the very least stay for the play that evening.

"I've been extravagant and rented a box, Luke," Jon said. "I insist you stay and help fill it."

"Who else ... ?" Luke asked, warily.

"Tom and Mary, of course, and Mary's sister and her husband, and a widow, Mrs. Brotherton, who lives nearby. I believe you know her?"

Luke knew Mrs. Brotherton, a widow some years older than himself who had, in the past, attempted to flirt with him. He grimaced.

Jon chuckled. "You will be safe, Luke," he insisted. "I have invited Mrs. Brotherton's current cicisbeo, you see, and will invite a widow for you who has not yet put aside her grief, although she is now out of blacks and into half mourning. *She'll* not importune you in any way. I promise!"

"Do stay," Beth encouraged and proceeded to give him just a hint as to the plot of the lighthearted play they were to see. "You see?" she exclaimed happily at his growing interest. "You do want to see it."

"It is true I love the theater." Luke compressed his lips, thinking. There was something in him which wanted, desperately, to get back to his own widow, but something equally strong feared to discover there was, as he'd previously believed, no reason his tutor's daughter had not returned to care for him. Nothing, that is, except her own selfish nature!

But Mrs. Weston was not a selfish woman. Surely that was certain?

Or was it? Luke sighed. What he really feared was that he'd discover the Mrs. Weston he thought he knew didn't exist at all but was only a dream he'd made up and, like a little girl dressing a doll, had "dressed" the person of Mrs. Weston in his dream!

"Luke?"

He would have to discover the truth, one way or another, of course. But he could delay the revelation, whatever it might be. Luke's lips smiled though his eyes did not. "Very well," he said. "I will indulge your great need to see more of me." He finished his breakfast amid their chuckles and took his leave after asking Beth if there were any commissions he could do for her.

"Jon," Beth said once Luke had departed, "what is the matter with him?"

"So you, too, noticed something? It is not my imagination then. I've no idea, Beth, and knowing Luke as we both do, I fear we are unlikely to learn. The man is not the confiding sort, me dear," he said warningly.

"No. He broods. It isn't good for him."

"Don't pester him, Beth. I don't want to lose his friendship."

She frowned a mighty frown as she spoke earnestly. "Jon, the way you scold, someone who did not know me would think I'm the hamfisted sort of driver who wades into deep waters with no notion that I might come a cropper, tossed like a rider to hounds on nasty shoals!"

"Beth," her husband said patiently, his eyes twinkling, "sometimes I think you mix your metaphors that way just to put me off my stride!"

"Did I do that again?" she asked innocently.

Jon's lips compressed and he eyed his wife. "Bethie," he said softly. "Come here."

"Why?"

"So I may turn you over my knee and give you a much deserved whack!" He sobered even as she chuckled. "Beth . . ."

"I swear I'll do nothing I should not."

"Why," he asked nothing and no one, "does that not do more to ease my concerns?"

Beth grinned and removed herself from the room. She went up the stairs to visit with her three youngest children and wished, very much, that the two boys now at Winchester were *not*. Not at Winchester, that is, but were home where she could cosset and play with them. She would, she decided, write each boy a letter once she was finished with the younger ones.

Still later she returned to the nursery, Luke in tow.

"You see how big she's become?" the proud mother asked, holding her youngest under the arms, the child's feet prancing against the floor. "She stands alone now." Beth coaxed the child into showing off her skill.

When the little girl was quite steady Luke brought the soft doll he'd bought her from behind his back. The brightly colored dress caught the tot's eye and she cooed and bubbled and grinned . . . and while both adults held their breath, took the necessary steps, three of them, to get her hands on her present.

"Wonderful," Luke breathed, his eyes shining. "I have never seen anything so wonderful. Not even watching a brand-new colt scrambling to its feet gives one quite that feeling." He looked up at Beth's sudden laugh. "You would disagree?"

"I am laughing, my Lord Manningford, because you have compared your goddaughter to a horse. Not even to a *mare,* now I think about it, but to a colt!"

Luke chuckled. "So I did. I suppose men are not taught the proper etiquette for dealing with the nursery set. Young Sarah," he said solemnly to his goddaughter, "I apologize if I insulted you. I meant it quite otherwise! In future I will remember *to compare you to a filly!*"

Again Beth chuckled. They remained with the child for a few more minutes, but it became obvious the lass was far more interested in attempting to remove the doll's clothing than in once again showing off her ability to walk.

"Poor Jon," Beth said as they removed to the ground floor parlor. "He has always before enjoyed coaxing their first steps from our children. He will be disappointed."

"You needn't tell him it has happened now. He can still have that joy if you do not. I am one who can hold his tongue."

Beth giggled. "How like you, Luke, to understand my intention without my having to explain!"

Luke chuckled. "I see I must spend much more time than I'd thought in my own nursery if I am ever lucky enough to have children. It will be the only way I may be certain my own wife doesn't perpetrate such frauds upon *me.*"

"I only do it because I love him."

"You needn't sound defensive! Having just experienced the wonder of seeing her walk, I know exactly why you do it. Did I, for instance, truly witness Sarah's first steps or have I, too, suffered from the care you take of those about you?"

"I swear you saw her very first steps. Or perhaps"— Bethie's eyes narrowed dangerously—"my *nurse* is as sly as I can be? Surely not! She wouldn't dare try such a stunt on *me.*" She turned a horrified look on Luke. "Would she?"

"I haven't a notion. Does it truly make a difference? If those weren't the child's very first steps, I mean? Would you feel differently about the miracle you have just witnessed if you knew it weren't the first time it happened? It is something of a miracle, is it not?" he added before she could answer. "The way a young thing grows and learns and develops and, if we are very lucky, gradually becomes a fully adult being?"

"With all the good and bad that involves? I suppose it

is a miracle, although I never thought of it that way. It is simply what happens, you see, so I never pondered the how or the why." She frowned. "And now I do, I think it much too deep a subject to take into luncheon. You will join me, will you not? It is such a long time to dinner even when, as tonight, we eat a little early so as to reach the theater for the first act."

Luke took a better look at his hostess. "Bethie, are you breeding again?" he blurted.

"Well . . ." She blushed, glanced down at her still slim figure and back at Luke. "Yes. But how did you know?"

"Because for so long as I've known you, which is since your marriage to Jon, you have become ravenous whenever you are"—He suddenly realized he was discussing something a man did not discuss with a woman—"well, *enceinte.*"

"Breeding. It is a perfectly good word and, after all these years and five babies, it does not embarrass me."

Luke, tipping his head and smiling, touched her rosy cheek.

"Well, not much anyway," she admitted. "Will you join me?"

"I'll drink a mug of ale while you eat," he agreed.

The afternoon passed pleasantly, and Jon arrived well in time to dress for the evening. The play was all it was promised to be, probably because this particular troupe of actors was quite skilled, unlike many traveling from provincial theater to provincial theater.

Luke even managed to enjoy the undemanding company of the quiet little woman at his side that evening. She was pleasant and made no obvious show of her grief, but it was obvious to an observant man such as Luke that she still, although now in half mourning, much missed her husband. He admired her for the depths of her love but hoped she'd not suffer too much longer. At least, not to such a degree.

On the other hand, once he said good night to her, he instantly forgot her.

He warned his host and hostess he meant to rise early

and be gone by the time they woke and said his thank-yous and good-byes before they went up to bed. It was still dark when he rose the next morning. He'd repacked his cloak bag the night before, ready to be strapped to the back of his saddle. Dressing quickly, he was ready to leave.

He made little noise going down the stairs and was certain he'd done the trick, rising without waking anyone, so it was a shock to arrive in the kitchen and find Beth cutting bread and slicing ham and making him up a packet of food.

"This is unnecessary, Beth!" He cast a horrified look at her middle. "You should still be in bed, should you not?"

"No I should not, and it *is* necessary. You've a long cold ride if you are to reach home today and I know I cannot tempt you to eat a proper breakfast. Which reminds me. There is hot chocolate on the back of the stove and porridge is in the kettle. You may eat a bowlful while I finish this."

Luke knew Beth. It would be far easier to obey than to argue, so he served himself. Digging in, he ate rapidly.

"You are in a hurry, are you not?"

"I've been gone a day longer than I meant, Beth, so, yes, I'm in something of a hurry."

His reluctance to face Mrs. Weston had disappeared sometime during the night. He was now in a hurry to return to her. In a rush to discover what explanation, if any, she had for staying away from her father. To discover if the woman he thought he knew was no more than a sham . . .

"What is it Luke?"

"What?"

"You were looking . . ." She shrugged. "I don't know, Luke. But what an odd combination of emotions I read in your face! Anger? Worry? Hope? I don't know, do I?"

"Perhaps someday I'll tell you." He finished his porridge and, rising to his feet, accepted the packet she handed him. "Right now I'm not certain myself, you see?"

She chuckled. "No, I don't, but you'll get it straight in your own head, whatever it is, and then you may explain."

"Perhaps . . ."

"Luke!" she said sharply when, after several moments, he didn't continue.

He blinked, looked at her.

"You have gone off somewhere in your head again!"

"Hmm? Oh." He smiled slightly. "Do I still do that? Jon used to become quite angry with me when I did it, did you not, Jon?" Luke sighed. "I had such good intentions. I meant to sneak out and leave you both sleeping the sleep of the righteous!"

"Now we know," Jon said, solemnly. "Bethie, what a terrible thing we have just discovered! Since we *are* awake, it must be that we cannot be numbered among the righteous!"

The jest lightened Luke's mood and he chuckled. "As soon as the weather improves you must pack up yourselves, the children, the children's nanny and all their needs and whatever I've forgotten and come out to Krilling's Woods."

"We'll plan to do just that," Jon said, taking his wife into a one-armed embrace and pulling her near. "The children love to come to Krilling's Woods."

"I enjoy having them," Luke said with the simplicity which indicated the truth of what he said.

"What you should do is wed and have a houseful of children all your own!" Beth scolded, and then was amazed by the two spots of color glowing along Luke's cheekbones. "Why, Luke . . ."

"Do take care on the road, Luke," Jon interrupted. He knew his friend well. If Luke were thinking of taking a wife but had not yet made a final decision, he wouldn't wish to be teased about it.

"I will. And now I must be off. Take extra good care of my Sarah," he said, smiling, and backed toward the door to the garden which led to the mews where his horse was stabled.

He breathed a sigh of relief that he'd managed to escape with nothing more said about his possible marriage. He couldn't possibly wed the despicable daughter of his beloved tutor—but if it turned out the wonderful Mrs.

Weston might have him? The trouble was, *which* woman lived in Rose cottage and how was he to discover the truth?

He rode along country lanes sorting through plan after plan, arriving at a method which he'd think possible only to find a flaw and so would craft another plan which would be still worse. He gave nary a thought to where he was going or, worse, to what the weather was doing, so it was an exceedingly unpleasant shock to find himself in the middle of a blizzard. Blowing snow whipped around Summer's Son to the degree he could see no more than a few feet ahead and that irregularly.

Swearing softly at his stupidity, Luke dismounted and, leading his horse, pressed forward. He tried to remember where he'd gotten to and, when he could not, prayed he'd not end up in a drift, himself and Summer's Son frozen to death. It seemed hours before, exhausted, he stumbled against a stone wall. Luke touched it, felt it, realized what it was, and a grain of hope lifted his spirits.

Besides, the wall protected them from the worst of the wind as they continued along to the main gate. Luke almost couldn't bring himself to turn into the long drive leading to Shevingham Hall. But there were ancient rhododendrons all along it which somewhat protected them, although nowhere nearly so well as the wall had done.

Sighing, Luke gave Summer's Son all the encouragement he could and, head down, stumbling through drifts, he led the tired creature up the drive. He didn't stop until, quite literally, he ran into the house.

Shevingham Hall was not a house he'd visited often and not at all for years. He forced his mind to function, forming some notion of how the buildings were laid out, and then, turning to the left, made his way around the house, never once ceasing to touch it. Finally he came to a wall he thought surrounded a kitchen garden. Beyond that he believed there was a hedge which would lead him to the stables. It wasn't far now. If only he could manage to keep his feet and keep going!

He did. Just.

A groom tending a mare in foal jumped from the loose

box out into the aisle, thoroughly outraged that some thoughtless person had opened the broad barn door to the elements. He swore roundly—until he saw a snow covered man sink to his knees and a weary horse, head hanging, just inside the opening. Having reached safety, Luke could, for the moment, do no more.

"Lord bless us. Here now. Samuel! Fenton! Move your stumps and come help, you fools. Where be ye?"

Slowly, Luke pushed himself back up to his feet.

"No, no. Sit yourself down, sir, afore you fall down!" the groom exclaimed.

The other two grooms tumbled down a steep, almost ladderlike set of steps. They took charge of the horse and the older groom saw to Luke. A mug of hot ale helped. Getting out of his greatcoat and wrapped in an itchy wool blanket helped, too, even if it did smell of horse.

Before too long, he was able to grin weakly at the worried groom and ask, "My horse?"

"He'll be just fine, my lord. The boys are working on him now and soon we'll be feeding him warm mash and the boyo won't even be remembering the storm at all. You'll see. Now you just sit there a bit while I'll send the lad into the house to have a room made ready and whatever else will be needed. That cloak bag all your luggage?" the man asked, handing it over to an urchin no bigger than a minute.

"No!" Luke struggled to his feet. "You can't mean to send that child out into that storm!"

"Easy now, sir. There's a hedge and a vine-covered walk that goes right up to the house like. You'll see when you've rested a bit."

"I'll be back, gov, afore the cat can lick her whiskers!" the boy said, a big cheeky grin showing a gap where front teeth had gone missing.

Before Luke could make another objection, the boy was gone. Luke sighed. If he'd been given a choice in the matter, he'd not have gone up to the house at all. He'd much rather remain in the barn than face either or both of the Shevinghams.

At a hopeful thought he looked up. "The family is in London?"

"My lord is. As usual. My lady's here." There was a momentary pause before the groom added, "Also as usual."

Luke was not eager to meet again the woman who so bluntly told him his face made him a monster in the eyes of any sensitive woman. Good manners suggested it was wrong to upset her; and then . . . well, the sight of her would bring back memories he'd spent more than a decade consciously forgetting!

"She'll like having company," the groom added, just the faintest of sly notes coloring his tone and a more obvious slyness to the sideways look he slid in Luke's direction.

"Lonely, is she?"

"She be one who likes her fun," the groom agreed, dryly.

Luke heard a muttered "fun" from the stall where the other two grooms worked on his horse followed by chuckles, but there was no time to wonder about the implication in that. A pair of tall footmen appeared and, politely but insistently, urged him to his feet. They tucked him into a dry coat which they'd brought for him and led him back out into the storm.

Except they left the stables by a small door near the tack room which Luke did not recall from the visits his family had made when he was only a boy. The door led to the promised walk. Luke refused the footman's offered arm, followed the one, the second following him, to the house. Again it was a door he didn't recall, but he and the other children had been housed in a far wing, and it was likely they'd used an exit more convenient to their rooms.

Although he was not covered in snow this time, the brief walk had chilled him all over again and he was glad when the Shevingham butler quietly informed him a hot bath awaited him. He was led up to his room by one of the footmen.

"Dinner will be served in two hours, my lord," the footman informed him, after inquiring whether he needed help with his shaving.

"Dinner . . ." Luke cast a longing look toward the bed and sighed. "Yes. Of course. Dinner. Do return to guide me down, please."

The two hours gave him time for the exceedingly welcome warmth of the hot bath and a much needed lie-down, but he was ready to descend to the dining room when his guide returned.

"Whom will I meet?" he asked, a traditional question when joining company unexpectedly.

"No one but my lady." The footman, a muscle twitching in his jaw, stared straight ahead. "Here, my lord," he added.

He paused before a door that Luke had a vague recollection led to a snug lady's parlor. He frowned, reached for the footman's arm, but was too late. Thrusting open the door, the footman intoned, "My Lord Manningford."

Now it was a muscle in Luke's jaw which twitched, but he stepped forward revealing none of his thoughts concerning the folly of such intimacy.

"My lady," he said, and bowed.

"My lord!" his hostess gushed. "What a delightful surprise. Do come in. You must be starved. You've come all this way through such an awful storm! You must have a little drink to warm your insides and then dinner will be served. Sherry? Brandy? What will you have?" The sprightly little woman who tripped toward him studied him avidly. "Come now, there is no need of formality between us is there? After all, we once knew each other very well—" She cast him a girlish, flirtatious look and giggled, mannerisms which sat ill with her age. "Did we not?"

"Did we?" asked Luke lightly.

He allowed himself to be drawn to the fireside wondering how her memories could differ so from his own. He hadn't known her at all. He'd reluctantly obeyed his father and, after discovering he was looked on as a monster or, at best, with pity, which was bad enough, he'd felt nothing but relief she'd said him nay!

"Brandy, I'm sure, would be welcome after your ordeal. What a miracle that you arrived safely at Shevingham, my lord." She stroked his arm and stared up into his face.

Curious, he stared back. He saw none of the flinching he'd have expected, and his curiosity grew. "Very lucky indeed," he said when he realized she awaited an answer. Mrs. Weston, he thought, his face a passive mask, would never behave in such an encroaching manner!

Lady Shevingham poured two brandies and sipped from the glass she picked up, turning it until the place her lips touched was toward him. She lifted it straight at him, but Luke, even more wary than he'd been before entering her presence but now for decidedly different reasons, stepped past her to the side table and picked up the untouched glass. He sipped.

"Very good," he said, giving the glass a startled glance. "Very good indeed. It has been years since I've tasted better."

Lady Shevingham giggled shrilly, and it occurred to him she'd indulged in one or perhaps several drinks before his entrance.

"Shall I tell Shevingham's supplier to drop off an extra keg on his next run, my lord?" she asked.

"Smuggled, is it?" Very gently and not without a bit of regret, Luke set down his glass. "No, thank you. I don't care to support the French in the war against us, you see."

Lady Shevingham pouted, sipped, and then giggled. "Still an old sobersides, are you not?" A bit of a bite entered her tone. "Haven't changed, have you? Still have your head up there in the clouds where it is too rarefied for us poor sinners."

"I haven't a notion what you mean."

She waved her hand, the brandy sloshing back and forth but, miraculously, not spilling. "Oh, you must remember. You sent a poem full of notions I'd never heard of and couldn't begin to understand . . . along with a bouquet, of course. A very nice bouquet, I seem to remember." She frowned, obviously trying to be certain. "You know. Before you came to ask for my hand."

Luke had a vague recollection of following his father's advice. He'd written the chit some sort of poetry. He now recalled what a difficult exercise it had been. After all, he'd yet to meet his intended!

"My governess explained it to me." She giggled again. "Very blue, my governess."

The doors opened and her butler entered, followed by footmen, all tall and well formed. The trays were deposited on the sideboard and chairs pulled out at an intimate little table set before the fire. Luke offered his arm and Lady Shevingham leaned on it with far more weight than he'd expected, her plump breast pressed into him and her eyes lifted to gaze up at him, her smile coy.

The meal, despite the informality, was a long one. The two spoke erratically, neither finding a topic the other could, or, as the case often was for Luke, that he *would*, respond to. Lady Shevingham's glass was constantly refilled, but Luke, having taken her measure, drank sparingly.

Her ladyship was one of those who did not know their capacity and would drink and drink until falling into a dazed sleep or they were sick with it! He feared her behavior, already shocking, would deteriorate still more. As it was, she was far too coming. More than once, she'd gone so far as to hint broadly that she expected him to warm her bed that night.

The meal ended and the footmen departed. With one last look to see all was as it should be, the butler also took himself away, closing the doors softly as he did so.

"Now . . ." Lady Shevingham cooed, coyly, an unlovely smirk on her face. "We'll not be bothered again this night, my lord." Unsteadily she rose to her feet and rounded the table toward him.

Luke rose when she did and, as she approached, moved away. It wasn't that she walked. More accurately, Luke thought, she *stalked*. He felt like an animal at bay and moved again.

"You've a lovely home, my lady," he said, desperate for

a topic which would catch her attention. "I remember it from when I was quite young."

She stopped, weaving. "You know my husband?" she asked sharply.

"He was some years our elder. It was his middle brother I knew best. Poor Tim. I was sorry to hear of his death."

She giggled.

Luke stared at her, shocked.

She was not so up in her altitudes she didn't realize he was outraged or *why*. "Oh, of course, I mean to say, poor poor Tim." She tried to remain solemn, but could not, and she almost seemed to purr as she peered up at him, smiling like a cat sated with cream. "Gone off to the wars for love of me, you know?"

Since Timothy had been army mad from his cradle, Luke rather doubted that and was ungentlemanly enough to say so.

"And you"—she ignored what she didn't wish to hear— "you poor dear man, have stayed single all these years, so in love with me you could not bear to wed another. Poor Luke," she finished complacently. Then her gaze sharpened. "But there is no reason," she added, prowling closer once again, "that you should suffer *entirely*. Is there?"

Luke rounded the table which had been moved back from the fire. "My lady," he said, edging toward the door. "I must leave you . . ."

"Call of nature?" She frowned and again waved the brandy glass, this time allowing a few drops to slosh over. She licked her knuckles. "Oh, don't poker up. You'd think I was missish or something." She pouted, finished off her drink, and flounced to where the decanters stood. "Don't be long now!"

Luke made no response as he let himself into the hall. He ignored the pain in his weak knee as he took the stairs two at a time, pulling himself up by the bannister. He tried two rooms before he found the one assigned himself where it took only moments to repack his bag. Then, checking that the hall was empty, he headed toward the back of the house where he hoped to find a secondary set of stairs or, if nothing else, a servant's staircase.

As he stepped into the ground-floor hall, Luke heard voices. He frowned, fearing his escape might be discovered, and ducked into an empty room where he waited. The chattering maids passed by. In the ensuing silence, he took another cautious look and, seeing no one, started out once more to find the door to the covered walkway and the relative safety of the barns!

Luke refused to spend the night under the same roof as Lady Shevingham. Even if he were to lock his door—a quick slashing grin creased his face—he feared for his virtue. There were, after all, additional sets of keys in any well-run household. Enjoying the touch of humor he'd finally discovered in the fiasco of the preceding hours, he didn't hear the approach of the butler. He turned a corner and they came face-to-face.

"My lord."

"Hmm . . . just wished to check on my horse before retiring," Luke said, thinking quickly.

The butler gave no more than a glance to the cloak bag before nodding. "This way, my lord. And what should I tell the mistress?"

Again Luke thought quickly. "Perhaps," he offered, "you might say I've come down with a streaming cold and think far too much of her to chance giving it to her."

"Excellent, my lord," the butler said softly. "My lady fears illness above all else."

The man pursed his lips, but Luke noted that his eyes twinkled. "I'll be gone at first light," Luke said cautiously, surprised the butler appeared to be on his side. He relaxed.

"Very good, my lord. Do be careful as you go. Although it's stopped snowing, the wind foretells bad drifting. I'll order the heavy horses out early to break a way along the drive and along toward the village, my lord."

"Thank you. And thank you for your care of me."

As hands met exchanging a small pocketbook full of coin, man and servant's eyes met. The servant bowed his head before straightening and turning to open the door they'd reached. "Thank *you*, my lord."

Luke wasn't sure if the thanks were for the *douceur* which would sweeten any servant's feelings or because he'd not be taking advantage of Lady Shevingham's . . . hmm . . . *generosity*. He didn't quite see how it could be the latter, however, since, to his mind, it was Lady Shevingham attempting to take advantage of *him* which was forcing him back out into the cold.

And the wind.

The butler was correct that, overnight, it would drift ferociously. Poor Summer's Son! They still had something over ten miles to go on the morrow just to reach the village. It was still farther to Krilling's Woods. Luke opened the small door to the stable and, quickly and quietly, shut it. It was a distance to the aisle where his gelding stood in a loose box and where, he feared, he'd find the groom nearby, still awaiting the birth of the foal. He'd no wish to meet that groom or any other!

Luke approached very quietly and heard the man talking soothingly to the mare. He wished he could join the man, could watch the birth of a new life as he'd done in his own barns many a time. He sighed softly. He did not wish to explain himself, his presence there, so he entered Summer's Son's loose box quietly. After pushing the gelding to one side, Luke piled straw into a corner, lay down in it, and, much to his surprise, nearly instantly slid into a very deep and restful sleep.

He didn't exactly oversleep, but there were stirrings on the floor above so he knew he must leave quickly—before someone arrived with a message from Lady Shevingham asking about his horse or, worse, himself. He saddled up, tying his cloak bag at the back and looked round for his saddlebags.

He found them hanging over the half-door and was surprised at how heavy they were. The one, of course, held Mrs. Weston's paper. The other, he discovered, contained a packet of food and a corked pottery bottle. He uncorked it and sniffed the steam rising lazily into the cool air. Hot soup! An excellent notion. He wondered who had brought the food to the barn and what they'd thought about his sleeping there.

Very likely they thought him a fool to have refused what her ladyship so obviously offered. He grimaced. Perhaps he was a fool. But he could not bring himself to support her delusion he'd remained unwed for love of her. Nor was he the sort to make love to one woman when he was so deeply and forever in love with another.

. . . In-love-with-another?

. . . *In love?*

Grinning like a fool, or so he suspected, Luke nodded sharply. It was true. Somehow it had happened.

Elation faded. Somehow he must discover why his love had been unable to come to the aid of her father. He was certain there *was* a reason. The woman he knew would have moved mountains to get to her father.

Move mountains, yes, he thought with a gentle smile, *but perhaps she was unable to swim oceans?*

Again he sobered. *Was* that the reason? That she couldn't afford passage home? Well, whatever it was, he'd discover it and he'd woo his Mrs. Weston and he'd win her and they'd live happily ever after.

Or else.

He sobered. Or else he'd be a truly unhappy man rather than merely a not-happy man, which was quite different. He sighed. That was a bridge he needn't cross just yet. With any luck at all he'd never have to cross it.

More cheerfully, he let himself and his horse out into the new day. The glowing pink of the sky in the east suggested an overly bright sun would soon be glaring off sparkling snow. The glare would, he knew, give him a headache. But if the old sailor's adage were correct and the rosy sunrise meant they should take warning of more bad weather to come, well, that, too, was something he'd worry about when it happened, which wouldn't be for some hours at least, and perhaps not until tomorrow.

Or maybe not at all. His leg, a weather predictor he carried with him since the accident with the half-broke horse, said the weather wouldn't worsen. Or was that a result of his good night's sleep? Another grin split Luke's face. Perhaps he should bed down in his own stable if it meant he'd wake up with no pain in his leg, something which happened far more often than he liked to admit.

The journey home was difficult for man and beast and, once or twice, he wondered at himself for not being sensible and remaining in the Shevingham barn another day or even two!

Still another thought and he ceased wondering. It wasn't a fear of Lady Shevingham's fantasies or her attempts to make them real. He could and would have avoided her ladyship's crude attempts at seduction.

No, his real reason for forcing a path through and around and over sometimes massive drifts was someone very different from Lady Shevingham! His true reason stood very little over five feet and was, perhaps, a little longer in the tooth than his sister would approve!

His sister, after all, wished her younger brother wed so he'd supply an heir of the direct line. Mrs. Weston's age showed in the white threads which laced dark hair and indicated she was beyond her best child-bearing years.

But she was a little lady with spirit and full of good humor and a willingness to take up the burdens of duty when and where they appeared. A little lady who, if she'd have him at all, would be true to her vows—unlike the one he was leaving behind at Shevingham Hall, meeting her again for the first time in years.

My father, Luke decided, *was a fool to wish that woman on his son. On* either *of his sons!*

The knowledge he came nearer and nearer to his love kept Luke searching out the easiest paths for Summer's Son, kept them moving in the right direction, and, even when his head felt as if it might explode from the expected headache, kept him moving right past the first houses in the village and down the street to the widow's cottage.

Only when he reached it did it occur to him he was too

tired to winkle out the truth, to discover what he must know and then, finally aware of whys and wherefores, somehow, somewhere, find the courage to ask her to wed him.

What if she could not do so? What if his face put her off? Or perhaps she still loved her husband? Or would his limp be a deterrent? A sprightly lady such as Mrs. Weston must love to dance, and, although he could walk for reasonable distances, he could not dance. Perhaps, after all, he should simply return to the Woods and try to forget Mrs. Carolyn Weston and her mischief-eyes and joyful head-on approach to life. Perhaps he should avoid being hurt far worse than Lady Shevingham's rejection hurt.

But Manningford remembered the paper he'd bought her. Dismounting, he removed it from a saddlebag. He carried it up the path and knocked at her door. At least he'd see her. If only briefly.

"My lord! You've returned!" she said, smiling up at him. "Are the roads better, then, than one would have thought? Do come in. I'll have Mrs. Williams make us a pot of hot tea?"

"Not just now . . ." Was there the slightest of wary looks to that smile of hers? A muscle jumped in his jaw. "The roads are close to impassable, but I prefer my home to anywhere else and came on despite the snow. Mrs. Weston . . ."

"Yes?" she asked when he didn't continue.

"Right now I must continue on to Krilling's Woods, but I would like to come see you . . . in a day or two?" Silently, he berated himself for the cowardly urge to postpone failure which had made him add that last bit.

"Yes. Please do. I've . . . a reason I'd like to see you, too, my lord." She smiled that smile which lit up her whole face. "I mean, beyond that I very much enjoy our talks."

"You enjoy them, too? Excellent," he added when she nodded. "Then I'll be off and return as soon as I may."

"Very good, my lord."

Holding close the knowledge she enjoyed his company, Luke forgot how tired he was. He turned his gelding's head toward home. For some reason, the lay of the land or perhaps less wind up in the tree covered hill country, he found there was less drifting and he and the horse arrived home with few problems, which was just as well.

Luke paid far more attention to daydreaming about his widow than he did to his path!

Two days later, Luke ducked as he stepped inside the widow's front door. Hat in hand, he studied her features, which seemed a trifle blurred. By tiredness, perhaps. His gaze settled on the dark circles under her eyes and the droop to her shoulders. Perhaps worse?

"What is wrong?" he asked sharply. "Are you ill?"

"What is wrong," Mrs. Williams said, standing at the back of the hall, her arms wrapped in her apron, "is that Mrs. Weston has not slept a wink for days. Not a wink."

"Now, Mrs. Williams," Mrs. Weston said soothingly, "that simply is not true. It is true, however," she added a trifle apologetically, "that I've not slept much." She smiled. "Do come into the parlor and Mrs. Williams will be kind enough to bring us tea and, perhaps, something on which we may nibble?" She turned as she said the last.

"Nibble! You'll eat a meal if I have to tie you to your chair and feed you." The woman glared, then glanced at Lord Manningford. "Hurumph," Mrs. Williams finished, embarrassed.

A trifle at a loss, Mrs. Weston turned back to his lordship. "She is, on occasion, a little above herself, but I fancy it is because she likes me and worries. Not," she added, moving into the sitting room, "that there is any cause. It is just that when I'm working, my scribbling, you know, it is difficult to pull myself away from it. I have tried in the past and, invariably, I lose something. Either my train of thought is broken and I cannot pick up where I left off or I forget to put in a crucial element for the plot which I must then go back and fit in. It makes the work too confusing so I've concluded that, when the story is flowing, I must let it flow. Do you understand at all?" she asked, turning to face him.

"I think so. It is rather like rousing in the middle of the night with a great thought, telling oneself sternly that one must *not* forget it, only to wake in the morning knowing there is something one should recall but which one cannot, for the life of one, do?"

"*Very* like, I think. I must thank you again for the paper. I had very nearly run out, and that would have been a disaster!"

"Surely the vicar would have loaned you some?"

She grimaced. "Yes. After I had explained why I wanted it."

He smiled. "I see. From what you said about his attitude toward the novel, that would not have done at all." Lord Manningford drew in a deep breath, forcing himself to begin probing into her past . . . only to remember Mrs. Williams would soon return and that perhaps it would be best—

He almost sighed from the relief.

—to postpone their talk until they were assured of privacy.

"I am to assume your work is going well, then?" he asked instead.

"Very well . . . except—" Along with a sidelong look, Mrs. Weston compressed her lips. "No. We will wait until after Mrs. Williams has brought tea and the food she insists I must eat. Will you join me, my lord?"

"Just tea, thank you. I rarely eat in midday."

"No, I don't, either. It is just . . ." She hesitated.

". . . Just," he finished for her, "that your schedule has become a trifle erratic thanks to your writing."

"Exactly. I am so glad you do not need everything explained to you, my lord."

"I know what you mean," he said, and grinned. "That awful question one hears. *But, my lord,*" he said in a falsetto voice, "*what can you possibly mean?*"

"Exactly! Except I hear madam rather than my lord!" Her smile faded. "I think," she said, musing, "that that was something which drew me to my husband. I didn't need to explain." She looked up. "I must have been surrounded by fools that that particular facet of his personality hid from me some aspects of which I should have been more wary."

"But not your father. Surely he knew the man for what he was?" Luke asked, startled into speaking too soon.

"My father"—she looked up sharply—"knew. Did you know him? My father?"

"I'm . . . not certain."

The door opened and Mrs. Williams backed in, a heavily loaded tray revealed when she turned. The cook bustled around the room, set the small table, and served the food, Lord Manningford barely stopping her from piling a second plate high for himself. "There," she said, when all was done to her liking. "I don't think I forgot anything. You just call if you need ought."

She turned and stomped to the door where she turned and glared at Mrs. Weston. Then she turned to Lord Manningford. "You, my lord. You see she eats proper like." With that order, she left the room.

Luke turned to look at his hostess and found her with her face covered, her back bent over, and she was shaking.

"Mrs. Weston? *Carolyn?*"

She looked up, her face brimming with laughter. "She never ceases to amaze me. Should I apologize for her forwardness?"

Finding she was neither embarrassed nor crying, he relaxed. "As you said, she worries about you. One cannot fault her for that. So, since I have been ordered to see you eat, then perhaps you should be seated?" He offered his arm and led her to the table. "Now, my dear, please do eat. I, too, am a trifle worried about you, you see."

"My father. He was a tutor, living in Oxford, my lord. William Lords."

"I thought it might be Lords. Yes, I knew him. He was everything my father was *not*. I loved him very much."

"Why do I not recall you? I knew most of the young men he tutored."

"I heard rumors his daughter eloped the previous year?"

She sighed, toying with a piece of chicken. "I was a fool.

But," she smiled wryly, "so was my father. He forbade me to see Lieutenant Weston. Which is, I fear, exactly how one goes about driving a couple together!"

"You wed . . . and went with the lieutenant to the Peninsula."

She nodded, stuffing a forkful of potatoes mashed with turnips into her mouth.

"It must have been"—he searched for the proper word—"interesting?"

She set down her fork, her expression the blank look of one seeing into the past. "Dirty," she said. "Often short rations. Impossible living conditions, terror during battles, horror afterward . . . Yes," she said judiciously. "I suppose one could say it was interesting."

He smiled at her wry tone. "And your husband? You loved him very much that you put up with all that?"

Faint lines appeared between her brows. "Love? Well . . . perhaps. At least to begin with. And by the time I realized the man I thought I loved didn't exist but was only in my imagination, well, it was too late, was it not?"

"Too late?" he asked sharply, relieved to learn she hadn't truly loved the man. "Was there nothing you could do?" He saw his opportunity. Almost slyly, he asked, "For instance, could you not have returned home?"

She grimaced. "I had made myself essential to his comfort. Even when . . ." She compressed her lips, looked at her food and picked up her fork.

Very gently, Luke took it from her. "Carolyn . . . I may call you that?" She nodded permission. "Even when . . . what?"

She seemed to collapse in on herself. When she looked up, it was again into the distance and at nothing at all. "I began to suspect, from his letters, that something was wrong with my father. I wanted, badly, to go to him. My husband informed me that a woman stayed with her man, no matter what. I hated him for that"—a bleak looked entered those staring eyes—"and I have sometimes wondered if I willed his death at that last battle . . ."

"No!"

She looked at him. "You cannot know."

"I do know. Wishing someone dead does not make them dead. Sometimes even attempting to *make* them dead does not kill them!"

She looked at him, shocked.

"My brother hated me. I never knew why. This scar"—he lifted a hand, sweeping fingers up the side of his face—"he tipped me into the hearth during a nursery fight. Deliberately. My sister believes it was her fault for removing the safety screen, but she didn't see his face when he lifted me and dumped me against the fire dogs."

"My lord . . ." Horror contorted her features and she rose to her feet. "Oh, but surely just a childish argument, a moment's . . ." She trailed off as he shook his head.

"The limp. That was because I stupidly took him up on a dare. We were somewhat older by then. He dared me to ride a certain horse, insisted I could not. As it turned out"—a rather wolfish but self-deriding grin slashed his face—"I *couldn't.* And"—he sobered—"it was over a year before I walked again. Actually, his taunts, when I was bedridden and it thought likely I'd be there the rest of my life, gave me the determination to prove them all wrong. But I still limp."

Luke cast Carolyn an anxious look. He now knew she had not been allowed to come to her father so that was settled. But what did she think of his scar, his limp? Did they put her off? Did they make of him something less than a man in her eyes? Someone who might be her friend but never her lover? Every muscle in his being tensed with the self-denying control that he *not* take her into his arms.

"My lord, each in our own way, we've suffered, have we not? Thank you for trusting me enough to tell me"—she bit her lip and just a touch of that mischief look appeared—"but I almost wish you had *not.* It is so much worse now," she murmured and sighed softly. "My lord, I didn't mean to do it, but I did, and I want you to see what I've done. Once you know, I'll abide by your wishes concerning the future of my work."

She was gone on the words and he heard her light step

on the stairs. He also heard Mrs. Williams approaching and glanced at the table. Mrs. Weston had barely touched her food. And his cup sat, untouched, across from her place. His lips compressed.

As the cook entered, he straightened, and with all the authority he could muster, he ordered, *"Not a word.* She will eat, but not until she is ready. I hope that will not be long now."

Mrs. Williams sniffed but held her tongue. She set a plate of tarts on the table, loaded up the uneaten food, and went out.

The kitchen cat scooted into the room, deftly avoiding the closing door. Partway across the room to the cushioned chair, the cat saw his lordship and froze.

The two stared at each other. "A two-penny kit, hmm?" Luke asked softly.

The cat's eyes narrowed.

"Hmm? More, maybe? You think you are already a four-penny cat? But you are not even full grown, I think!"

The cat blinked, stalked nearer, and, only then, Luke realized the one animal carried another. A dead mouse was laid at his feet, and he was given a green-eyed, glaring, "so-there" look before the cat jumped up into the chair.

"All right." Luke grinned as he opened a window and threw the mouse out. "I will concede that, if you are not yet, you will be a four-penny cat."

The cat responded with a purr.

Luke lost interest in the cat when Mrs. Weston opened the door and entered, a stack of paper clutched to her bosom. She stared at him and he thought her just a trifle wild-eyed. "My dear! What is it?"

"I want you to do something."

"Anything."

"I want you to sit down and read and not say a word until you've read . . . oh, at least fifty pages?"

"Fifty pages may take some time."

"I will be very quiet."

"May I ask *why* I am to read them?"

"Because of what I've done! You'll see. And please, don't

make a judgment until you've read enough to understand.''

"Understand . . . ?''

"Oh, *the devil,*" she exclaimed. She bit her lip, looking
up at him warily only to discover he smiled at her impropriety. "I should not have said that. I could, I suppose, explain,
but, truly, I'd rather wait until you've read enough you'll
understand? At least, I hope you will?''

"Mrs. Williams was unhappy that you'd eaten so little.
While I read, will you eat a tart or two?''

"I'm too nervous. Please, my lord?''

"Very well.''

Luke picked up the cat and settled into the chair, putting
the cat on his lap where gentle stroking soon had the
animal purring, claws extending and retracting, occasionally pricking him through the wool of his trousers. He
began reading, only to feel something. He looked up. It
wasn't *something.* It was Mrs. Weston. Her eyes, staring at
him, looked painfully wide.

"My dear,'' he chided gently, "I will do much better if
you could find something to do. I am put off by your
watching me that way!''

Mrs. Weston moved to the window where she stared out
at the snow instead. Luke returned to his reading. After a
moment, his hand stopped petting the cat. His brows
almost meeting, he stared at Mrs. Weston.

"What the devil!''

"You promised to read.''

He hadn't, but he hadn't said he wouldn't, either. "I
don't understand.''

"Just read! Oh, *please* do.''

He read on. Suddenly he realized the scarred man in
the story was *not* the villain. "The *hero?*" he muttered.
"But how can he be the hero?''

"*Read.*"

She was, he thought sounding a trifle desperate. "Yes.
Of course.'' Besides, he was intrigued. How *could* any
author make him—

He canceled that thought.

—Make the hero a scarred man?

Well over an hour later, Luke looked up, smiling. "Well?"

"Well . . . what?"

"Well . . . where is the rest? You surely do not mean to leave me with our heroine trapped in a well holding on to the well rope for dear life and our hero still miles away riding, *ventre à terre,* to her rescue. I must know what happens, how he finds her, how he rescues her"—he picked the cat up and set him on the floor—"and if"— he rose to his feet and moved toward her. "the beautiful maiden actually really truly can love such a badly flawed man."

"You don't mind?"

He stopped. "Don't mind? What is there that I should mind?"

"That I used you as a model for my hero, of course."

Mrs. Weston might, he thought, almost have stamped her foot. He smiled. "Did you think I would?"

"But . . . so presumptuous of me and you'll never believe I didn't know about your brother, didn't know what I was doing. I didn't even know I'd used you for my hero until . . . well, until that day you stopped here before going on to Bath and then it suddenly . . ." She blinked when his hands clasped her upper arms gently. "Lord Manningford?"

"I believe," he said, staring down into her bemused face, "that I mean to be more presumptuous than you could ever be." Very slowly, giving her every chance to object, he lowered his lips to hers. When she didn't object, he savored their softness, their wonderful warmth, wondering if he were dreaming, that he would wake . . . and praying he would not!

"My lord?" she asked a trifle shyly when he lifted his face from hers.

"Will you marry me? Will you be my wife?"

"Me?" She shook her head. "I mean I? But surely you don't mean—"

He nodded his head firmly.

"—you do?"

"I want it more than anything I've ever wanted, my dear."

"But ..." Carolyn gently released herself. "I never thought of marriage. I thought perhaps you ... we ..." Embarrassment turned her neck a painful red. "Well ... you know?"

"You are very prettily flushed, my dear. But why would you think I'd take you for my mistress and not for wife?"

"I'm too old," she wailed softly. "I'm not of a station from which you *should* choose your wife. I'm not ugly, but not particularly pretty. And worst of all, I've almost nothing in the way of dowry!"

"I have sufficient for our needs, so a dowry or the lack of one is unimportant. I admit I've seen more beautiful women. Most of them," he continued thoughtfully, "are spoiled rotten, thinking only of themselves. They are not particularly interesting once one tires of looking at them. You, my dear, are not hard to look at, but far more important, you are truly interesting. You have a love of life, of living, of doing and being, and those things shine in your eyes and actions." He chuckled. "Whom else have I ever met who could talk me into flying down a hill on a sled?"

"But surely ..."

"My dear, I want you to teach our children, if we are lucky enough to have them, that same joy, that wonderful freedom to live and enjoy life that doesn't conflict with a willingness to do one's duty or, as you do, *more* than one's duty!"

"I don't know what to say."

She looks as flustered as she probably is, Luke thought, and lost the last of his own concern that she could never love him.

"Am I not too old to have children?" she asked. "I am twenty-eight, my lord, and never once conceived when married. It is very possible I cannot have children."

"I would like children and I admit it, but I'll not repine if we do not have them. I have a somewhat distant cousin whom I've assumed would be my heir, not having met you, you see! Before you, it was my intention that I never wed, so I am already resigned to producing no heir in his place. Children . . . they would merely be an extra dollop of love, would they not?"

"Oh dear. I simply don't know what to do for the best. I cannot believe—" She shook her head. "It isn't possible that—" Agitated, she moved a few steps to the right just as the cat moved across her path.

Luke jumped more quickly than he'd moved for quite some years and just managed to break his love's fall. Instead of landing on the floor, she fell against him, clutching him and staring up at him. Luke didn't even think about it. His arms went around her and he pulled her into a close embrace. His head came down.

This kiss was far more heated than the first, rapidly deepening to something beyond a mere kiss. For long minutes each clung to the other. Then Luke gentled his clasp to something far more tender and, finally, broke from her.

"My dear," he said once his breathing was somewhat more even, "I think that four-penny cat may have been trying to tell you something."

"Four-penny cat?" She looked bewildered.

He smiled. "I have this funny notion that she *deliberately* tripped you, forcing me to catch you, placing you in my arms where we could show each other once and for all just how sincerely we each want what I have asked? That we become man and wife?" He grinned a wicked grin which made his scarred face quite handsome. "*Soon?*"

"I know how I feel about you, my lord. That was never in question. I just don't want you to feel you've been made a laughingstock for wedding the designing widow in the village, caught in her snare, lost your wits over a skirt— all the awful things people will say."

"No one who becomes acquainted with you will think any such thing. And what the others think . . . do you care?" He gestured at his face and, a trifle bitterly, added, "People have whispered behind my back for years. And some have said things to my face. I gave up worrying about it years ago. I find it amazing you saw anything in me that suggested I be your hero!"

"Oh, no, that part was easy," she insisted. "Inside where it counts, why, *there* you are all hero, my lord. And that is what I tried to show in my story, that one must look beyond the surface and see what is true and strong."

"I suspected there might be a proper moral at the end of your tale." He smiled at her tenderly. "Can there not," he asked wistfully, "also be a proper ending for the two of us, my dear?"

He watched Carolyn draw in a deep breath. She hesitated only a fraction of a moment more. Then, looking him in the eyes, she said, "I will find the courage to face down the gossips whom I fear will hurt you. I will say . . . yes."

Luke gave a whoop and scooped her up, carrying her to the one comfortable chair in the room. "Move, cat," he said. "I want that place."

Before the cat had finished stretching and jumped down, the door crashed open. "My lord!" Mrs. Williams exclaimed.

Luke swung around, grinning. "You may be the first to congratulate me! Mrs. Weston has agreed to wed me." He smiled down at the woman cuddled in his arms. "And, Mrs. Williams, you are to take that miraculous cat to the kitchen and feed him a large bowl of cream. I do believe, if it were not for him, my one true love might have said me nay! Oh yes, indeed! *Tuppence is surely a four-penny cat.*"

LOOK FOR THESE REGENCY ROMANCES